I0653675

UNQUIET SOULS

PROJECT DEMON HUNTERS:
BOOK ONE

CHRISTINE POPE

Dark Valentine Press

UNQUIET SOULS

Copyright © 2019 by Christine Pope

ISBN: 978-1-946435-20-0

Published by Dark Valentine Press

Cover art by Christian Bentulan

Ebook formatting by Indie Author Services

Prologue

Michael Covenant stared down at the single name on the piece of paper he held and told himself to count to ten before he spoke. Voice remarkably steady, he said, "Audrey Barrett wasn't on the list I gave you."

Colin Turner, the producer of *Project Demon Hunters*, shrugged, looking completely unconcerned. "She should have been. Don't know why you left her off. Master's in psychology, post-grad work with the Rhine Institute—she's the real deal when it comes to parapsychology." Wearing a knowing grin, he added, "Besides, she's a hell of a lot more photogenic than any of that lot you suggested."

Unfortunately, Michael couldn't really argue with any of those completely valid points. He'd had his own reasons for keeping Audrey Barrett off the short list of potential co-hosts for the show he and Colin had been pitching to various cable networks, reasons he needed to conceal from his producer. When Colin messaged him earlier in the day to tell him that they'd been given the green light by a travel cable network, Michael had guessed there had to be a catch.

And it sounded as though Audrey Barrett was that catch.

"She doesn't have any experience actually working out in the field," he said, still doing his best to sound calm and unruffled. Inwardly, though, he could feel himself already tensing. If he ended up being forced into this....

"What 'field'?" Colin scoffed. Even after more than a decade in Los Angeles, his Manchester accent was decidedly obvious—probably an affectation more than anything else at this point. He always looked slightly rumpled, fair hair untidy, skin too pale for your usual Angeleno. "Wandering around in old houses with those little ghost-detecting whatchamacallits?"

"EMF meters," Michael said, an automatic response. "There's a bit more to paranormal investigations than merely wandering around old houses, you know."

"If you say so."

There wasn't much point in pressing the issue, because Michael knew Colin was in this simply to cash in on the current craze for ghost-hunting shows. They'd come up with a slightly different angle, one that promised plenty of jump scares to keep the audience on their toes, and the cable network was interested enough to offer them a limited six-show series to start airing this coming October.

Because really, what were ghosts compared to actual demons?

"Have you contacted her?" Michael asked. "Audrey Barrett takes herself seriously, you know. I have no idea whether she'll even say yes."

Colin tilted a sandy eyebrow, clearly unimpressed by his co-producer's concerns. "Who's going to say no to a lead spot on a reality TV show?"

While Michael knew not everyone wanted to be on television, he guessed that Colin would only scoff at such an assertion. Actually, Michael himself had been reluctant when Colin first approached him to act as host and co-producer of *Project Demon Hunters,* mostly because the thought of such widespread exposure was troubling on many levels. It was one thing to work the paranormal circuit, the lecture halls and the conferences and the guest appearances on various fringe podcasts and radio shows. But to have your face beamed into millions of households each week? The chances of having his carefully constructed identity torn apart were very small, and yet he still wasn't sure he wanted to take that risk, not when he could lose everything if the truth about his past was ever revealed.

But Colin had worn him down, arguing that he was the leading voice in demonology today, and the sort of person a demon-hunting show needed.

The money hadn't been bad, either. Even on a cut-rate cable show, the pay scale was a lot higher than what he'd been getting from his various convention and seminar appearances. While he was comfortable enough, he knew he would have been foolish to pass up that kind of cash infusion.

"Audrey Barrett is *exactly* the sort of person who would say no," he remarked. "She's not in this for the fame and fortune."

"Which is why I need you to talk to her," Colin said reasonably. "Expert to expert. She'll understand that."

Michael had his doubts, but he knew if he continued to dig in his heels, Colin would wonder why he was being so stubborn. On the surface, Audrey Barrett was exactly what *Project Demon Hunters* needed—someone smart, articulate, and photogenic as hell. Never mind that Michael had done whatever he could to stay out of her orbit, not always an easy thing to do in a field as small and fringe as the paranormal, even though the topics they focused on were very different.

Well, it looked as though he wouldn't be able to avoid her any longer.

"All right," he replied. "I'll get in touch with her tomorrow."

Colin corrected him at once. "*Today.* Glendora's only an hour drive from here, and the execs want a commitment ASAP so we can get production started now. I'm already getting the crew put together—I don't want to waste any time."

Probably because February and March tended to be two of Southern California's gloomiest months, and so any location shoots set here would look properly foreboding. There was some money for travel in the show's production budget, but not enough to travel out of state for each episode. They'd have to pick their locations wisely. Luckily, he already knew exactly where they needed to start…a place that was almost around the corner from Audrey Barrett's house.

"On my way," he said, since he knew he'd only be wasting time if he attempted any more arguments. He got up from his seat across from Colin's glass and steel desk. "I'll call you as soon as I have Ms. Barrett on board."

"Take these," Colin said, handing over a manila folder. "Contracts."

There probably wasn't any point in saying that

Colin was getting ahead of himself, so Michael took the folder without comment, lifted his free hand in a brief gesture of farewell, then left the office. As he waited for the elevator to take him down to the building's parking garage, he tried to reassure himself that everything would be fine.

After all, he'd been hiding the truth about himself for more than ten years now. He'd just have to keep doing it for a little while longer.

Chapter 1

THE KNOCK ON THE DOOR TO HER OFFICE startled Audrey, mostly because her work wasn't the sort of thing that lent itself to drop-in visits. Her clients found her mainly through their insurance directories, or, much more rarely, through her website, and in general they set up their appointments online so they wouldn't have to talk to an actual person. Well, at least not until they actually set foot in the office itself, but by that point they probably figured the die had been cast.

She got up from the chair behind her desk and went to answer the door. The place was too cramped to have a reception area, was only a plain square room with a window that overlooked Glendora's small main street in the historic part of town. Just as well that it wasn't any bigger, because she couldn't afford to pay a receptionist anyway.

The man standing in the hallway outside Audrey's office shared with the other micro office suites on the building's second floor looked vaguely familiar, although for a second she couldn't place where she'd seen him before. Then his identity seemed to fall into place—the shaggy, sandy blond hair, the scruff of beard, the piercing eyes in an unusual golden-gray hue.

Michael Covenant, self-proclaimed demonologist and frequent guest on shows like *Coast to Coast* and *The Paranormal Podcast.*

What he was doing here in tiny Glendora, at her office, she had no idea. Or rather, she had several ideas, none of which were particularly appealing.

He spoke before she could close the door and back away. "Audrey Barrett?"

"Yes," she said reluctantly, since she guessed he knew exactly what she looked like, and so there was no point in trying to deny her identity.

"Can we talk?" he asked. Those gray-gold eyes were fixed on her, piercing. She wanted to look away, but for some reason found herself unable to. Some kind of hypnotism? That might explain all the people who paid good money for his books or to attend the conferences where he was a featured speaker.

However, Audrey hadn't lost herself so much

that she couldn't reply crisply, "We're talking now."

His head tilted to one side as his eyes narrowed at her. "You know that's not what I meant."

"Come in," she said, since she guessed the best way to get rid of him was to let him speak his piece and then tell him she had a client coming in and couldn't afford to spend any more time in discussion. Besides, as much as his approach to the paranormal annoyed and sometimes down-right offended her, she didn't want to be rude.

A small smile touching his lips, he entered the office, then waited for Audrey to close the door before he sat down in the chair opposite her hand-me-down desk. There was another chair off to one side, placed there for those times when she had a couple in for counseling, but it felt safer to sit down behind the desk, thus giving herself the illusion of authority despite her unease at his presence here.

Since she guessed there was no reason to pretend ignorance of his identity, she asked, "How can I help you, Mr. Covenant?"

He didn't even blink at her off-hand use of his name. Was he arrogant enough to think he was instantly recognizable? Minor celebrity on the paranormal circuit didn't exactly provide the same sort of star power as acting in films or TV, but, despite being a psychologist, Audrey really didn't want to speculate as to what might go on in Michael Covenant's brain.

"It's more how I can help you, Ms. Barrett."

"Audrey is fine," she said. It wasn't so much that she wanted to be on a first-name basis with him, more that she disliked being called "Ms."—it only reminded her of how she'd been forced to stop after getting her master's degree, hadn't been able to go on and earn a Ph.D. in psychology. Right then, even though she knew it was petty, she probably would have derived a certain small pleasure in telling Michael Covenant to call her "Dr. Barrett."

He leaned against the back of his chair, hands resting on the knees of his dark trousers. The day was dank and damp, not rainy, but with a fog that had never lifted, and so his usual uniform of black jacket with black T-shirt underneath—the same outfit he seemed to wear in every publicity photo —didn't look as out of place as it might have on a typical sunny Southern California afternoon. "Audrey, then. I'm currently developing a show for a cable network with producer Colin Turner… you might have heard of him."

She had, just because his sensational one-off specials tended to clutter the cable offerings during October, when one could usually find hour-long shows like *The 10 Most Haunted*

Places in America and *Serial Killers Among Us* to binge on if the usual horror fare of slasher flicks and alien invasions wasn't enough to satisfy a viewer's appetite for the macabre. Anyway, Audrey's personal opinion was that dropping Colin Turner's name probably wasn't the best way to pique her interest in the project.

"Yes," she said briefly, and left it there.

Michael Covenant was probably many things, but stupid wasn't one of them. His smile vanished, and he sat up a little straighter in his chair. "The show is called *Project Demon Hunters*."

Her response was immediate. "No."

His brows—much darker than his hair—drew together. "I haven't told you anything about the show, Audrey."

"I think the title tells me everything I need to know," she returned. "If you want someone who's into the sensational, why don't you contact Raymond Shipley? Your show sounds like it would be more up his alley."

This suggestion only made Michael's frown deepen. Raymond Shipley had a fairly successful ghost-hunting show a few years back, and he also had a singular talent for turning the faintest creak or electrical malfunction in a house into clear-cut evidence of a haunting. None of his so-called "evidence" could have ever held up in a court of law, but he did know how to keep an audience from changing the channel.

"The execs at the network don't want Raymond Shipley," Michael said. "They want you."

"Why?" Audrey asked frankly. "I study the paranormal, not the supernatural."

"Same thing."

Was he being deliberately obtuse? Tone sharpening a bit, she said, "In my opinion, they tend to be two different things. My field of expertise is extrasensory abilities, not hauntings and possessions…or demons."

She didn't bother to add that she really didn't believe in demons or ghosts or other supernatural entities. So far, her research had generally proved the hypothesis that most unexplained phenomena of their ilk could be attributed to the peculiar powers of the human brain, and nothing more.

"But that's exactly *why* they want you," Michael told her. Now he was leaning forward, extraordinary eyes fixed on her face. "They want you to be the scientific, skeptical side of the team."

"They want Mulder and Scully," Audrey replied, doing her best to make her indifference clear. She had no desire to play the straight man on a cut-rate cable program. "I'm really not interested in rehashing that dynamic."

"It was very successful."

"On a fictional show. My work at the Rhine Institute was all about trying to make the paranormal more mainstream, not sensationalizing it for ratings."

For a moment, he didn't say anything, only sat in his chair and gazed at her with an expression so neutral, she couldn't tell what he was thinking. Then he said, "One hundred thousand dollars."

Audrey blinked. "Excuse me?"

"One hundred thousand dollars for six episodes. If they renew the series, then of course you can renegotiate for more money." A pause, and he added, "Although at that point, you might want to consider getting an agent."

Now it was her turn to be quiet. Although she hated to admit she might be swayed by the promise of filthy lucre, a hundred thousand dollars was a lot of money. She could pay off the remainder of her student debt, possibly get herself a better office…

…not have to worry about the looming tax bill on the house that had once been her parents' and had come to her after their deaths nearly fifteen years earlier.

Also, the exposure would probably be helpful. She could rail against the subject matter and the distasteful reality that the network execs had probably zeroed in on her because she was more camera-friendly than some of her peers, but the cold truth of the situation was that appearing on such a show would very likely get her more clients, something she desperately needed at the moment.

"Six episodes?" she asked, and he nodded. "How long would filming take?"

Now his smile returned, as if he knew he'd already sealed the deal, even though she hadn't yet said yes or no. "About six weeks. We're still scouting locations, although the one for the first episode has already been chosen."

His remark surprised her. After all, homes being oppressed by demons didn't tend to be all that thick on the ground. "It has?"

"Yes." Michael leaned forward in his chair, still smiling. "In fact, it's right here in Glendora."

Audrey felt her eyes widen. "I hadn't heard about any supernatural phenomena occurring here."

A shrug. "Well, the people involved wanted to keep the matter quiet."

"So putting it on national television is keeping it quiet?"

"By the time the episode airs, their problem will have been solved. Besides, we'll be discreet—a fictionalized name for the town where the incident has occurred, aliases for the owners."

That made sense, just because amateur ghost

hunters tended to descend whenever they had a new location to investigate. If the house was distinctive enough, it probably would still be found eventually, but Audrey supposed that was the owners' problem. Better a bunch of looky-loos to contend with rather than a horde of demons.

Not that she believed in demons, of course.

"I'll need to think about it," she said, which she knew was a cop-out. She just didn't want to agree right then and there.

"Take your time," Michael replied, then took the manila envelope he'd been holding and set it down on her desk. "Just don't take *too* much time. Colin wants to start taping the show next week."

Next *week?* While it would have sounded good to say that she needed much more time than that, had to rearrange her clients' appointments to accommodate the production schedule, that would have been a complete lie. At the moment, Audrey had a grand total of ten patients, none of whose issues were anything remotely paranormal. Thank God her master's degree and the certification she'd received from the state of California allowed her to practice psychology, which might have paid the bills well enough if she'd had any skills at marketing herself, or the necessary dedication to make counseling her one true calling.

As it was....

"I think I can manage that," she said calmly. "I

just want to have my lawyer look over the contract before I sign anything."

"Of course." A certain glint in his eyes seemed to indicate he knew she was bluffing about the lawyer. She certainly didn't have an attorney on retainer, especially one who specialized in entertainment law.

However, Audrey's best friend Bettina was a paralegal at a local law firm, and she knew she'd give her a hand by looking over the contract. Maybe it wasn't the same as hiring some pricey Hollywood lawyer, but better than her trying to puzzle the thing out on her own.

"End of day tomorrow?" he went on, and that was when Audrey knew she'd really committed to this thing, despite her reservations. Being free of her ever-nagging concerns about her finances was just too alluring. "You can scan the signed contract and email it to Colin. His email address is on the letterhead. Unless you want to bring it to his office in Hollywood, that is."

The off-hand way Michael had made the suggestion seemed to indicate he knew she wouldn't take him up on that particular offer. Maybe driving into Hollywood would have proven her dedication to the project, but she knew she wasn't that dedicated. She just wanted the relief—and breathing space—that kind of money would provide for her.

"I'll scan it," Audrey said. "I have clients tomorrow."

His expression was so bland that she could tell he'd seen through the lie. However, to her relief, he didn't call her on it, only said, "I'll let Colin know to keep an eye out for your email." A very brief hesitation, and he went on, "I'm looking forward to working with you, Audrey. Once we have the signed contract, then you can meet with me and Colin, and we'll go over some details with you."

"Sounds like a plan," she responded, although inwardly she could feel herself wince. It sounded as though she'd be heading into Hollywood in the near future despite her best efforts to stay safely here in the San Gabriel Valley.

Michael got up from the chair then, hand extended. She took it, was a little reassured by his firm grip. At least it felt straightforward and confident. "Until then," he said.

After that, he let himself out of her office, quietly closing the door behind him. Audrey stared at it for a long moment, at last experiencing some very nervous butterflies in her stomach.

Just what in the world had she gotten herself into?

"An additional forty hours of promotion, including but not limited to, participation in local radio programs, interviews on podcasts, and in-person appearances," Audrey's friend Bettina intoned, reading aloud from the contract she'd given her to inspect. One French-manicured finger was twirling an expertly highlighted strand of hair as she spoke; she'd come over to Audrey's house as soon as she got off work, and so she still wore her silk blouse and pencil skirt, although she'd kicked off her sling-backed high heels.

"No extra pay for that?" Audrey inquired.

A brief glance over the contract's contents, and Bettina shook her head. "Nope. Although really, you're getting a hundred grand for about six weeks' worth of work, so I'd say it's still pretty fair, all things considered."

Well, that was true. Audrey picked up her glass of pinot noir and took a sip, using her free hand to knead away at the knot of tension at the back of her neck. It didn't seem to help much.

Bettina also drank some wine before returning her attention to the contract. Audrey had bribed her with pinot noir and takeout lasagna from Spaghetti Eddie's, since she didn't have anything monetary to offer. Usually, the sight of the soothing blue-gray of her living room walls and the comfortable, well-worn furniture only helped her to relax. Now, though, all she could do was look at those walls and remember how that tax bill of $10,427 was due in six weeks…and how she had less than half that amount in her savings account, with nowhere near enough coming in to make up the difference.

Except for the pay outlined in the contract, of course. One third as an advance, one third paid at the midway point of the shooting schedule, and the final third due when filming was complete. It would definitely be enough to keep her going, since her parents' life insurance policy had paid off the mortgage and the tax bill was now her biggest operating cost besides her ever-present student loan payments. Yes, there was the rent on her office, but that was only five hundred a month, and her therapy clients' fees covered that and her utilities and food…barely.

"A lot of this is boilerplate," Bettina went on, putting down her wine glass. "Residuals, that kind of stuff."

"Do cable networks even have to pay residuals?" Audrey asked. Her grasp of entertainment industry pay standards was admittedly shaky.

"Yep. And a lot more than you might think, because the rates were renegotiated a few years back. If the show's popular, you might get a nice passive income for a while."

It was nice to think that she would still be making money from the show in the future, even if all they ever did was shoot those first six episodes. Of course, she still had to find a way to survive that process, something she really wasn't looking forward to.

Bettina must have picked up on some of her misgivings, because she said, "Are you really sure you can do this, Audrey? You're not exactly what I would call the TV-show type."

No, she wasn't. She hated public speaking, even while she understood all too well the psychology which lay behind that particular phobia. However, this wasn't quite the same thing. It wasn't as though she'd be on stage speaking her piece in front of hundreds of people, but in a closed environment with a small crew, filming on location in haunted houses. Or possessed houses, she supposed, although technically the correct term when you were dealing with demons wasn't possessed, but infested.

"I think Michael Covenant will carry most of it," Audrey replied. "I'm sure they just want me there to be his sidekick."

"I suppose so." Bettina didn't say anything else; she really didn't need to. Although Audrey knew her friend wasn't what you could call a believer in the paranormal, she at least respected Audrey's evidence-based approach to the subject. Bettina knew she wasn't the sort to chase after every woo-woo theory that crossed her path, but rather believed there could be physiological and psychological rationales behind a lot of those phenomena.

Unfortunately, Bettina also knew Audrey wasn't a fan of Michael Covenant's, probably because of a rant she'd gone on about the way he blithely attributed clairvoyant talents to intervention by extra-dimensional entities. As if the human mind, in all its intricacy and power, wasn't capable of manifesting abilities that went far beyond what most people would consider "normal."

Audrey sipped her wine as Bettina read through the contract again. At last she straightened, then got up out of her chair, took her own glass of wine, and came over to where Audrey sat on the couch. She gave Bettina an inquiring look, and she said, "I don't see any red flags. The part about the show providing medical/liability insurance is a little out of the ordinary, but I suppose if you're going to go tromping around in haunted houses, the production company wants to make sure they have people ready in case you fall down a flight of stairs, or whatever. They do require mediation in case of a workplace injury, but again, that's the sort of clause most companies ask for these days."

"Good," Audrey replied, hoping she sounded cool, although those damn butterflies were fluttering around in her stomach again. She hadn't even thought about the possibility of being injured somehow during filming—after all, this wasn't an outdoor adventure show or a *Survivor* type of scenario—but she supposed it would have been strange if the producers hadn't done whatever they could to plug those sorts of loopholes.

"Demons." Bettina shook her head, peach-glossed lips pursing slightly. "I thought you didn't believe in that kind of thing."

"I don't," Audrey said at once. "All of the reported cases I've studied have shown that the behaviors which manifest themselves in supposed cases of demon possession or oppression can be attributed to a variety of physiological and psychological issues. Anyway, it's TV. They're just going to be filming jump scares for the benefit of the audience at home, while Michael Covenant and I bicker about the real reasons behind what everyone is seeing."

That all sounded very calm and matter-of-fact. And it was nothing more than the truth. All the same, the nervous sensation in her stomach translated itself into a creepy-crawly sensation along her spine, as if her body knew more about the subject than her conscious mind wanted to admit.

"And you're really okay with working with him?" Bettina drank some of her pinot noir and then lowered her wine glass, although she didn't set it down on the coffee table. Blue eyes speculative, she watched Audrey for a few seconds before adding, "I mean, it just seems that what he does is pretty much the antithesis of all that post-grad work you did."

She was right, of course. Audrey had spent a frustrating six months working at the Rhine Institute, which had carried on the research first begun at Duke University, exploring the extrasensory powers of the human mind. She'd interviewed and tested those with clairvoyant abilities, and had done her damnedest to get the grants which would allow her to continue that line of research. Unfortunately, her efforts had come to naught, which was why she was doubly glad she'd put in the required three thousand hours of supervised counseling after she got her master's, just in case she had to go into regular counseling rather than pursue her dream of adding to the field of the paranormal. The work gave her something of an income stream, although Audrey knew she should have been working harder to build her client list. The most she'd done was jump through the requisite hoops to get her name added to the list of approved providers for several insurance companies. Unfortunately, her heart just wasn't in it.

Maybe if she'd been more dedicated, the job offer from Michael Covenant wouldn't have seemed so appealing. However, she knew she couldn't blame her current situation on anyone other than herself. Once her work at the Rhine Institute had ended, she'd found herself adrift, not really sure what she wanted from herself or her life. It had been easy to come back to Glendora because she had a home and something of a life here…or at least people who recognized her in the checkout line at the supermarket. Where else, really, could she have gone?

"I know Michael's theories and mine don't jibe," Audrey told Bettina, then drank the last swallow of wine in her glass. "Which is why I'm really looking forward to proving him wrong."

Chapter 2

THE MEETING WITH MICHAEL COVENANT AND Colin Turner, his producer, was surprisingly anticlimactic. The three of them assembled in Colin's office in a high-rise on Sunset Boulevard, where both Michael and Colin stated they were glad to have Audrey on board, and Colin informed her that she'd need to meet with their hair and makeup people, and the woman in charge of wardrobe.

"I can't wear my own clothes?" Audrey asked, a little surprised. After all, this was supposed to be a reality show, wasn't it?

Colin gave her an indulgent smile. When she'd first met him, she hadn't liked the way his gaze raked her up and down, apparently cataloguing her various assets and flaws, but then Audrey realized that was all part of his producer schtick and did her best to ignore it. Possibly he'd seen her stiffen in indignation, because after that he'd poured on the charm, his north-of-England accent becoming even more pronounced as he said she had perfect bone structure for the camera —whatever that was supposed to mean—and that he knew she would do fine.

Audrey almost inquired acidly as to whether his certainty was based on his appraisal of her bone structure, but she decided to let it go. There was no point in trying to fool herself; she knew that a large part of the reason why Colin had selected her was because he thought she would look good on camera. Deep down, she had to admit that her dark hair and eyes would provide a good contrast to Michael's sandy-blond hair and oddly hued hazel eyes, providing some additional visual interest.

"No," Colin said, still smiling. "That's just our policy. Don't want to be responsible for some sentimental favorite of yours getting ruined or anything."

"That's a possibility?" Again, Audrey didn't quite see how standing in a haunted house and riffing on the nature of the strange noises emanating from the attic would pose much of a risk to her wardrobe.

"You'd be surprised," Michael put in. Unlike Colin, he wasn't smiling, instead looked deadly serious. "I've been vomited on, covered in mud, splashed with blood—"

"That's quite enough," Colin said hastily, probably because he must have seen the way her eyes widened at those revelations. "Not that we think anything like that is going to happen during filming, but better safe than sorry, isn't that right?"

Audrey glanced from him to Michael, who'd settled back into his chair but was giving her another of those speculative glances, as if still trying to determine whether she'd really be able to handle what this show might throw at her. Once again, she looked forward to the chance to prove him wrong.

"Yes, I suppose so," she said. "But I want practical clothes. No skirts or heels."

"No, nothing like that," Colin responded, looking relieved that she hadn't commented on Michael's remark about blood and vomit. "Jeans and boots, that sort of thing. We'll need your sizes."

About the last thing Audrey wanted was to blurt out her pants size in front of Michael Covenant, of all people, but she knew she didn't have much choice. "I'm a size six in most things," she said, "but of course clothes vary from brand to brand. And a size seven for shoes, mostly, unless they run small."

"I'll let Kathleen know," Colin said, adding by

way of explanation, "the wardrobe gal. She'll put some things together for you."

In a way, it was sort of fun to contemplate the notion of getting new clothes to wear, even if they were borrowed and not really hers. And who knew —maybe they would let her keep some of the wardrobe if they didn't have another use for it.

"When?" Audrey asked.

"Friday morning," Colin replied. "The production offices, which are actually in Universal City. I'll email you all the particulars."

She nodded, although inwardly she could feel herself groan. Yet more time spent in traffic, going to and from Glendora. She wasn't naïve enough to think she wouldn't waste several hours of her life sitting on the 210 Freeway going back and forth to the company's production offices, no matter what time of day it might be.

But, as Bettina had pointed out, Audrey was getting paid a lot of money for what would be a relatively short period in her life. At least she didn't have any counseling sessions scheduled for Friday morning, just one at three o'clock that afternoon. She'd have to make sure she was back in Glendora by then.

"All right," she said, then glanced over at Michael. "Since you have my signed contract and NDA, can you let me know where we'll be filming on Monday?"

"No," he replied flatly, and Audrey stared at him, wondering if he'd misunderstood her question.

Colin, as seemed to be his pattern, rushed in to smooth things over. "What he means is, it's better if you go in fresh, so to speak. Don't want you coming at the problem with any preconceived ideas."

Annoyed, she thought if that was really their goal, then they should have hired someone else. Audrey already had plenty of ideas about demon hunting, none of which were what one might call favorable. But if Michael was really worried that she'd spend the days between now and Monday sneaking around the property, trying to get a read on the place in order to have an advantage when they started shooting, so be it. She wasn't going to argue, or try to convince him that she had much better things to do with her time.

"Sure," Audrey said. "I can understand that. Then I guess I'll be in Universal City on Friday and on Monday—"

"On Monday, I'll come pick you up," Michael cut in.

That prospect didn't appeal very much—at least if she had her own car at the shoot, she'd feel somewhat more in control of the situation—but she'd signed the contract. She was committed to this thing now, and if Michael Covenant wanted to throw in odd stipulations and demands, so be it.

Committed is right, she thought. *You probably should be committed for agreeing to this…or at the very least be subjected to a seventy-two-hour psychiatric hold.*

However, Audrey was determined not to allow him to see that she harbored any misgivings about the project, mostly because she feared he would see her unease as a sign of weakness. She smiled and said that sounded great, and soon afterward she made her escape to get her car out of hock from the parking garage under the building where Colin's office was located. As she'd feared, she had to sit in traffic all the way back to Glendora, but what difference did it really make? It wasn't as though she had anyone waiting for her.

And whose fault is that?

Hers, mostly. It was easier to live a hermit-like existence than get far enough along in a relationship where she had to explain what had happened to her parents. The few times Audrey had made herself tell the truth, the men she'd been seeing had quickly found a reason to break off the relationship. These days, no one wanted to deal with baggage.

Neither did she…but she hadn't been given any choice.

Monday rolled around, after a weekend in which Audrey quite ferociously did nothing of any importance at all. Usually, she would have tried to go hiking, or met up with Bettina to go to the movies or at least lunch and window shopping, but instead she got caught up with laundry and housework, pulled weeds in the garden, and finally hemmed that set of curtains she'd been meaning to get to for months.

Possibly an outside observer would have commented that she was trying to get all those odds and ends done in case something really did happen to her during the filming of the first episode of *Project Demon Hunters,* but Audrey refused to look at it that way. These were all tasks that needed to be handled, and it wasn't as though she could afford to hire someone to take care of them for her. The house was the one tangible thing she had to remind herself of her parents, and she wasn't about to let anything happen to it...not even if it meant appearing on some half-baked reality show in order to prevent a tax lien. She'd already gotten one extension and knew she couldn't ask for another. The show was her one chance to get her precarious finances in order.

Michael had texted her that he would be out front at six-thirty Monday morning, which would have sounded early except that she knew they both had to go to hair and makeup before they could even set foot in the supposedly haunted—or infested—house where they would be filming. Pride prevented Audrey from leaving the house completely bare-faced, so she put on a little lip gloss before going out onto the front porch to wait for him.

The morning was cool and foggy, the mois-ture-laden air making odd little circles of light around the orange-toned street lamps. Although she'd put on a sweater, Audrey still shivered. So much for sunny Southern California.

A pair of headlights raked through the fog, and she saw an ancient Toyota Land Cruiser pull up and stop in front of the house. Looking at it, she couldn't help but frown a little. So, even with all his appearances on the conference circuit and the books and the DVDs, he couldn't afford anything better than that?

Audrey told herself she shouldn't be a snob. After all, she drove a seven-year-old Toyota Corolla. But....

Pulling in a breath, she made herself go down the front walk and then open the Land Cruiser's passenger door. Michael was sitting inside, his over-long hair looking more disheveled than ever, a scruff of beard on his cheeks and chin. A pair of Starbucks cups sat somewhat precariously in a cardboard carry-out container on the front seat, since of course a vehicle that old didn't have anything as handy as a cupholder.

"Thought you could use some coffee," he said, his tone almost too casual. "It's black, but there's some sugar and cream in that bag."

"Black is fine," Audrey replied, settling herself in the passenger seat so she could fasten the seatbelt. "Thanks—I didn't have time to make some for myself this morning."

"These shooting schedules can be brutal," he said as he pulled away from the curb.

"Well, I did some work as an extra when I was in college, so I was ready for that part of the gig."

He turned his head to regard her briefly before returning his attention to the road. "Really? I didn't know that."

Audrey shrugged. "It's not like it was something I would have put on my CV. I had a friend in college whose mother was a set decorator, and they needed some college-age kids to fill in on a TV pilot they were shooting. It was a fun way to spend a couple of days, but—"

"But it wasn't something you wanted to do full-time." His mouth quirked a little. "And now you're doing that very same thing."

"A six-week shoot isn't exactly a full-time job," she pointed out.

"Maybe not exactly, but it's full-time while

you're doing it." Once again, he swiveled his head to take a quick look at her, and then turned back to keep an eye on their foggy surroundings. "How did you handle the schedule with your clients, anyway?"

"I moved their appointments to the weekend," Audrey replied. It hadn't been something she'd really wanted to do, but it was better than trying to find new counselors for them for just a few weeks. In addition to her very real fear that they might not come back after the six weeks of shooting were done, she also worried that assigning them new therapists would reverse some of the progress they'd made, as the fragile trust they'd created would have to be rebuilt all over again with someone else. Luckily, all her clients had been accommodating—and also interested in what she would be doing with her weekdays. She hadn't gone into too much detail, except to say she was helping with a show that would be out the following autumn. And really, she couldn't have told them much more than that anyway, since she'd had to sign a nondisclosure agreement that stipulated she wouldn't share the subjects or the locations of any of the shoots she'd be doing.

"It's going to be rough, not giving yourself any time off."

Was that a real note of concern in his voice, or was Michael simply worried that she'd be using energy better spent on the show? Audrey certainly didn't know him well enough to tell for sure, although she had a feeling it was more the latter than the former.

"It'll be fine," she said. "I'm used to long days. I had to work the whole time I was getting my counseling certification."

"Ah."

That was all he said, which could have meant anything. She realized then that she didn't know much about his own bona fides. He'd sort of appeared on the scene out of nowhere about five or six years back, and something about his flamboyant style and brooding intensity had kept people from looking too closely at his background. She'd seen one conference program note that he had degrees in both theology and physics, which seemed like an odd combination, at least on the surface.

They were heading north, toward the foothills above Glendora, and the road climbed gently with them. In general, Audrey didn't spend much time in this part of town, since the houses here were far beyond her limited means—and beyond her parents' means back in the day. The house she lived in was modest, a refurbished Craftsman-style cottage her parents had bought when she was just in kindergarten. Up here were houses that stretched into the millions.

After crossing Sierra Madre Boulevard—whose sign she could just barely make out through the fog—Michael turned onto a secluded little street, and then into the driveway of an enormous house that seemed to suddenly loom up at her through the gloom. Here was an unexpected flurry of activity, with people moving portable lights from oversized vans and into the home, someone setting up a small pop-up tent to one side, probably for craft service, and a woman wheeling a rack of clothing into what looked like a second, smaller house on the property.

Michael had apparently followed Audrey's gaze, because he said, "The owners are letting us use the guest house for wardrobe and makeup. Come on—I'll show you."

He undid his seatbelt and she followed suit, then got out of the Land Cruiser and went with him to the guest house...which didn't look all that much smaller than her own home, which was a modest 1,500 square feet. If there had once been furniture here, it had all been moved out of the way. To one side were several low tables with mirrors bolted to them and canvas-backed director's chairs placed in front. The other side of the room was where the rack of clothes had ended up; Audrey recognized Kathleen, the wardrobe supervisor, from her meeting with her the previous Friday.

Kathleen came over as soon as she spotted Audrey standing next to Michael. "Morning, Audrey," she said briskly. "We might as well get started." A pause as she looked over at Audrey's companion. "I suppose you're wearing that."

"Yes, I am," he said, unperturbed.

Which didn't surprise Audrey all that much. Today, just like the other days she'd seen him, he was wearing black trousers and a black jacket with a black T-shirt underneath. She wondered if he had multiple iterations of the same outfit. It would certainly cut down on the time he spent choosing his clothes every morning.

Apparently, Kathleen wasn't surprised, either. "As I thought," she said, then returned her attention to Audrey. "It's going to be a cool day, so I thought we'd go with a leather jacket and T-shirt, some jeans and boots. Casual but put together. Come along."

To her relief, while they were talking, someone had set up a couple of folding Japanese screens to hide one corner of the room and serve as a makeshift dressing area. Audrey took the clothes Kathleen handed her and went behind the screens to change into them. To her surprise, everything she'd been given fit perfectly, which meant that there really wasn't any need for all the clothes Kathleen had brought along. Of course, Murphy's Law being what it was, if she hadn't provided a range for Audrey to wear, the one outfit she would have been given probably wouldn't have fit.

That task taken care of, she went over to the makeup and hair side of the room, and sat down in the empty chair. A pretty Hispanic woman about her own age was fussing with Michael's hair, although Audrey couldn't quite tell what she was hoping to accomplish. It still looked disheveled and windblown, and possibly as though he'd cut it himself. Then again, maybe that was the look he'd been going for all along. She didn't like admitting it to herself, but the too-long hair brought more attention to his wide cheekbones and unusual eyes, made you want to look twice at him.

Or maybe more than twice.

Once the stylist was done, Michael got up out of his chair and went back outside, leaving her to transfer her attention to Audrey.

"I'm Daniela," she said as she wrapped Audrey's hair around a big-barreled curling iron. "You're Audrey, right?"

She nodded.

"Well, you're in good hands with me," Daniela said. "Gotta look your best while those demons are chasing you, right?"

That remark made Audrey lift an eyebrow. "Do you really think there are demons?"

Daniela shrugged. "I don't know for sure, but I'm glad I'm in here and not up there." With one shoulder, she gestured toward the mansion Audrey had spied through the fog. All the while, though, Daniela's deft fingers were busy, setting big waves in Audrey's hair with a speed and economy of movement she knew she'd never be able to copy, no matter how hard she tried. "And I've got my crucifix in my pocket, just in case."

Maybe Audrey should have chuckled at her superstition, but again she experienced one of those chills down her spine. She told herself it was only the damp, gloomy morning, especially since it didn't seem as though anyone had turned on a heater in here, and the little house felt as dank as the air outside.

"I'm sure it will be fine," Audrey assured her. "This is just a TV show. There aren't any demons."

Daniela's shoulders lifted slightly. "If you say so, *chica.*"

Audrey's hair done, Daniela set down the curling iron, went over to a rolling cart laden with several large cases, and retrieved an impressive set of makeup brushes, along with an even more impressive kit containing more makeup than Audrey had probably owned in her entire life. She held herself still as Daniela applied foundation and blush and contour, eyeshadow and liner and mascara, dark powder on her brows and semi-gloss lipstick on her mouth. When she stepped away, she gave a satisfied nod. "What do you think?"

To be honest, Audrey wasn't sure what to think, except that she knew she hadn't worn this much makeup since her senior prom, now more than ten years in the past. "Well, it's...."

"It feels like a lot, I know," Daniela said, bending in to brush more highlighter on Audrey's brow line. "But you need it, or you'll disappear under those lights." She stepped back a pace and eyed her critically. "You look great. Natural, but done."

Natural? Audrey wanted to laugh but realized Daniela wasn't joking. Possibly under the lighting they were using for the show, it would appear natural and not like the makeup of a girl who'd gone crazy with her mother's cosmetics when she wasn't looking.

"You have a great face," Daniela went on. "You're really not an actress?"

Audrey shook her head. "No, just a psychologist."

"Well, Ms. Psychologist, you're good to go. One of the P.A.s will show you where Michael is waiting for you."

Audrey thanked her and got out of the makeup chair, then went outside. The day had brightened a bit; the sun must have come up while she was getting groomed, but the morning was still gray and foggy, feeling as though it might not clear up at all.

As Daniela had promised, a production assistant—a girl who barely looked old enough to drink, her fair hair pulled back in a messy ponytail —came up to Audrey as soon as she emerged from the guest house/cum makeup trailer. "Ms. Barrett? Come this way, and I'll take you to Mr. Covenant."

So formal. She wasn't really used to that; her counseling clients addressed her by her first name. Still, Audrey didn't bother to protest, but followed the girl as she led her along the brick walkway to a side door that opened into a sort of conservatory room all made of glass. Michael was waiting there, his back to the two of them as he stared into the interior of the house.

"Mr. Covenant?" said the P.A. "She's ready."

He turned. If he noticed the difference in Audrey's appearance, he didn't give any evidence of it. "Thanks, Brooke. You can tell Chris and Susan that we'll be ready in a few minutes."

"This is an impressive place," Audrey said, since she wasn't sure what kind of comment she should make. "What's the story?"

Now Michael smiled, and she noticed how the shift in expression lit up the gold-gray of his eyes, relaxed the usually tense set of his features. Although he was probably only a few years older than she was, he already had a permanent frown line engraved into the skin between his brows. "The house was built in 1911. It's gone through a number of different owners, as you can imagine. In fact, it's had quite a bit of turnover for a property with its price point. No one wants to stay for very long."

"Because it's haunted," Audrey ventured.

"I think we've gone beyond haunting here," he replied, the smile vanishing as if it had never been. "As you'll soon see. The current owners are desperate, which was why they were willing to have us film here. Anything to protect their investment."

"Which was…?" Maybe it was crass to ask, but curiosity had gotten the better of her.

"Three and a half million dollars," he replied. "So you can see why they're eager to get the house cleared. Right now, the owners are staying at their condo at the Escena Golf Club in Palm Springs, but of course that solution can't be a permanent one."

Of course not. After all, who would want to rough it in a luxury condo on a golf course any longer than they absolutely had to?

Since she had the feeling that a comment along those lines wouldn't go over very well with him, Audrey decided it would be better if she just nodded. And really, her thoughts hadn't been very charitable ones. It had to be upsetting to feel as though you couldn't live in your own house, millionaire or not.

"What we're going to do is walk through the house," Michael went on, suddenly brisk. "I've already shot some intro stuff over the weekend—basically what I just told you—so now it's more about reaching out to feel what's here, and communicating those feelings to the camera. But if you feel anything yourself, make sure you let me know. Just talk to me, not the camera. Pretend it's not there. I want this to feel genuine."

She wanted to tell him that she'd been in plenty of houses where supposed "supernatural" phenomena was taking place and hadn't felt a thing, but she knew that wasn't the complete truth. There had been that one odd experience in New Orleans....

Right now, though, Audrey felt as if something was missing from the equation. "What about EMF meters?" she said. She didn't profess to be an expert ghost hunter, but she knew enough about the basic tools of the trade to realize Michael hadn't mentioned them at all.

"No point," he replied. "We're not tracking ghosts. Demons don't register in the electromagnetic frequencies the way spirits do."

He sounded completely matter-of-fact. Was he right? Not having studied the finer points of difference between ghostly manifestations and demon infestations, Audrey couldn't say for sure. While she didn't like to admit her ignorance, she had to realize he was the expert here.

"All right, what if we both feel something?" she asked.

"Then the next step is to determine what it is. The easiest way to dispel a demon is to know its name, but of course it won't be eager to give up that information. You have to trick it into giving it to you. Failing that, there are a number of prayers and charms that can be used to drive them off."

"Of course," Audrey said, deciding she'd better leave her reply at that. They didn't have time to get into an argument over whether demons were really just a manifestation of human psychoses, and therefore not real at all.

Michael shot her a sideways look, as if he knew she wasn't really buying into his commentary about demonology. "I know your opinion on the subject of demons, Audrey," he said. "But I'm also asking you to keep an open mind. I've dealt with this sort of thing before."

"Successfully?"

"Yes." He hesitated, then went on, "I don't generally advertise this, but I'm an ordained minister in addition to being a sensitive. I have the toolbox to handle the situation, as long as you don't get in the way."

Get in the way? "So I'm just window dressing?" she asked. She didn't make much effort to keep the irritation out of her tone.

"No," he said, apparently not offended by her question. "More like...the control in a scientific experiment."

If that was supposed to make her feel better, it really didn't. But this was his show, and she was just the co-host. The control. The photogenic skeptic.

Fine. Audrey had to hope that if he got really dramatic about confronting an unseen force or whatever, she wouldn't burst out laughing. She doubted that sort of reaction would play well for the cameras, although of course they could edit out whatever they had to. This wasn't a live show, after all.

"All right," she said. She knew she needed to choose her battles. "Can you tell me anything about the owners?"

"Robert and Rebecca McGrath," Michael replied. "At least, those are the aliases we'll be using to protect their privacy. However, we will be telling the truth about their backgrounds. He's a developer from Orange County. His wife is originally from Louisville, Kentucky. Apparently she got tired of living in brand-new houses and wanted something with 'character.'"

"So they bought this place." From where they

stood, Audrey was able to see into the conservatory, take note of the wicker furniture and potted plants that filled the space. It did look very genteel and Southern, something that might appeal to someone from Kentucky…and definitely not the norm in this part of the world. The San Gabriel Valley actually did have its share of vintage homes, probably more than a lot of people might believe, but mansions like this one were pretty rare. "How long have they owned the house?"

"A little over six months. They lived here in the fall and into the holidays, but after the first of the year, things started to become unsettled. About a month ago, it all got to be too much, and they left." Michael's eyes glinted at her. "Ready to go in?"

"Sure," Audrey said, hoping she sounded steady. More than anything, she wanted to ask exactly what he'd meant by "unsettled," but she had a feeling he'd evade the question, since he probably wanted her to go in without any preconceived notions.

"It's all right," he told her, a flicker of a smile playing around the corners of his mouth. "The crew's already inside, and so far, they're all fine."

As assurances went, that wasn't much of one. Even though she could feel tension begin to knot in her stomach, Audrey nodded, remaining silent as he reached out to open the door to the conservatory. However, she couldn't help but notice the way the P.A. who'd escorted her here hung back. Staying out of the way because she'd been told to do so, or simply afraid to go in?

Of course, Audrey couldn't ask, so she followed Michael into the conservatory and past the wicker dining set there, then through a pair of French doors that opened into the living room. It was a huge space with a conversation area at one end and a piano tucked into one corner, with coffered mahogany ceilings and a large fireplace with a marble surround. The furnishings were very traditional and slightly stuffy-looking to her California-bred eyes, but she supposed they fit the house. What didn't fit the house were the studio lights set up on tripods, banishing shadows with their glare. Now she began to understand why Daniela had piled on the makeup.

The crew was already here, standing in front of the fireplace. There were only two of them, actually—a scruffy-looking man with a Steadicam assembly, and a fair-haired woman, probably in her early forties, holding a boom mike. They immediately began to track Michael and Audrey as they entered the room. He stopped in front of the fireplace, and she paused next to him, trying not to look too ill at ease. This was mostly a recap, because she knew they'd filmed a few intro pieces over the weekend without her, but she listened intently. The formal opening sequences would be filmed later; Colin's plan seemed to be to throw her right into the action in order to make her responses seem more authentic.

"The Whitcomb mansion," Michael proclaimed. "Built in 1911 by a railroad tycoon who lost his fortunes in the crash of 1929. Since then, the house has been bought and sold many times, with most of the residents staying no longer than a year. Reports of strange sounds and smells…cold spots and voices in empty rooms. All the classic signs of a haunting, but the latest owners began to fear they were dealing with far more than a ghost." A pause, those glittering, gray-gilt eyes fixed on the camera. "And that is exactly what my colleague Audrey Barrett and I are here to discover."

Audrey knew she shouldn't smile, so she settled for giving him a sober nod, all the while wondering if she looked as foolish as she thought she did. So far, she hadn't gotten any kind of feeling at all about the house, except for wishing that she could be somewhere far, far away from here. She and Michael had only been filming for a few minutes, and already she wanted to kick herself for agreeing to be on the show. Somehow, she knew it was all going to be manufactured scares and hyperbole, just like every other ghost-hunter program she'd ever watched.

Michael began to move and Audrey followed along, doing her best to look purposeful and composed despite her inner turmoil. The camera operator and the sound technician came with them, staying a few steps ahead. Their progress took them from the living room into the dining room, which was also huge in scale, with an enormous table that had twenty chairs grouped around it. Fussy wallpaper, and a patterned rug to match. The overall effect was a little overwhelming, and Audrey could feel her temples begin to pound, although that could have simply been from the smell of dampness that surrounded her, making her wonder how long the house had been closed up.

"Some of the most startling incidents were observed in this room," Michael went on. "Chairs piled on top of the table, plates actually moving from where they'd been set even as people watched. So far, our research hasn't been able to come up with a definitive reason for why such phenomena would be concentrated here rather than elsewhere in the house."

That wasn't just the smell of a damp house that had been closed up for too long—it was mildew, concentrated, powerful, like a shower that hadn't been scrubbed in months. It was so strong, Audrey could feel herself growing dizzy, even though she knew she shouldn't show any sign of my discomfort, needed to stay calm and strong in front of the camera.

A wave of dizziness. No, scratch being calm and composed—she had to grab hold of something. She stepped away from Michael and clutched the back of one of the chairs, hoping that would steady her.

"Audrey?"

She couldn't tell whether the concern in his voice was real, or whether he was faking it for the cameras. For some reason, she couldn't speak. It almost felt as though there was an invisible hand wrapped around her throat, squeezing. From somewhere in the distance, she heard sharp, hissing laughter that grated on her ears.

"Audrey!"

With her free hand, she tried to reach out to him. The invisible pressure on her throat increased, and the floor seemed to tilt beneath her feet, as if she stood on the deck of a ship on a stormy sea rather than solid ground more than a hundred miles from the ocean. Terror flooded through her, zinged along her nerve endings.

The laughter increased, shredding her eardrums.

Then merciful darkness fell.

Chapter 3

STRONG ARMS HELD HER, AND AUDREY FOUND herself wanting to remain in that embrace. It provided a feeling of security she hadn't experienced for a long time, a sense that she finally wasn't alone. A pleasant scent surrounded her... something woodsy and masculine. Her eyelids fluttered, and she found herself staring up into Michael Covenant's face. His brows were drawn together, but an expression of relief passed over his features as soon as she was able to open her eyes and really focus on him.

Then she realized he was the one holding her as he knelt in the dining room, with the cameraman and sound technician hovering in the background. Just behind them was the young P.A., who somehow managed to look both worried for

Audrey's well-being and scared out of her mind at the same time.

"Audrey, are you all right?" Michael asked, his tone urgent.

"I'm fine," she said, knowing she sounded irritated rather than frightened. And she *was* irritated with herself for fainting like some heroine out of a gothic novel. Where the hell had *that* come from? She'd never passed out before, not even that one time in high school when she'd been stupid enough to donate blood on an empty stomach. There had to be a rational explanation for her faint. Managing a rueful smile, she added, "I guess I didn't eat enough for breakfast."

From the way his eyebrows lifted, Audrey guessed he wasn't buying her story. "That's it…low blood sugar? You didn't hear anything? Feel anything?"

"I—" Part of her wanted to lie, to ignore the strange sounds and smells that had assaulted her right before she fainted. But that would have been cowardly. She needed to tell Michael the truth. That was why they were here, after all—to discover exactly what was happening at the mansion. "There was an overwhelming smell of mildew. It seemed to come from nowhere, but it was all around me. And then there were the voices."

"Voices?"

"Laughing. Evil laughter. It was high-pitched."

"Like a child's voice?"

"Not exactly." Audrey hesitated before adding, "It really didn't sound human."

He was silent, then, to her surprise, he looked up at the cameraman. "Did you get all that?"

A huge grin that split the man's dark beard. "Everything."

Annoyed, Audrey pushed herself out of Michael's arms and staggered to a standing position. Her knees didn't feel that stable, but she could use the wall to steady herself. She sure as hell wasn't going to let him keep on holding her. "You were filming all that?"

"Of course," he replied, unperturbed. "The faint —the way I was able to catch you—it was all gold. The viewers are going to eat it up."

"I wasn't faking," Audrey said, her tone flat.

"I know you weren't. That's what makes it even better."

Anger flared, but she held her tongue. This was TV, after all. She knew what she was getting herself into. Or rather, she'd thought she'd known.

What Audrey hadn't been expecting were those voices. That smell, worse than anything she'd ever experienced. Even now, her stomach churned at the memory.

But it was all gone. She couldn't exactly call the room she stood in ordinary, but it didn't feel haunted, or possessed. However, if this sort of thing happened here on a regular basis, she could see why the owners had bolted for their Palm Springs condo.

Her eyes not quite meeting Michael's, Audrey said, "I need some fresh air."

He nodded, then glanced over at the cameraman and the sound technician. "Chris, Susan, let's take five."

"Sure thing," the cameraman—Chris?—said, and promptly left the room.

Audrey did so as well, heading back through the living room and conservatory so she could stand on the brick patio outside and take in deep breaths of the cool morning air. In the distance, she heard the sound of traffic passing by on Sierra Madre Boulevard and remembered there was still a real world out there, no matter how creepy and cloistered the mansion felt.

As she sat down on the edge of the brick planter that bordered the patio, Michael came outside and shut the door to the conservatory behind him. "You're angry."

"No," she said. "I knew I was signing up to have everything filmed. Just part of the game, right?"

She'd expected him to agree with her, or possibly make a noncommittal shrug. Instead, he replied, "This isn't a game. What you experienced in there was real."

"But you still made sure you captured the whole thing for the show."

"Of course I did. That's part of the deal. Colin would have my head if he found out I tried to suppress valuable footage like that."

Tilting her head, Audrey asked, "What's your goal with all this, Michael?"

His fingers plucked at the hem of his jacket. He looked so uncomfortable, so fidgety, she just had to ask. After all, she'd seen that kind of nervous twitch before.

"When did you quit smoking?"

"Is it that obvious?"

To most people, probably not, but Audrey knew that when you were used to working with clients fighting addictive behaviors, it was easier to notice the tells. "I'm a shrink, Michael, remember?"

He chuckled. "Right. It's been ten months. Most of the time I can power through it, but every once in a while, the urge catches me off guard."

She could imagine. Nicotine was highly addictive, worse than heroin on some levels. "If you've made it this far, you can stay with it. Usually it's the first month or so that's the worst."

"That's what I keep telling myself." He

reached in his jacket pocket, pulled out a piece of gum, and put it in his mouth. Chewing contemplatively, he said, "That mildew odor you experienced—the owner's wife smelled the same thing. So did the woman who lived here before her. But none of their husbands were ever able to sense it."

"You didn't smell it?"

"No."

That was strange. True, olfactory acuity varied from person to person, but that mildew odor had been so strong, everyone in the room should have been able to detect it, even if not at the level at which Audrey had experienced the smell. Had she suffered some kind of hallucination?

"It's often how they work," Michael continued. "Demons, that is. They tend to choose one person in a house to target, to do what they can to weaken them. That person often tends to be female, simply because our society still doesn't put as much stock in testimony by women, often treats them as lesser."

Audrey wanted to bristle at his words, but unfortunately, she knew he was only speaking of a sad truth. "What's their goal, though? To drive someone to mental imbalance?"

"Basically, yes. What they really want is to torment you to the point where you consider taking your own life, just because by doing so you commit your soul to eternal damnation."

Had he really just said that? Eyes narrowed, Audrey stated flatly, "You can't believe that's true."

Looking grim, he replied, "It's not a matter of what *I* believe, but of what the demons believe. They thrive off our mental torment, drink it like fine wine. The anguish a person goes through at the moment they take their lives...that's something they want to savor."

Audrey shivered. She could have blamed the dank, chilly morning, but she was wearing a jacket, and it wasn't really that cold out. "Have you encountered a lot of them?"

"Enough to know they're real." Michael came over to her, extended a hand. "It's rough the first time. You're confronted by something completely *other,* completely evil. It hits your world view upside the head."

"I still don't know those were demons," she protested, even as she let him help her up to a standing position. Her knees were still shakier than she wanted to admit. "I could have manufactured the whole thing in my head, just because I was expecting there to be something in this house."

He offered her a sad smile. "It's easier to think that, I know. But you'll come around. In the meantime, we have a show to shoot."

The last thing Audrey wanted was to go back inside that house, but she didn't have much choice. She'd signed up for this, and she needed to see it through. After her failure to get more grants for her psychic research, after settling for a private practice even though that wasn't what she really wanted, she needed to have some kind of victory.

No matter what.

Michael didn't take her back to the dining room, though. Instead, he sat her down on the sofa in the living room and questioned her again about the "attack." His words, not hers; she hadn't really thought of the incident in those terms, but the more they discussed what had happened—with the camera recording every tense moment—the more she realized it *had* been some sort of an attack, albeit not a physical one. As to why it had been focused on her…she wasn't sure if she wanted to know the answer to that question.

Once they were done with the interview, Michael asked Audrey if she was ready to go upstairs. She really didn't want to go farther into the house, but she knew she needed to suck it up and do her job. Anyway, she'd already survived one attack, and now she knew a little more of what to expect. Of course, she was frightened, but she wouldn't let that stop her. She'd survived the deaths of her parents; she could survive this as well.

"Let's go," she said, and he gave her a satisfied nod.

"We're moving," he told the cameraman and the sound technician, and they all headed up the stairs.

Audrey didn't think they were actually all that spooky, mostly because there was a big window above the landing that let in a good amount of light. At least they were doing this in the daytime; Michael and Colin had apparently decided they didn't need to go for cheap scares with shadowy corners and the two co-hosts blundering around in the dark armed only with flashlights. The contract had stipulated that there might be some night shoots, but either Michael had decided this place was scary enough in broad daylight, or the plan was to start slow and end on a high note with the really terrifying stuff.

Neither prospect was terribly reassuring.

They passed several medium-sized bedrooms and ended up in what had to be the master suite, which really didn't look too frightening, thanks to the windows on three sides and the light-colored bedspread and serene landscapes that hung on the walls. The studio lights sitting on tripods on either side of the door also did a lot to dispel her lingering sensation of unease.

Michael glanced over at her. "Feel anything?"

Audrey shook her head. "I'm not psychic, remember?"

"You don't think you are," he replied. "There's a difference."

About all she could do was lift her shoulders. As part of her research in parapsychology, she'd had a fellow researcher administer a Zener psychic test on her—the test that used a series of cards with symbols on one side. Even though most parapsychologists acknowledged that the tests were far from accurate, it was still fun to give it a try, just to see what happened. Audrey's score had been inconclusive at best, which was fine by her; she'd wanted to study psychics, not actually be one.

Michael looked at the camera, not at her, as he spoke. "A far greater proportion of the population has psychic talents than most people think. These talents can lie buried in us, but are then brought out in moments of stress. There was a reason why the demons made Audrey the focus of their earlier attack—they saw some kind of threat in her."

She found that claim hard to believe. What did the demons think she was going to do… psychoanalyze them into oblivion?

But she didn't bother to contradict him. For some reason, she was drawn away from where he stood, toward the large dressing area, which had a pair of mirrors hanging above a wide, granite-topped vanity, and a door in the wall, which she assumed must lead to a walk-in closet.

Just looking at the closet was enough to send a cold shiver down her spine. She glanced away from it, toward one of the mirrors. Reflected in it was her face, which looked pale and pinched and tense, as though all the makeup Daniela had so carefully applied a half hour earlier had somehow managed to erase itself.

That wasn't the worst, though. Behind her reflected self, Audrey thought she detected a large, shadowy figure growing, coming closer toward her. She startled and looked over her shoulder, but all she could see was Michael walking into the dressing area, Chris and Susan a few paces behind him, recording everything.

Audrey could feel herself frown as she turned back toward the mirror—only to see a strange, cloudy darkness roiling within it, tendrils reaching out to wrap themselves around the gilded frame. The screeching laughter sounded in her ears again, although, judging by the way she was the only one who flinched and took a terrified step backward, no one else could hear it.

Behind her, Michael muttered a curse, then came over to stand squarely at her side. "Stand your ground," he said clearly. Was he enunciating for the cameras even now?

Stand her ground? She was ready to run and keep on running. But no, she couldn't do that. She needed to stay here at Michael's side and pretend to be brave for the cameras.

"This is not your home," he went on, now addressing the entity in the mirror. "This is not your place. Go now!"

The laughter only grew louder, even as the tendrils began to stretch across the wall, reaching for the other mirror, which so far seemed blessedly empty. Since they stood behind Michael and Audrey, she couldn't see either Susan's or Chris's expressions, but she noted how Michael's eyes narrowed and his shoulders hitched slightly, and wondered if he'd finally heard that inhuman laughter.

To her dismay, he stepped forward, moving closer to the mirror. She wanted to grab his arm, drag him back, but it felt as though enormously heavy weights held her in place, preventing her from doing anything but watching in horror.

Slowly, he reached into his pocket and drew out a small vial. Holy water? If Audrey hadn't been so terrified, every limb cold and as heavy as though her bones had suddenly turned to stone, she might have found herself laughing nervously. Holy water was for horror movies, wasn't it?

Apparently, Michael didn't think so, because he pulled the stopper out of the vial and said,

"This place is not yours. You have no claim on it. The light will not allow you here."

And he splashed the contents of the vial on the dreadful, smoky figure that clung to the mirror's frame and the wall next to it.

For a second, nothing happened. Then the laughter turned to a high-pitched screech, so shrill Audrey thought for sure it had blown out her eardrums, that if she'd had the strength to put her hands up to her ears, her fingertips would have come away smeared with blood. Even as she winced, the frame of the mirror bowed oddly, behaving more as if it was made of rubber than painted hardwood. And then it snapped back into place, the glass it held shattering into a thousand pieces.

That paralyzing weight now gone from her limbs, Audrey threw up her hands to protect her face, expecting to feel all those tiny shards of glass needling their way into her skin. But even as she tensed against the onslaught, it was gone. She stared at the wall, not sure of what she was seeing, while her heart pounded in her chest and every nerve ending seemed to shrill with an overload of adrenaline.

The mirror was whole and untouched, as if it had never held that horrible shadow, had never been broken by a supernatural force she couldn't begin to comprehend.

Michael turned toward Audrey, smiling slightly. He slipped the now-empty vial into his pocket, then looked past her shoulder to address his crew.

"You get that?"

They sat at one of the metal tables that bordered the pool. Despite her earlier misgivings about the weather, the sun had come out, was now shining brightly enough that normally Audrey would have taken off the leather jacket she wore, finding it too warm.

Not now, though. In that particular moment, she wasn't sure she would ever be warm again. Her hands still shook, and there was a core of cold in her body that the sun couldn't touch.

Brooke, the blonde P.A., had fetched them coffee. Chris was off to one side, watching the playback on his video camera and smiling slightly. Audrey didn't know where Susan, the sound technician, had disappeared to, but she knew if she were in Susan's place, she would have been well on her way to the least haunted place she could find…preferably one that offered alcohol.

Michael watched her with some concern. "Are you all right, Audrey?"

"Define 'all right.'" She sipped her coffee,

wishing someone had thought to slip some whiskey or cognac into it. Even though she didn't normally drink hard liquor, right then she thought she'd try anything to steady her nerves.

"It can be a little startling the first time." He drank some of his own coffee, then set the steel travel mug down on the patio table. "And, to be fair, I wasn't really expecting something quite that…spectacular."

"What *were* you expecting?" Audrey asked. She didn't bother to keep the accusation out of her voice; it was pretty clear to her that he'd been keeping some important particulars of this case close to the vest. In order to surprise her, make sure her reactions were genuine?

Oh, they'd been genuine, all right.

"I didn't know for sure." His eyes met hers, clear, earnest. The sunlight seemed to sparkle in the gold flecks in their depths. "You need to believe that, Audrey. People don't always keep the best records when it comes to hauntings or possessions. They don't want others to think they're crazy. A lot of this stuff gets swept under the rug."

"But there were cold spots, and smells, and strange voices."

"Yes, all those things. Auditory manifestations are rarely recorded, though."

"Did you get them this time?"

He nodded. "Oh, yes. Susan's very happy about that."

"I'm glad someone is," Audrey muttered, then took another sip of coffee. "So...what now? I mean, you've gotten some pretty spectacular footage, but I don't see how this brings us any closer to clearing the house of...whatever is in there."

"I'll analyze the footage, consult my library. If necessary, there are a few experts I can call."

"I thought you were the expert."

Michael gave her a thin smile. "I'm a jack of all trades compared to these guys. But they don't want to be on camera, don't want to be known as going on the record. Still, they should be able to offer some insights, if it comes to that."

Audrey didn't bother to hide the hopefulness in her voice. "Does that mean we're done for the day?"

"I think so. I told the owners that we'd need to be here for at least two days, possibly three, so we have some time." Now his gaze was appraising, although not in the way she was used to. "You probably need this time to assess and adjust. It can be hard, coming to terms with the realization that the universe is a much bigger place than you thought."

That was one way of putting it. Part of her brain still didn't want to acknowledge what she'd just seen, was trying to come up with plausible ways that the specter in the mirror could have been a trick. Audrey would be the first to admit that she didn't know a lot about movie magic, but it seemed to her that the shattered mirror and the fog that had boiled out of it would have required some fairly sophisticated practical effects. Yes, it would probably be easy to pull off that sort of thing with CGI, but she'd been there. She'd seen it for herself, heard it. Maybe there was a way to create all those phenomena without resorting to computers, but she didn't see how.

Which meant…it was all real?

"I'm not sure I'm ready to go there quite yet," she said, then drank some more coffee. It was strong and hot, doing its best to melt the chilly core of dread that seemed to be coiled in her belly.

Michael's eyebrows lifted. "Really? After what you just saw?"

"It was pretty spectacular, but I'm not sure it *proves* anything. You and your crew could have set all that up to get a rise out of me. Like you said, it looked great on camera."

Now he appeared downright angry, golden glints flashing from his eyes, lips thinning. "You don't really believe I would do something as low as that, do you?"

"I don't know," she said frankly. "Your history makes it pretty clear that you're not above a bit of showmanship if that's what it takes to get people to buy your books or DVDs, or subscribe to your YouTube channel."

His free hand, the one not holding the mug of coffee, clamped down on the tabletop. "You're pretty cynical for someone who studied at the Rhine Institute."

"Just because parapsychology interests me doesn't mean I'm willing to believe that demons lurk around every corner," Audrey shot back. "Scientific exploration of the outer limits of the human mind is a very different thing from believing in some sort of Old Testament version of good and evil, complete with demon hordes."

For a long moment, Michael didn't say anything, although she could tell from the way his chest rose and fell, his tight grip on the handle of his coffee mug, he was still angry. When he spoke, his tone was controlled but cutting. "I would think you'd be one of the first people to recognize there is very great evil in the world."

Audrey winced. Then she pushed out her chair and stood. She knew if she stayed there, she might say something she would regret later. As frightening as the day's events had been, she knew she needed to stick this out, and that certainly wasn't going to happen if she allowed herself to get in a knock-down argument with Michael Covenant.

Still, that didn't mean she couldn't leave. He'd already told her they were done for the day.

"I'm going to call a Lyft," she said distinctly, then turned on her heel and stalked away.

He didn't say anything, or try to stop her.

Somehow, she knew he wouldn't.

Chapter 4

No one else tried to keep Audrey from leaving, either, which meant Michael must have spoken the truth when he said he needed to take a breather, consult his books, maybe talk to some experts if necessary. She took her purse, which she'd left in the guest house they were using for the wardrobe and makeup room, and then got out her phone, opened the app, and called for a Lyft to come get her. Belatedly, as she was climbing into the driver's Toyota Camry, she realized that she was still wearing the clothes Kathleen had given her from the show's wardrobe, but since no one had stopped her, she figured it wasn't that big a deal.

Just as well. She didn't think she could handle the delay.

It felt strange to walk into her house, look at

the little metal clock on the mantel, and realize it was only one-thirty in the afternoon. So much had happened since she left this morning, it felt more like an entire day had passed.

Now that the sun was out, bright daylight streamed through the windows, gleaming on the restored oak floor. All was quiet except for the ticking of the clock, and the scolding of a pair of jays somewhere in the backyard. A serene, prosaic scene, and yet Audrey still felt cold, even though the T-shirt she wore under her borrowed leather jacket seemed to stick to her skin. She hadn't realized she was sweating that much.

Usually, if she had some spare time and needed to relax, she would draw a bath, let herself lie in the warm water and breathe in the scent of her favorite bath bomb—the one with the cucumber/melon scent—and maybe have half a glass of white wine to unwind. Now, though, the very thought of lying naked and exposed in the tub made another shiver pass over her.

Don't let him get to you, she told herself.

Unfortunately, it was probably too late for that.

She went to the kitchen and poured herself a glass of water, then drank half of it in one large gulp. When it hit her stomach, she realized she hadn't eaten anything since the toast and yogurt she'd hurriedly wolfed down at five-thirty that morning. However, despite her physical hunger, Audrey could tell that she really didn't want to eat anything. Her nerves jangled and her hands felt shaky, although that could have simply been from too much caffeine and not enough food.

Michael Covenant's words kept echoing in her mind, no matter how hard she tried to push them away.

I would think you'd be one of the first people to recognize there is very great evil in the world.

Never mind that good and evil were slippery concepts, and not ones that someone with her background liked to throw around with abandon. A therapist was supposed to say that while actions could be evil, people weren't. They were simply acting out their own neuroses, their own world views.

And yet, Audrey still had a hard time believing that the man who'd killed her parents wasn't evil. He'd never said why he did it. There hadn't been a note, or a manifesto left behind. He'd allowed himself to be arrested, and then was found dead in his cell three days after capture. No sign of any trauma, no obvious evidence of a heart attack— which would have been odd, since he was only in his early twenties—no poison, nothing.

The media called it the Waikiki Massacre, even though technically the gunman had fired down from his room on the eleventh floor of the

Hyatt Regency onto crowded Kalakaua Avenue and not onto the beach itself. Not that it mattered —by the time he was done, forty-two people had been killed, including Audrey's parents.

They'd gone to Hawaii to celebrate their twentieth wedding anniversary. At the time, she was fifteen years old. Her aunt Deb—her mother's older sister—was staying with Audrey while her parents were out of town…and she ended up staying through the whole ordeal and afterward, renting out her own house so her niece could stay at her high school and be surrounded by her friends, could have something of a normal life despite the tragedy that had struck, seemingly from nowhere. Her maternal grandparents made some token protests about taking her in, but they'd just sold their home in Murrieta and bought a condo in Scottsdale for the winter months and an RV for travel in the summer, and weren't in any real position to act as her guardians. And Audrey's paternal grandfather was dead, and her grandmother in a fifty-five-plus community in Florida, so that meant Deb was the only real choice.

In some ways, the gunman fit the typical profile of a mass shooter—he was a white male, a little younger than most mass shooters, but the difference wasn't terribly anomalous. His parents proclaimed that he'd never shown any interest in guns, had never exhibited any traits that might have been warning signs. In a way, despite her grief, Audrey had felt almost sorry for them, for their utter bewilderment at the tragedy that had hit their family as well. The shooter apparently had younger siblings, but the whole family went into hiding not too long after the massacre, concerned for their safety.

As for Audrey, her aunt Deb kept her from spiraling into her own anger and sorrow. She made sure her niece saw a therapist, did everything in her power to ensure Audrey wasn't permanently scarred by the event. Because she was a minor when the shooting occurred, she was off-limits to reporters after both she and her aunt made it clear that they didn't want to be interviewed. Besides, there were plenty of other angry surviving family members who were more than happy to talk to the press, to lobby for better gun-control laws. While Audrey understood their anger and the way they were channeling it, she didn't get involved. She graduated from high school, went to Pomona College in nearby Claremont. Audrey had always suspected that her aunt had something to do with that—she was an English professor at Scripps, another of the Claremont Colleges, and so it was entirely possible she'd pulled a few strings to make sure her niece was admitted, even though she was a good student, if not a stellar one.

At any rate, Audrey had done her best to put the past behind her. Possibly her parents would have been surprised by her interest in parapsychology, but she guessed they would be proud to know that she'd gotten her master's degree, had graduated without as much student debt as many of her peers, thanks to scholarships and grants and the part-time jobs she worked the entire time she was in school. Of course, it also helped that her parents' life insurance had paid off the house, which Deb ceded back to her once she was out of college and working full-time.

Well, mostly working. Audrey knew she needed to do a little better on that front. If she'd screwed things up with Michael Covenant by storming away from the Whitcomb mansion today, then she'd have to get her act together and start hustling for clients for real.

The roof creaked slightly and she startled, nearly dropping the water glass she held. Through the open window, she heard the rustling of the willow tree in the backyard, its fronds trailing over the small pond with its miniature waterfall her father had so carefully constructed when she was fifteen.

Just the wind. Audrey knew she really needed to get herself together, because she couldn't be jumping at every noise, every shadow. That was no way for an adult to function.

Even so....

She went upstairs to the master bath, stared at her overly made-up face, and grimly started the water running so she could wash it all off and start over. At the same time, she couldn't help shooting furtive glances at that mirror, wondering if something dark and foggy would start to loom somewhere in its depths, something that would begin to climb out and reach toward her—

Stop it, Audrey told herself. *Just stop it. Right now.*

She grabbed a towel and dried her face, then calmly applied moisturizer, mascara, and lip gloss. There. That looked more like her real self staring back from the mirror, which showed nothing except her own face and the innocuous water-colors of pansies and roses that she'd bought at a local craft market, hanging on the wall behind her.

Turning away from the mirror, she went over to the closet and extracted a few empty hangers, then took off her borrowed clothing and hung it up before getting into an outfit that wasn't too dissimilar, except that the T-shirt was white instead of gray. No need for a jacket, though, not with a cheerful sun shining down from overhead, seeming to laugh at her fears and the faint, creepy sensation she couldn't quite get rid of.

She'd cleared her calendar, and Audrey knew it would look very unprofessional to reach out to any of her clients to see if they wanted to come in for their sessions this afternoon after all. No, she'd just have to work through next weekend as she'd planned, and figure out something to do with the free time that had unexpectedly landed in her lap.

The problem was, she'd already done most of the little chores she'd been saving for when she had some idle time. She supposed there was no reason why she couldn't just go back downstairs to the living room, turn on the TV, and let a few hours of mindless programming do their best to erase the morning's events from her brain.

No reason except that it felt like a very bad idea.

Again she heard the roof creak, and again she looked out the window, making sure nothing was moving out there except the leaves on the trees and the birds flying overhead. It was a mild, lovely day, typical of Southern California in late February. There was absolutely no reason for her to be jumping at every sound, her heart beat speeding up even though her senses tried to tell her that her flight responses were way out of whack.

But she'd seen that entity emerging from the

mirror at the Whitcomb estate, had heard that frenzied, shrieking laughter throbbing in her ears. All those terrible phenomena had occurred only a mile or so from where she now stood.

It would have been better if she weren't alone, but the friends she'd made in high school and college had slowly drifted out of her orbit as people got married and moved away or simply became absorbed in the minutiae of surviving everyday life. Bettina was the only one who'd hung on, maybe because her duplex was only a few blocks away from Audrey's house…or maybe because she worried about what would happen to her friend if she were ever truly on her own.

However, since Bettina was at work and Audrey certainly wasn't about to bother her because she had a raging case of the heebie-jeebies, she knew she needed to come up with some other way of distracting herself. Something to make her feel a little better about the nightmare she'd witnessed earlier that day.

Something to protect herself.

An idea came to her then, one she wanted to dismiss as absurd, except that she knew ritual could be soothing, even if one didn't entirely believe in it. She'd encountered something other-worldly, and although she had no reason to believe it had followed her home, that didn't mean she couldn't create her own kind of shield.

Audrey wondered whether maybe she should smudge the house.

As soon as the thought crossed her mind, she wanted to laugh at herself. However, even if going through with the ritual turned out to be a complete waste of time, at least getting the materials together would give her something to do, would get her out of the house for a little while.

That seemed to settle it.

She picked up her purse and went out, locking the door behind her as she paused on the front porch. Her destination wasn't far, and it had turned into a lovely day, so she decided to walk.

Glendora's historic downtown was small, four or five blocks ranging along a street that bore the same name as the town itself. Sisters We was a metaphysical bookstore and depository for all sorts of mystical goods, ranging from various decks of Tarot cards to crystals and jewelry. Audrey had been in a few times because their book selection was actually fairly good and because she liked to support local businesses when she could. At any rate, she'd noticed that the store carried smudge sticks in various sizes, along with the abalone shells often used as fireproof bowls during smudging rituals, so she knew she would find what she wanted there.

She just had to hope she wouldn't run into anyone she knew while she was shopping. Her clients knew that she'd done some studies into the paranormal, but she'd always described her research in the most clinical terms possible. Just because she'd written papers on neurological anomalies in those claiming to be clairvoyant didn't automatically mean she was the type to load up on crystals and amulets and rune stones.

A scent of incense surrounded Audrey as soon as she entered the store, but something sharp and aromatic, not cloying like patchouli or nam champa. Soft harp music played in the background. She didn't see anyone else shopping, which suited her just fine. With any luck, she could be in and out of there before any other customers appeared.

"Can I help you?"

She turned and saw Rosemary McGuire, the youngest of the three sisters who owned the store —hence the name "Sisters We"—standing a few feet away from her. She had long brown hair that fell in wavy spirals almost to her waist, and she was wearing a tank top and a patchwork silk skirt. Audrey thought Rosemary was probably around her own age of twenty-nine, but her pixie-pretty features made it difficult to tell for sure.

"Hi," Audrey said, then faltered. So much for being in command of the situation.

Then she told herself to buck up. If she could face…whatever that was…this morning and live to tell the tale, then she should be able to handle a simple shopping transaction.

The words came out quickly, as though she'd realized the best thing to do was blurt it out and get it over with. "I need a smudge stick and a bowl."

"Sure," Rosemary said. "They're over here. We have several different sizes."

Audrey followed her to a shelf off to one side, where there was a pretty display with smudge sticks ranging from bundles of sage not much bigger than her pinky to oversized specimens that wouldn't have looked out of place in a Cheech and Chong movie. "Does the size matter?" she asked, then wanted to bite her tongue.

Somehow, Rosemary managed to maintain her serious, yet earnest expression. "Not really," she replied. "It depends on how often you plan to smudge your house. Obviously, you'll run through the smaller ones faster, so I tell the people who smudge a lot that they might as well get a bigger one to start. Same goes for the abalone shells—it's not like they're going to get used up or anything, but obviously you want one that's proportional to the size of the smudge stick you'll be using."

"Um…a medium one should be fine," Audrey said. Since she hadn't done much study on the subject, she hadn't realized that smudging was something you had to do on a regular basis. She supposed she'd been hoping that she could do it once, and that would keep the bad juju away permanently. "And a matching bowl."

"Do you have a white candle?"

"Candle?" she repeated, feeling a bit confused. Was that part of the ritual?

Rosemary gave her a patient smile. "You need something to light the smudge stick. Some people use a lighter, but the ritual has more strength if you use a candle to light the stick, and then keep the candle burning a bit after you're done smudging to let the positive energy linger a little while longer." She paused, head tilting as she studied Audrey, the tiny diamond in her nose piercing glittering in the sunlight from the display window at the front of the shop. "I can show you, if you want. Izzie's coming in to spell me so I can take a late lunch."

"Oh, no," Audrey said hastily. "I should be able to figure it out."

"It's really not a problem." A pause, and then Rosemary added, "You've been around something today, haven't you? Something...dark."

Audrey wanted to protest, but that cold, crawling sensation had returned. Now it felt as though the hair on the back of her neck was starting to lift. "Maybe," she allowed. "I'm still not sure exactly what it was. But I thought it couldn't hurt to surround myself with some positivity."

"It's a good idea," Rosemary said. "But if you're a beginner, you want to be careful. I really think I should help you."

"Help with what?" That was another woman's voice, just a bit deeper than Rosemary's. She came around the corner of some freestanding bookcases and paused a few feet away from where Audrey and Rosemary stood, head tilted in the same inquisitive way as her younger sister. At least, Audrey guessed this must be Isabel, the oldest sister, even though she'd only seen her name and hadn't met her before this. Like Rosemary, she had wavy brown hair, except she had it pinned up in an intricate mass on top of her head that managed to look effortlessly boho and probably would have been ridiculous on Audrey if she'd ever attempted such a look.

"Smudging," Rosemary said. "She brushed up against something pretty nasty today, and we want to make sure it doesn't follow her home."

Isabel studied Audrey for a moment. Then, without asking permission or saying anything at all, she reached out and laid a hand on her shoulder. Her eyes widened, and she shook her head. "What were you doing at the Whitcomb mansion?"

"How did you know that's where I was?" Audrey demanded, then realized by asking the question, she'd effectively prevented herself from protesting that she'd never heard of the place. As for Isabel being able to deduce her activities from earlier that day just by touching her shoulder… well, Audrey figured she could put that aside to ponder later.

The sisters exchanged a glance. "Glendora's not so big that it has an abundance of haunted mansions," Isabel said. "Not that the Whitcomb place is precisely haunted…it's much worse than that."

"How much worse?" Damn it, was that a slight quaver in her voice? Probably. Well, Audrey couldn't do anything about it now, although more than ever she wanted to curse Michael Covenant for not telling her up front exactly what he was getting her into.

"Let's go to your house," Isabel suggested. "We'll make sure the place is cleansed, and then—"

"And then we'll tell you about the Whitcomb mansion," Rosemary finished for her.

"What about the store?"

"Oh, it's not a problem," Rosemary said. "I already told CeeCee that she needed to come in."

Audrey could feel her brows lifting. "But I didn't see you call or text her—"

"No, you didn't," Isabel said briskly.

Telepathy? There were quite a few documented cases of siblings being able to share that kind of silent communication, although it was more common in twins or triplets, which clearly the McGuire sisters were not. Audrey itched to ask them more questions, but she knew they had more urgent matters to deal with at the moment.

From the small smiles both Isabel and Rosemary wore, she could tell they'd more than guessed at her internal questions. Giving an inward shrug, Audrey said, "Let's go to my house."

The sisters stood in the middle of the living room, slowly looking around, not speaking. Right then, Audrey was glad she'd gone on her cleaning spree over the weekend, because that meant the place was about as presentable as it was ever going to be.

They'd put the smudge stick and abalone bowl and candle on the coffee table, but they hadn't shown any sign of preparing for the ritual. Instead, they'd asked Audrey to wait off to one side as they reached out to feel the house's vibrations.

The Audrey Barrett of a few days ago might have scoffed at such a request. Now, though, she could only be glad they were here, since Michael Covenant apparently didn't care that she'd been rattled enough to walk off the set. She didn't even know whether he still wanted her to return to the mansion the next day, although, to be fair, she hadn't dug her phone out of her purse to see if she'd missed any messages.

"It's not here yet," Rosemary said, her voice dreamy, faraway. Her eyes were half closed now, hands hanging limply at her sides.

Audrey wanted to ask, *Yet??*, but didn't think it would be a good idea to disturb the other woman's focus or trance or whatever it was.

"No," Isabel said. Just like her sister, she had her eyes nearly shut, her clean, elegant features utterly still. "Its energies were disrupted by the TV crew, I think." Her eyes opened then, and she fixed Audrey with a bright blue stare. "You're lucky." A glance at her sister, and she added, "It's safe to begin now."

Rosemary nodded. From a pocket in her voluminous skirt, she produced a blue Bic lighter, so prosaic that Audrey couldn't help smiling a little as she looked at it. She placed the white candle on one of Audrey's soapstone coasters, then lit it. Once it had a good flame going, Rosemary picked up the sage smudge stick and passed it over the tip of the flame several times. It caught, and a wisp of smoke rose from it. Within a few seconds, it was releasing more smoke, enough that Audrey had to fight to keep from coughing.

"*Air, fire, water, earth. Cleanse, dismiss, dispel,*" Rosemary chanted, going to each corner of the living room. Isabel followed, murmuring the words as well. Since Audrey didn't quite know what she was supposed to do, she stayed where she was. Once they were finished with that room, however, Isabel gestured for her to follow them.

"We have to do the whole house," she said in an undertone, and so Audrey went with them as they walked from room to room on the first floor, then trailed in their wake when they made their way upstairs, where they repeated the ritual in the master bedroom, the guest room, and the office, which had once been Audrey's childhood bedroom.

Throughout all of this, Rosemary's voice never flagged, although Audrey reflected it was a good thing the house really wasn't all that big. A place as huge as the Whitcomb mansion would take forever to cleanse.

Although I have a feeling it would take a lot more than a few sticks of sage to clear that place out, she thought as she followed the sisters back down to the living room, where Rosemary carefully tamped out the smudge and laid it in its abalone bowl. The white candle was still burning, and she paused for a few moments, hands cupped around it, eyes closed, before she blew it out as well.

"There," she said, opening her eyes to look at Audrey and her sister. "I think that should do it."

Isabel nodded, although her response wasn't exactly reassuring. "For now, at least."

"'For now'?" Audrey echoed.

"You should do that every morning," Rosemary said. "And probably every time you go out someplace where you're surrounded by a lot of people. Crowds can really sap your psychic energy."

"It's all right," Audrey told her. "I don't have any concerts or Lakers games on the docket right now."

"Maybe not, but it's still good to be careful."

She nodded. "Can I get you some water? Now that you're done with the smudging, maybe you can tell me what's really going on at the Whitcomb mansion."

Rosemary and Isabel exchanged another of those glances, and once again Audrey got the impression that they were sharing some kind of nonvocal communication. Right then, she wished she had access to the equipment she'd used at the Rhine Institute, because she would have loved to get a look at their brainwaves while they were engaging in such activity.

"You told me you would," she added, an edge creeping into her voice. "I'm kind of surprised I never heard anything about it, considering I've lived here all my life and never heard any of my friends mention anything being wrong with the house."

"Oh, the various owners did their best to make sure word never got out," Isabel said. "Or rather, the thing living in that house made sure."

"Then how did Michael Covenant find out about it?"

"We don't know," Rosemary replied. "It could be that the current owners' desperation was stronger than the entities' desire to stay hidden."

"'Entities'?" Audrey repeated. That didn't sound very reassuring.

"You should probably sit down," Isabel said. "And thank you for the offer of some water, but we're fine."

Audrey nodded and began to head toward the armchair to the left of the sofa, only to be interrupted by the sound of the doorbell. Startled, she looked over at the two sisters, but they only lifted their shoulders. Obviously, whatever might be living in the Whitcomb mansion, it probably wouldn't waste time by doing something so polite as ringing a doorbell.

Shooting them an apologetic smile, Audrey went to the door and opened it.

Standing on the doorstep was Michael Covenant.

Chapter 5

EVEN THOUGH THE DAY HAD WARMED UP considerably, he still wore his black jacket. Unsmiling, eyes fixed on hers, he said, "We need to talk."

"Yes, you do," said Isabel, who'd appeared behind Audrey's left shoulder. "It seems as though you haven't been entirely truthful with Ms. Barrett."

Judging by the way his jaw set, Michael wasn't very happy to see her. "What are you doing here, Isabel?"

"Giving Audrey some much-needed help," Rosemary chimed in as she came over to stand next to her sister. "Since you left her high and dry."

"I can explain," he began, and Audrey cut him off.

"Yes, I think that's exactly what you should do."

"Alone," he said, gray-gilt eyes narrowing.

She really didn't think he was in a position to be demanding anything, but she knew she ran the risk of him leaving if she didn't agree to a private conversation. Maybe she should have simply told him that their professional association was at an end, but if he came at her with his entertainment lawyers for breach of contract, she'd be in a world of hurt. That kind of lawsuit wasn't the sort of thing her friend Bettina could help her with, and she knew she couldn't afford to hire an actual attorney.

"Fine," Audrey replied, although she made sure that her tone indicated the situation was anything but fine. Wearing an apologetic smile, she turned toward the two sisters, who both stood in almost the same pose, hands on their hips, disapproving expressions on their faces. "Thank you so much for all your help, but—"

"But His Highness requires an audience," Rosemary broke in. "I get it. Come on, Isabel."

Audrey almost expected Isabel to protest, but she wore a resigned expression, as if she knew she had done what she could and needed to let matters run their course. As she moved past Audrey and onto the front porch, she said in an undertone, "You know how to find us. If you need help, don't hesitate to reach out."

About all she could do was nod. Rosemary, not as restrained as her sister, snapped at Michael, "You'd better tell her everything, or we'll know!"

He didn't respond, only stood there in stony silence as Isabel took Rosemary by the arm and led her down off the porch.

Audrey could have done without that particular confrontation, but she supposed it could have been worse. "Come on in."

He entered the living room, and she closed the door behind him. Almost at once, his gaze moved to the spent smudge stick in its abalone bowl, the white candle sitting next to them. The sharp scent of burned sage still lingered in the air. "That's what they were doing here?"

"Yes," she said crisply, "since it seemed obvious that you had more important things to deal with."

Once again, his lips thinned. "You were safe."

"Can you guarantee that?"

Since she'd been trained to observe people's responses, she noticed right away how his gaze slid away from hers. "'Guarantee' is a strong word."

"Hmm." Her throat was dry—possibly from the lingering smoke scent in the air, even though the windows were open—and so she said, "I need a glass of water. You want one?"

"Sure."

Audrey left him standing by the coffee table in the living room and went to fetch some water. Since she kept a pitcher in the fridge, it was nice and cold. She took a few sips from her own glass, steeling herself for the upcoming conversation, before she went back out to where Michael was waiting for her. He still stood where she'd left him, hands jammed into the pockets of his trousers, a faint frown pulling at his brows.

"Here," she said, and handed him his glass. "And please sit down."

He didn't protest, but took a seat in the armchair. Deprived of her favorite spot, Audrey sat at the end of the couch closest to the chair.

Once they were both settled, she asked, "Did you really have to consult some 'experts,' or were you just using that as a ploy to give yourself some time to think?"

Now he smiled, although his expression had little humor in it. "You're a very perceptive woman, Audrey."

"I take it that's a yes on the second option."

Michael took a sip of water, then put his glass down on one of the unused coasters on the coffee table. "I'll be honest—I wasn't expecting that kind of an attack right away. Usually, the house likes a bit of settling-in time before that sort of thing happens."

"'The house'?" she echoed. "You're saying it's the house and not something else?"

"No. I phrased that badly." He rubbed his hands on the knees of his trousers. "It's just that most of the manifestations have something to do with the house. They don't appear out of nowhere—they come out of the mirrors, or the closets, or from under the beds."

In a confirmation of just about every childhood nightmare Audrey had ever had. Fighting back a shudder, she said, "Maybe you should start at the beginning."

A long pause, and then he gave a reluctant nod. "I don't have all the details," he began, as if he knew he needed to preface his explanation with some kind of warning. "We're talking about more than a hundred years of history, after all. But, from what I've been able to tell, the place has been cursed from the beginning. Three workmen died during its construction, which was unusual even in the days before OSHA. And the people around him said Jeffrey Whitcomb began to change almost as soon as he moved into the place."

"That soon?" she asked, startled. "And he still lived there for more than fifteen years? You told me earlier today that he lost everything in the stock market crash."

"Yes, but he wasn't living in the house by that point. His concerned children moved him to a sanatorium some five years earlier, in late 1924. Apparently, he began to show some signs of instability within a few years of taking up residence in the house, to the point where his wife left him—it was quite a scandal at the time—and took the children with her to raise them on her own. They were all too glad to sell the house when the time came, although they were very tight-lipped about exactly what had gone on there."

Audrey crossed her arms. "What exactly *did* go on in the house?"

Michael leaned over and picked up his glass of water, drank some more. "Jeffrey Whitcomb became obsessed with the occult. He had a steady stream of mediums, swamis, and all sorts of charlatans—the words of his associates, not mine—coming and going. I think that was when Alice Whitcomb finally picked up and left. She actually died in 1920, and so it was the children who oversaw their father's removal to the sanatorium. They were also the ones who had the house redone before it was sold…but they couldn't quite keep the workmen from talking about what they saw."

"What did they see?" Audrey asked, even though she wasn't sure whether she really wanted to know the answer to that question.

"The carpets in some of the rooms had been pulled back, and strange circles and symbols had been painted on the wooden floors beneath,"

Michael said. A sideways look from those glinting eyes, and he added, "Spell circles, that is. Spells of summoning, spells to give the caster power over those around him."

"Summoning demons?"

"Yes. You might be thinking that Jeffrey Whitcomb's wealth was a result of those practices, but he was rich before he ever came to California, and, as far as I've been able to tell, he had absolutely no interest in the occult until he moved into the house. It was working on him, rather than vice versa...or at least, that's what seems to have happened, based on the evidence."

"Oh." Once again, her spine prickled, and the flesh on her scalp crawled. Maybe at some point she'd get used to hearing about these sorts of things, but she doubted it. These weren't stories told to frighten her, but only a recitation of facts. She knew what she'd seen in that mirror. That hadn't been a story. It was real.

Michael hesitated, as though he expected Audrey to say something else. When she remained silent, he shrugged slightly, then continued. "The first buyers were here less than a year. They never really said why they left, although the general belief was that Glendora was too quiet for them, and they were moving back to San Francisco. After that, the place changed hands about every three or four years, as far as I've been able to tell.

The person who lived here the longest was a man named Abner Crawford—he stayed for more than a decade. But then his children found him hanging from a beam in the master suite, and the revolving door started up again."

That image made Audrey want to shudder again, partially because she'd walked under those very same beams only a few hours earlier. What if she'd looked up and seen a ghostly image of the dead man hanging there in the same place where his children discovered him all those years ago?

Then again, it wouldn't have been any worse than what she'd actually experienced....

"Is it something about the land?" she asked. "Was the house built on an old Indian burial ground or something?"

Michael shook his head, one corner of his mouth twisting slightly. "If only it were that easy. There's no record of anything like that on the site, but I suppose it's possible there was something else, some kind of relic or artifact that draws negative energy to the place. There aren't any ley lines —what some call rivers of supernatural energy— anywhere near the house. Maybe it all really does go back to Jeffrey Whitcomb. The seeds of his madness could have been planted years before he moved here, but they only blossomed once he was in the right place."

"So...what are we talking about here, really?"

Audrey sat up a little straighter, her hands wrapped around the tall glass of cool water she held. "And no bullshit this time, Michael. I mean it."

From the way his eyes flared slightly at her remark, she could tell she'd startled him. That was the first time she'd sworn in his presence, but if what had happened in the master suite of the Whitcomb mansion was only a harbinger of things to come, it sure as hell wouldn't be the last.

"The rituals Jeffrey Whitcomb performed found their audience," Michael said slowly. "When you open yourself to those sorts of energies, you have to understand that there are entities who will answer. Only they're not coming to do your bidding. They're coming to find a weakness, to exploit you any way they know how. A skilled practitioner of black magic, of summoning, knows how to close the gateways he's opened and seal them so those entities can't return, but that's not what happened here. When Whitcomb's children took him away, they didn't allow him to close the loop, so to speak. The gate stayed open."

"And things kept coming through it," Audrey said. Suddenly, the glass she held felt freezing cold instead of pleasantly cool, and she hastily set it back down on its coaster.

From the way Michael's gaze flickered toward the glass, she could tell he hadn't missed any of that. However, he didn't comment, only replied, "Yes, things keep coming through it. What we need to do is locate where the gate is, so we—or rather I—can close it once and for all."

"You're an exorcist, too?" she asked, her tone clearly skeptical.

"Not exactly," he replied. "We aren't dealing with possession here, but rather a demonic infestation. Like I said, usually it takes a while for the demons involved to start ramping up their activity. In this case, I think they recognized us as a threat and therefore mounted an attack as soon as they detected our presence."

"I don't know why a demon would see me as a threat," Audrey said, wishing she didn't sound so shaky. She was supposed to be the cool, calm, rational one, wasn't she?

"I didn't understand it at first, either," Michael said. He leaned back in his chair as he watched her, his expression brooding. "But after seeing the way you fainted, hearing you describe what you experienced, clearly you're far more psychic than you believe."

She wanted to laugh, but her throat felt too dry for that. However, she knew he had to be mistaken. She'd spent too much time around people who truly were psychic, had taken enough tests of that sort of ability to know that she simply didn't have that kind of talent.

Her skepticism must have shown on her face, because he said, "I can tell you don't want to believe me. Why? Are you afraid of being the subject after so many years of being the researcher?"

"No," Audrey replied. "That's not it. I just know I'm not psychic. I think it's more that the demons targeted me because they wanted to mess with my head."

"Well, that is something they enjoy doing. But I think we're dealing with more than that here." He rubbed at the dark gold scruff on his chin. "Have you ever had any experiences like the one you had earlier today in the Whitcomb mansion? Hearing sounds that weren't there, odors that didn't seem to have any physical cause?"

She wanted to say no. But....

His voice lowered slightly, became almost coaxing. "Tell me, Audrey."

She glanced away from him, partly because it suddenly felt too intimate with only the two of them there in her living room, and partly, for some strange reason, because she could suddenly recall how it had felt with him holding her after she had fainted, the strength of his arms, the soothing rise and fall of his chest as he breathed. For a moment—a second, really—she'd felt safe, which was just ridiculous. No one was safe inside the Whitcomb mansion.

To stall for time, Audrey reached over and got her glass of water, took a couple of swallows. Was she really going to confide in him? She'd kept this story to herself for her entire adult life, mostly because she knew no one would believe her. But Michael did believe in this sort of thing…and he also seemed to believe there was more about her than met the eye.

Finally, she said, "When I was fourteen, my parents and I went to New Orleans. We did the typical tourist stuff, but I was going through a sort of goth phase at the time, and I wanted to go on one of those ghost tours. You know, where they take you around to various haunted sites."

Voice still calm and quiet, he replied, "Yes, I know what ghost tours are."

Of course he did. For all she knew, he'd guided a few of them in his time. "Right. Well, for most of it, I didn't really feel anything at all, even though the tour guide was doing his best to give everyone the creepy crawlies in every place we visited. But then we started walking toward one particular building, and I started to feel nauseated —really sick. I told my parents I couldn't go any closer, and I went to stand across the street so I wouldn't vomit."

"And what was it about the building, Audrey?"

She stared down at her hands in her lap, at the French manicure she'd gotten so she would look polished and put together on camera. "It belonged to a man back in the 1830s, something around then, anyway. He was supposed to be a doctor, but he performed all sorts of horrible experiments on slave women. No one really knows how many of them died in that place. The tour guide thought I must have been feeling some of the psychic residue from their pain and suffering."

That all sounded absolutely preposterous when she said it out loud, even though she knew that getting strange vibes from a particular location was really quite common. She risked a glance over at Michael, and for once he wasn't frowning. Instead, he looked almost pleased.

"More evidence that you're a sensitive," he said. "Or at least, sensitive to negative vibrations and atmospheres. No wonder the Whitcomb mansion affected you so much. Is there anything else?"

"Nothing like the New Orleans experience," she answered, hedging. The last thing she wanted to do was relive the worst moment of her life.

But he wouldn't let it go. "It doesn't have to be exactly like that particular incident," he said, his tone reasonable, persuasive. "Anything out of the ordinary that happened to you, that didn't seem to have a rational explanation."

"I—" Once again, her mouth felt dry, and she sipped some more water. "It was the day my parents died. That is, at the time, I didn't know they'd died. We—we didn't get the phone call until hours later. But...."

His face looked pale. He pressed his lips together, then said quietly, "They died in the Waikiki Massacre, didn't they?"

"How did you know that?" she demanded, feeling somehow violated that he'd been privy to something as terrible and secret as the way her parents had died, something she'd done her best to keep in the past.

"It was in your background check," he said, tone still calm, almost soothing, as if he'd guessed she'd be upset that he knew such a thing about her. "Colin does one for anybody he's considering using in one of his shows. Even though you were a minor at the time, it's still public record."

This explanation sounded reasonable enough, but Audrey still hated that his producer had gone digging through her personal history. It should have had absolutely no bearing on her ability to appear on the show.

"Right." She pulled in a breath, then another. God knows she'd discussed that terrible event enough times with her own therapists that talking about it now with Michael shouldn't be that big a deal.

Only...she'd never told anyone what had

happened the day they'd died, not even her aunt Deb.

"We were just about to have dinner," Audrey said. "My aunt Deborah was staying with me while my parents were on vacation. She'd decided to give me a treat, so she'd ordered pizza for the two of us. I remember that she was at the door, paying the delivery guy. And then…." The words trailed off. Even after so many years, she still wasn't sure she trusted herself to describe what had happened next.

"And then…?" Michael prompted, still in that gentle tone which barely sounded like his own voice.

"This terrible, knifing pain went through my head. I was standing by the dining room table—I'd just put down the plates and napkins for dinner. I guess I thought I was having a stroke or an aneurysm or something. I grabbed the back of the chair and hung on, because I was worried that I was about to fall to the floor. Then the pain was just…gone. By the time my aunt came to the table with the pizza, I'd gotten ahold of myself enough to pretend that everything was okay."

"But it wasn't."

"No," Audrey said. "I did the math later, and it turned out I'd experienced that blinding pain in the very moment my mother was killed. The bullet hit her here." She raised a hand to briefly touch her right temple. Not looking at him, she added, "I've never told anyone that story."

So gentle, so quiet. "Why not?"

"Because I didn't want to sound crazy. I mean, I'd experienced it, and it seemed crazy even to me. Later on, I tried to tell myself that the timing had to be off, that I'd just attempted to manufacture a story to make it sound as if something paranormal was going on. For a while, I almost convinced myself." Her gaze still focused on the trees outside the window, she said, "But not for very long."

"That's because you knew it was true, that it had really happened to you." For a moment, he was quiet, hands still resting on the knees of his dark trousers. "Unfortunately, it's a common story. Not what happened to you exactly," he went on, as if he knew Audrey was about to protest that her experience was anything but common, "but how you felt compelled to hide it from everyone. There's such a taboo in our society about admitting to any kind of psychic talent."

She knew that just as well as he did, thanks to her studies in the field. Modern American culture was almost relentlessly focused on the prosaic, on things that could be easily measured. Psychic ability didn't fit in the box, so to speak, which was probably why it had become the subject of such ridicule. While she knew that her own strange experiences had been part of the reason for her wanting to explore the world of the psychic, she wasn't sure she wanted to admit that she possessed any of those gifts herself.

"It never happened again," she said, still trying to explain her behavior. "And nothing like the incident in New Orleans, either."

"Because you didn't encounter anything that might evoke that sort of response. Until today, anyway," he added. His gaze met hers, and for some reason, she found it hard to look back at him. Was it only that she'd just given him a little piece of herself, something no one else knew?

Or maybe it was that she still couldn't quite erase the sensation of lying in his arms, which was ridiculous. Michael had offered her assistance, nothing more. They were colleagues, and besides....

"Are you still angry with me?" he asked.

The question made Audrey's eyes widen a bit. They'd been sidestepping around the issue the whole time he'd been there at her house, but he knew just as well as she did that she'd marched away from the Whitcomb mansion while practically seething with anger.

"I don't know," she said honestly. "I don't appreciate being used like that. But since you were willing to sit down and tell me the truth about the Whitcomb place, I'm not quite as angry as I was a few hours ago."

"Good," he replied. "Because I'd like you to go back there with me."

Had he lost his goddamn mind? She stared at him, wondering if maybe she simply hadn't heard him correctly. "Excuse me?"

A smile, one that seemed to acknowledge her incredulity while trying to give her a reason to ignore it. "I know it sounds crazy. But I'd really like to be with you to watch your reactions. Just the two of us. No cameras, no crew. No gimmicks."

"I don't see what purpose that would serve," she told him. "We've already proved that the entities in the house don't react positively to me."

"True, but it's exactly because you reacted so strongly to the negative energies in the house that I want to see how you'll do without so many distractions." He shifted in the chair so he was turned toward her, bent slightly forward, his expression earnest. "I promised the owners of the house that we would clear it for them, but even though I've walked through the place several times, I still haven't been able to detect the source of the evil, what exactly is still drawing the demons there."

"Try the bathroom mirrors," she said with a shaky laugh.

Michael didn't smile. "They might have been using the mirrors as gateways, but something else is bringing them to the house. It's sort of like… like an airport."

"'An airport'?" Audrey repeated, brows lifting.

"I know it sounds strange, but bear with me." Now he actually got up out of his chair and went to the window, pausing so he could peer outside for a few seconds. "The mirrors were functioning like runways, for lack of a better term. However, it's the air traffic controllers in the tower who help to guide the planes in, and so there has to be something else in the house, something that's acting basically like the tower at an airport, showing the demons where they're supposed to go."

His explanation made some sense, but she didn't bother to tell him that. "Haven't you already been over the entire house?"

"Yes, but clearly, I missed something. I'm hoping that your senses will detect something when mine couldn't."

Audrey hesitated. After all, it was bad enough to have been in that place when accompanied by a film crew, knowing that other people associated with the production were still on the grounds somewhere, even if they weren't in the same room that Michael and she had been in. But to go there alone with him, with no help, no backup? That sounded like a recipe for disaster.

The coaxing voice was back. "It will be fine," he said. "Didn't I protect you last time?"

Well, using the word "protect" might be stretching things a bit. Yes, he'd driven back the demons, but it wasn't as if he'd stepped in front of them and offered to meet them in single combat to defend her honor or something. Not that she really expected anything of the sort, but....

"Say I do go back there with you," Audrey began, then held up a hand as an eager glow appeared in his gold-gray eyes. "I'm not saying I will, but if I do. You made it sound as though Colin wanted my reactions to be as realistic as possible, that I was supposed to be experiencing everything fresh, so to speak. If we go there together now and we do locate the source of the negativity, so to speak, then we'll have to do it all over again for the cameras."

Michael appeared singularly unconcerned by that prospect. "I'm not worried about it. We'll put on a good show. Really, there's going to be a percentage of those watching the episode who will think everything is fake. That episode with the mirror—it was terrifying for us, but one of those skeptics seeing it six months down the line is just going to dismiss it as CGI. Pretty decent CGI, but still."

She couldn't argue that point with him, mostly because she'd thought close to the same thing at the time, even as shaken as she was. Even so, was she mentally prepared to go back there?

A horrible suspicion crossed her mind. "You're —you're not luring me back there to scare the shit out of me and capture it all on hidden cameras, are you?"

"Of course not!" Michael exclaimed. He looked genuinely offended that she would even think such a thing, but really, after what had happened earlier in the day, it wasn't outside the bounds of possibility. Voice a little calmer, he went on, "I understand why you might not want to trust me, but there are no hidden cameras. No tricks. I just want to see what you can do with your talent when you allow it to guide you."

Privately, she wasn't sure her "talent" amounted to much, but....

If it really existed, was as strong as Michael Covenant seemed to think it was, shouldn't she do whatever she could to develop that talent? It might be something that could help protect her against the entities infesting the Whitcomb house. Ignoring such a gift now wouldn't serve any useful purpose.

"All right," she said after a long pause. "Let's go back to the mansion and see what we can find."

Chapter 6

As Michael pulled his ancient Land Cruiser into the driveway of the Whitcomb house, Audrey reflected it would be hard to tell that a film crew had even been there earlier in the day. All of the cars were gone, and it looked as though both the driveway and the paths leading from it had been carefully swept. Possibly the support crew wasn't as affected by the negative energies in the house as she had been, or maybe they'd been relatively safe because they hadn't actually gone inside.

Now, with the sun out, the place looked serene enough, front lawn green and smooth under the blue sky, the palm trees that edged the grass rustling faintly in the breeze. Off to one side, a fountain played quietly, the sound soothing.

Or rather, it should have been soothing. Right

then, Audrey found herself irritated by its irregular splashing noises because they could have been masking something much more frightening, more sinister.

"Are you okay?" Michael asked as he came around the front of the SUV.

"So far," she replied.

"You're not getting anything out here?"

She shook her head.

"Okay, we'll go inside—through the conservatory, just like we did last time."

Following him as he headed down the pathway, Audrey asked, "Why don't you ever go in through the front door?"

"The current owners specifically asked us not to. They thought we'd attract less attention coming and going from the side entrance."

Well, maybe that was a valid concern, although anyone driving by on the street where the driveway was located would have known something was up as soon as they saw all the vehicles parked there. Even now, with just Michael's Land Cruiser in the drive, they'd have to know something was going on—for no other reason than anyone who could afford to live in a place like this would probably own something a little more impressive.

The conservatory looked the same as well, no sign at all that the crew had been in here earlier.

Michael closed the door behind him and Audrey. "Anything here?"

She held herself still, wondering if she was going to be assailed by the overwhelming odor of mildew, or whether those cacophonous shrieks were going to once again start up inside her head. Then again, she really hadn't experienced anything out of the ordinary until they went into the dining room.

"No," she said. "I don't feel anything at all."

Well, nothing except a creeping sense of unease at being here in the first place. She had to fight the urge to stand closer to Michael. Not that his was the most comforting of presences, but because she knew he was the only thing standing between her and an attack from those…things.

He didn't reply, but led her through the living room, barely pausing there before he went on to the dining room. She'd guessed he would bring her there because that was where the first assault occurred.

"What about here?"

Once again, Audrey made herself stand still and do her best to reach out to whatever entities or energies might be lurking here. Now she felt nothing. No mildew smell, no unearthly shrieks. For the first time, she was able to really focus on the room, on the long table with its ranks of matching chairs, the white-painted wainscoting, the truly unattractive floral wallpaper.

"Still nothing," she said, and shrugged, trying to seem casual although her whole body was tense, waiting for the next blow to fall. Trying to sound flip, she added, "Although that wallpaper is a crime in and of itself."

His lips twitched slightly. "Duly noted. However, they didn't hire us for our interior decorating skills."

"Too bad. This place could use it."

And it could. Audrey hadn't paid much attention to how dated the furnishings and interiors actually were, because at the time she'd been basically scared out of her wits. Now she could see that, despite its very high price tag, this place was going to need some major updating.

Not her problem, though. The only thing she needed to worry about was the unearthly presences in the house.

They could be tricky little bastards, though. She hadn't done much research in demonology, but she'd hastily read through a few books over the weekend, trying to get herself mentally prepared for whatever might lie ahead. One of the demons' favorite tactics was to fool a person into thinking they were gone, that an attack had been a one-time thing.

Well, based on what Michael had told her

about the history of this house, Audrey knew that sure as hell wasn't true.

Slowly, she walked out of the dining room and into the kitchen. This space looked as though it had been updated fairly recently, judging by the expensive pale, polished granite of the counter-tops, the enormous stainless-steel Jenn-Air appliances. She also didn't get any kind of a feeling from the room, except possibly a small stab of envy for people who could afford a kitchen that was bigger than a postage stamp. Her parents had taken excellent care of their renovated Craftsman, but they'd never had the money to knock out walls and enlarge the hopelessly tiny kitchen there.

"Still nothing," Audrey said.

Michael didn't seem too concerned. Hands in his pockets, he looked around the kitchen, then gave a small nod. "Let's go downstairs."

"'Downstairs'?" she repeated, not sure she'd heard him correctly. "Aren't we already on the ground floor?"

"Yes, but the house has a basement. I think originally it was used for storage, but one of the owners in the '60s turned it into a game room."

She really didn't like the idea of going down into a basement, even one that had been reno-vated and used for something entirely innocuous.

"It'll be fine," he assured her. "Over here—the steps downstairs are through this doorway."

They'd passed the door as she and Michael walked down the short hallway that separated the dining room from the kitchen, but she hadn't paid it much attention at the time. It did look perfectly innocuous, painted white and with eight recessed panels. However, as soon as Michael opened it, a ripple of cold went through her body.

She didn't think she'd made any kind of a sound, but he paused by the open door and gave her a searching look. "Did you feel something, Audrey?"

"I—I think so," she replied. "A wave of cold."

"That's promising."

"'Promising'?" she repeated, not sure she'd heard him correctly.

"Well, just in that it indicates there might be something down there."

As remarks went, that one wasn't terribly reassuring. Right then, Audrey wished she had her smudge stick with her. Maybe she could have waved it in the air around her body and created some sort of a shield.

No, on second thought, one of those toy guns that lobbed water balloons. Water balloons filled with holy water.

Michael put his foot on the top step, then turned and looked back at her. "Come on,

Audrey. I'm here. I'm not going to let anything happen to you."

Famous last words, she thought. But she'd agreed to come here. She could have said no, told him that they needed to wait until they had the full backup of his crew. Then again, none of them were experts in the occult. It wasn't as though they would have been able to offer any real assistance.

And she wanted to prove to him that she was just as tough as he was, even if she was scared out of her mind.

Putting her foot on that step was one of the hardest things Audrey had ever done. She forced herself to do it, just as she'd forced herself to get on that "gravity drop" ride at a local amusement park when she was in high school, despite the churning worry in her stomach. Michael had turned on the lights, so at least it wasn't pitch black down in the basement, but as she followed him, step by step, she experienced a sensation of building pressure, almost as if something was pressing down on every inch of her body. Her ears began to ring, although she didn't hear the evil laughter that had assaulted her earlier in the day. There was no smell of mildew. Just the sensation of somehow entering a heavier atmosphere than what she was used to.

"Do you feel that?" Michael asked. His face

was strained and pale; a sheen of sweat stood out on his forehead.

"Yes," Audrey said, fighting to inhale enough oxygen to force the words out. "It's pretty bad."

"Almost there."

They came down from the bottom step and into the basement proper, which was a large, rectangular space that looked as though it had been decorated in 1968 and then left here to molder as a spectacular example of what not to do when updating your house. The carpet was shag in an ugly olive-green shade, and sticky-looking wood paneling covered the walls. Scandinavian-style teak furniture—probably hideously expensive back in the day—and an enormous console television up against one wall, the kind of TV she'd seen in the background of photographs of her mother and her aunt Deb when they were little girls.

Abruptly, the pressure stopped. Michael and Audrey looked at each other.

"Is that a good thing?" she asked.

"I doubt it," he said.

No sooner had he stopped speaking than the huge console television in its faux-wood cabinet began to rock back and forth, banging against the wall and knocking chips out of the wood panel-ing. She gasped, but Michael pulled a vial of holy water from his pocket and splashed some of its contents onto the television. It subsided, but Audrey got the feeling he'd only subdued it temporarily, that it was biding its time like an angry dog that knew it could break its chain any time it wanted.

Her hands were shaking. She clenched them into fists and made herself stand in the center of the room, reaching out as best she could with a talent she really didn't believe she possessed. The cold was back, seeping up through that ugly shag carpet, through the soles of her boots, and right up into her limbs. She ignored it, telling herself it wasn't real, was only another weapon used by the demons to keep her off-balance.

Well, if that was their plan, they were doing a good job of it. Her teeth began to chatter, and she found it almost impossible to focus. The TV console started to shift once more, but in a sullen way, as if it knew Michael would splash it with holy water again if it got too out of hand.

"Audrey?"

She shook her head, guessing that she wasn't capable of speech right then. The only way she could stop her teeth from chattering was to clench her jaw. That helped a little, but the cold never stopped, kept flowing up into her legs until they felt the way they had that one time when she'd camped out to watch the Rose Parade and overnight temperatures had dropped into the low forties…icy, numb, as if they belonged to someone else.

Nevertheless, she found herself stumbling on her nearly frozen limbs over to one wall, almost as if something outside her body was guiding her there. Before she truly realized what she was doing, Audrey had dropped to her knees and was scrabbling at the hideous green shag carpet, pulling it away from the baseboards.

Beneath the carpet and its padding—which basically disintegrated beneath her fingertips—wasn't cement, but wooden floorboards. However, the first one she touched felt loose, as if it hadn't been firmly nailed down…or something had tried to pull it up. As she pried it loose, she finally came across the concrete substrate beneath.

It was covered—at least the portion she could see—in strange runes and symbols, overlapping circles and triangles. Audrey couldn't begin to guess what they all meant, but she had a pretty good idea why they were there.

"M-Michael!" she called out, teeth still chattering.

At once he was next to her, peering down at what she'd uncovered. "This is it," he said, his voice grim. "This is what's been calling them here."

"C-can you get rid of it?"

"Yes," he replied. "But we're going to have to pull up the whole floor. If—"

He didn't get a chance to finish the sentence, because in the next moment, all hell broke loose, the oversized television flinging itself away from the wall, the Danish modern coffee table and chairs all taking to the air and flying toward them. Audrey screamed, flattening herself against the vomit-green shag carpet, while Michael crouched next to her, doing his best to shield her from the flying furniture. The pressure and the cold in the room increased to the point where she wasn't sure whether she would have been able to lift herself from the floor even if she'd wanted to.

"Stairs," he murmured in her ear, which had begun to ring again from all the pressure being exerted on it. "Come on."

Sobbing in terror, she began to inch her way across the game room to the basement stairs, which now felt about a thousand miles away. Michael followed her, murmuring something she couldn't quite make out, but which sounded like Latin. Some kind of spell or invocation to keep the furniture at bay? She didn't know. The only thing she did know was that somehow, miraculously, even though those objects continued to circle the two of them like oversized birds of prey, none of them touched either her or Michael, although she could feel her hair ruffling in the breeze caused by the passage of one of the chairs.

A lifetime later, they reached the bottom stair and began to crawl upward. A few steps further, and walls were safely around them, partially shielding Michael and Audrey from the onslaught of the demonically propelled furniture. However, that didn't prevent the entities wielding those objects from trying to get in one last lick, as the console TV smashed into the entry to the stairs, glass and wood and its internal components spraying everywhere.

At once, the pressure that had been bearing down on Audrey disappeared. She got to her feet and ran up the rest of the steps until she reached the relative safety of the kitchen hallway. Michael was only a pace or two behind her, and he slammed the door shut as soon as he emerged from the stairwell.

They stared at each other for a few moments, both of them panting from exertion, and then, incongruously, he began to laugh.

"Are you fucking insane?" she demanded, staring at him in disbelief.

"Sorry," he said. "I just wish I'd gotten that on camera, because I know Colin isn't going to believe me when I explain it to him."

She shook her head. "Can we get out of here, please?"

"Of course."

They hurried into the kitchen, then went out through a door she hadn't noticed previously, one that led directly into the backyard. Once she was outside, with the sun shining down on her and the sound of a distant fountain helping to cover the traffic noise from Sierra Madre Boulevard, Audrey felt a little better. Not a lot, but some. At least her heart no longer felt as if it was about to pound its way out of her chest.

Michael glanced over at her. "You okay?"

"Define 'okay.'" She took a deep breath, glad that the air was cool and clean. It helped—if only a little—to scrub away some of the residue of that terrible encounter.

"You're here, and you're safe. I'd define that as okay."

"Then I guess I'm all right." She straightened her jacket and sent a frightened little glance back at the house, but everything seemed to be quiescent...for the moment. "So, what do we do next?"

He ran a hand through his over-long hair, which glinted dark gold in the sunlight. "I'll need to do a dispelling ritual, but I'll have to get permission from the owners to tear up the floor in the basement so I can erase all those summoning sigils."

"That's what they were?"

"Yes. Pretty dark stuff."

"Do you think Whitcomb put it there?"

"Maybe. Probably." Michael paused and glanced up at the house, at the white-painted exterior that hid such darkness within. "I do know one thing, though."

"What's that?"

"I need a drink."

The town's one and only wine bar—Glendora Terroir—was located just two doors down from Isabel and Rosemary's metaphysical bookstore. As Michael and Audrey walked past the storefront of Sisters We, she stole a surreptitious glance at the window, wondering if the two of them were inside, observing hers and Michael's progress and sharing disapproving looks. However, she only caught a glimpse of an older man perusing one of the bookshelves, with no signs of any of the three owners.

She'd have to remember to ask Michael why Rosemary and Isabel had been so openly hostile toward him. That is, she could guess at some of the reasons why, but she was still curious.

At a little before three on a weekday afternoon, the wine bar wasn't very busy. A couple who looked like they might be retired sat at the bar, but the tables and the little conversation area with its low sofa and matching chairs were all empty.

Michael sat down on the sofa, probably because it was located at the far end of the space and therefore was least likely to lend itself to eavesdropping. Not that the man and woman at the bar seemed very interested in the newcomers; they cast an incurious gaze in Audrey's direction, but turned back to their own glasses of wine as soon as Michael and Audrey had settled themselves and picked up a couple of menus to peruse.

After a brief inward struggle, she'd sat next to Michael, mostly because it would have looked strange for her to take a seat in one of the chairs, leaving him alone on that big sofa. It was a little odd to have him so close to her, although Audrey told herself that he'd been this close when he'd been shielding her with his body just a few minutes earlier…or when he'd held her as she was recovering from her faint that morning.

And once again she did her best to push that image out of her mind. She didn't need to waste mental energy on that sort of thing, not when they had so much else to worry about.

"I'm going to have the petit verdot," Michael said, then set down his menu. "What about you? It looks like I'll have to go up to the bar to order."

Since Audrey had been here before, she knew that Candy, the woman who worked at Glendora

Terroir most weekdays, would have gotten to them eventually…very eventually. But after what they'd been through, waiting that long for a glass of wine really wasn't an attractive option.

"The GSM blend," Audrey told him. Grenache, syrah, mouvedre…a classic-Rhone-style wine. She'd had it before, and liked it.

"GSM." He nodded and got up from the couch, then went over to the bar, where Candy turned away from the older couple she'd been chatting up, her blue eyes suddenly sparking with interest. He smiled at her and spoke, although Audrey couldn't hear what he was saying.

She tried to tell herself that the flash of jealousy she'd experienced while watching the bartender was completely foolish. Michael could flirt with anyone he wanted, although Audrey didn't know where he found the energy, considering he'd been fending off demon-propelled furniture not a half hour earlier.

However, his flirting—if that was even what he'd been doing—seemed to accomplish its goal, because he returned to the sofa, a glass of wine in either hand, in a remarkably short amount of time. After handing Audrey the Rhone-style red blend, he sat back down on the couch and took a sip of his own petit verdot. The wine was so dark it looked nearly black, a fitting drink, considering what they'd uncovered in the basement of the Whitcomb mansion.

"What's our next step?" she asked, doing her best to sound brisk and businesslike despite their decidedly unbusinesslike surroundings. And then, because she didn't want to wait any longer, she sipped at her wine, glad of the faint flush of warmth it sent down her midsection as she swallowed. It might have been a warm day outside, but she hadn't quite gotten rid of the chill from their foray into the basement game room.

"I'll call Colin. He's the liaison with the owners—I haven't actually spoken to them directly. I don't think it'll be too difficult to get their permission to do whatever we want with the basement. They would have ripped all that out eventually anyway."

True. Audrey doubted that anyone who'd paid three and a half million dollars for their house would willingly hang on to vomit-green shag carpet. She nodded, and Michael continued.

"Once we have the go-ahead to get at the floor beneath the carpet and the wood, then we'll go back with the crew and film the removal of the demon-summoning glyphs."

"Are we all going to wear body armor?" Audrey asked, only half joking. She still didn't know how he'd managed to keep the furniture from hitting either one of them. Wouldn't it be even more difficult for him if he had to worry about protecting Colin and Chris and Susan, and whatever other crew members might be in the immediate vicinity?

Michael drank some of his petit verdot and offered her a tight smile. "No, I don't think that's going to be necessary. I'm not saying the demons won't try to put up a fight, but they're going to direct their ire at me, since I'm the one who'll be removing their express route to this dimension."

How was she supposed to respond to that? "What do you need me to do?"

"Offer moral support, more than anything." He shifted on the couch so he faced toward her, rather than the coffee table where he'd just set down his glass of wine. Now it felt even more awkward, being this close, but she did her best to look back at him calmly, with no shift in expression. "Your reactions to the entities in that house have made it pretty clear to me that you must be a sensitive of some sort, even if you don't believe that about yourself. It's very likely that you'll be able to feel an imminent attack and provide some warning."

He sounded completely confident in her abilities, whereas Audrey was anything but. And she hadn't exactly put in a good performance down there in the basement. Yes, she'd been able to find the spells of summoning on the subfloor, but she'd screamed like a little girl and had been crying from fright as she dragged herself to the stairs and safety. A warrior against the forces of darkness, she most definitely was not.

The jury was still out on exactly how much of a mind reader Michael Covenant actually was, but he clearly picked up on her doubt, because he said, "You did very well."

"I did not. I was a mess."

"You might think that, but you didn't bolt at the first sign of something wrong down there. You looked, and you found it. A lot of people would have run for the stairs as soon as they felt that cold and pressure. Don't be so hard on yourself."

He sounded so reassuring, Audrey wanted to believe him. "How do you do it?"

A lift of his shoulders before he reached for his wine glass. "Because I have to."

"A real crusader?"

"Something like that." The corners of his mouth lifted slightly, but his expression remained somber. She wondered then what it was that had sent him down this path. The brief bios she'd read about him were fairly vague—they only said that he'd exhibited psychic abilities from an early age and had grown up somewhere on the East Coast before traveling through Europe and the Americas to train his peculiar talents, but there weren't any real particulars, any anecdotes that explained why he had ended up here in Southern California. And she didn't feel as though she knew him well enough to ask.

Not yet, anyway.

Audrey glanced over at the bar. The older couple sitting there now looked as though they were paying off their tab, so in a minute or two, she and Michael would be the only occupants of the wine bar. Well, except for Candy, who kept shooting glances in their direction, as if she couldn't quite figure out what the two of them were doing there.

Good question.

Well, aside from the most obvious. After that nightmarish encounter, they'd both needed a drink, and getting one at a public place like this seemed a lot less fraught than going back to her house. Audrey realized then that she didn't have any idea where Michael lived; his biographies all said he lived in Los Angeles, but L.A. was a big place. His house could be anywhere from Pacific Palisades to the funky hillside residences in Mount Washington, east of downtown.

"So…." she said, drawing out the syllable, since the couple at the bar was now on the move, headed toward the front door. She waited until they were gone to say, "You get rid of the demons, I provide moral support, and the owners can move back into their house. All's well that ends well."

"That's the plan." He smiled, a genuine-looking one this time. "Then we'll move on to the next location."

"Which is?"

His gaze shifted away from hers. "We're working on two possibilities at the moment. Colin should have one of them locked down by midweek."

Audrey realized then that it was still Monday. Hard to believe that only about eight hours had passed since Michael picked her up at her house in the dark fog of an early morning. "Local?"

"One of them is in Santa Barbara. The other is in Tucson."

Both of those locations didn't seem as though they would be likely possibilities for a demon infestation, but then again, you could say the same for sleepy little Glendora. Darkness lurked wherever it wanted, it seemed.

Inwardly, Audrey hoped they'd end up in Santa Barbara. The seaside town might be a three-hour drive away, but at least it was still technically in Southern California. And yes, Tucson was probably just about twice that distance, and yet going there felt like a much bigger commitment.

She didn't really want to think about how she'd just mentally committed herself to doing that show. Of course, she was under contract to appear, but it was almost as though knowing she had abilities that might be of some use had only cemented her resolve to continue.

Since she didn't feel like voicing those sentiments out loud, she settled for a noncommittal, "Got it," and sipped at her wine. It was starting to feel a little sour in her stomach, probably because she hadn't eaten anything since her skimpy breakfast. The wine bar offered small plates, but she didn't think ordering food was a good idea. That would make this meeting feel uncomfortably like a date.

However, Michael didn't seem to share those reservations, because he picked up the menu card again and turned it over, looking on the reverse side at the bill of fare. "Should we get a cheese plate or something? We're both almost finished with our glasses of wine, and if we're going to have more, we should probably eat something."

A second glass of wine seemed like an even worse idea than ordering food. "No, that's all right," Audrey said hastily. "One glass is about my limit on a weekday, especially if we're going to have an early call again tomorrow."

Disappointment flared in his eyes, but then he shrugged. "You have a point. Besides, I need to call Colin. Once I have that squared away, I'll know better what the schedule is going to be."

"Sounds good," she said, and picked up her

wine so she could swallow the last mouthful. "Thanks for the drink, Michael."

"Of course." An automatic response, one offered without him really meeting her eyes. "I'll pay the bill, and then I'll drive you home."

"Oh, no need for that," she told him. "I'm only a couple of blocks away from here."

For a second he appeared puzzled, as if he was trying to figure out why she would turn down an offer of a ride. But then he seemed to brush his concerns aside, saying, "Okay. I'll be in touch as soon as Colin has everything worked out with the owners."

"Sounds like a plan." Because it felt as though she should say something else, she said again, "Thank you for the wine."

And then she was giving him a smile in farewell, moving toward the exit so he couldn't try to offer another ride home. As she pushed the door open, she glanced back to see him already at the bar, wallet in hand, as Candy beamed at him and looked far too happy about the way Audrey was leaving the bar without him.

Good luck with that, she thought. *You might not find him so attractive once you find out what he does for a living.*

Then again, maybe Candy would find the whole demon-hunting thing appealing, if for no other reason than the low-level celebrity it afforded him.

For herself, Audrey was glad of the chance to walk outside in the sun, to allow herself to be surrounded by Glendora's relentlessly normal main street, from the small shops and boutiques to the stationery store/cum post office. When she walked past the building where her office was located, she experienced a pang of guilt, just because it felt wrong to be out here enjoying the sunshine when she normally would have been seeing clients.

For about the thousandth time, she reminded herself that feeling guilt about something she had no control over wasn't a good use of her mental energies. The clients had been rescheduled, and she'd just experienced something fairly traumatic. There was nothing wrong with allowing herself a little time to relax and mentally prepare for the next stage in the process.

The scent of sage still lingered in the house. After going inside, Audrey set her purse down on the coffee table and stood in the middle of the living room for a moment, doing her best to reach out and try to sense whether anything felt wrong about the place.

No, everything was calm, as far as she could tell. Even so, she picked up the white candle and lit it, then got the smudge going. Holding it and the abalone bowl, she walked from room to room, thinking of the bright golden warmth of the sun and doing her best to bring that light in here with her.

She had no idea whether she was doing any real good, though.

At last, she returned to the living room and flicked on the television. Having it on in the background helped make her feel a little less alone, but she still startled at every creak of the house, every whisper of the wind in the trees outside. Was this state of permanent unease what she had to look forward to now that she was working with Michael Covenant?

The day grew darker as the hour approached six o'clock, and Audrey had to restrain herself from turning on every single light in the house, settling for the two table lamps in the living room and the dark bronze chandelier in the dining room. She had the makings for a salad in the fridge, but that didn't sound very appealing. What she really wanted was some comfort food—a big gooey grilled cheese sandwich, or some corn chowder or quiche.

She didn't want to admit to herself that maybe her desire for food she didn't have on hand was a pretense for getting out of the house. Besides, no matter what excuses she might come up with to get herself out of there for a few hours, sooner or later, she'd have to come back to sleep.

Just as she was about to force herself into the kitchen and make that damn salad after all, the doorbell rang. She muted the TV and got up from the couch, doing her best to ignore the foolish excitement rising in her, speculating that it might be Michael, coming over to tell her about the next day's plans in person.

When she opened the door, however, it was Rosemary McGuire standing on the front porch, a pizza box in one hand. Her blue eyes laughed up at Audrey.

"I had a feeling you might need some company."

Chapter 7

"So, what is it with you and Michael Covenant, anyway?" Audrey asked, feeling much more relaxed after two pieces of pepperoni pizza and a glass of pinot noir.

Rosemary wiped her fingers on her napkin, then set it back down in her lap. "It's not just me. Isabel and Cecily don't like him very much, either."

While Audrey could see why Michael might rub people the wrong way, Rosemary's antipathy seemed a bit more personal than a mere clash of personality types. "But why?"

She reached for her glass of wine, took a sip. "It was at a psychic fair a couple of years ago. The three of us had a booth there. We weren't even doing readings, just selling stuff from the shop."

"You do readings?" Audrey asked, somewhat

surprised. As far as she could remember, she hadn't seen any signage in Sisters We that advertised those sorts of services.

"Yes," Rosemary said. Hands wrapped around the bowl of her wine glass, she leaned against the back of the chair and sent her dinner companion a speculative look. "Not formally...well, not exactly anyway. We don't advertise. But if people ask, then we'll do a reading for them. Cecily and I work mostly with the Tarot, and Isabel does palm reading."

"How long have you known you were psychic?" Audrey asked, genuinely curious.

Although a lot of people might have been put off by such a question, Rosemary seemed to take it in stride. "Since...forever, I guess. It runs in the family, in case you hadn't noticed. Our mother is psychic, both our grandmothers...I think it would have been weirder if we *hadn't* been born with any talents."

That was probably true. Audrey's research seemed to show that strong psychic ability had some kind of genetic component. Where hers had come from, though, she had no idea. As far as she could remember, her mother had never mentioned having any kind of talents in that area. But then, even if she had, Audrey wondered whether her mother would have ever said anything. She'd always thought of her parents as having an ideal relationship, because they'd been best friends as well as husband and wife, but her father was a very down-to-earth person. He needed to see facts and evidence before he'd believe something—and since he'd taught biology at the local community college, she could see why he would have that sort of mind set.

Unfortunately, though, his wasn't the sort of personality that lent itself to believing in psychic powers...or ghosts and demons, for that matter. He'd been troubled by his daughter's reaction to the haunted building in New Orleans because he could plainly see that she was in distress, but he'd been inclined to blame her malaise on the gumbo she'd eaten for lunch. As for her mother, she'd been sympathetic, but as far as Audrey could tell, that place with its very dark history had had no effect on her.

"And you're having to come to grips with yours, aren't you?" Audrey stared at Rosemary, wondering how the other woman had guessed that she was grappling with her own burgeoning abilities, and she smiled and said, "Oh, I thought I could feel something earlier, but I wasn't sure. Now, though...it feels like it's beginning to shine out of you." Rosemary drank some pinot noir, then set down her glass and quirked an eyebrow at Audrey. "He convinced you to go back to the Whitcomb place, didn't he?"

"Yes," she said shortly. "And we think we found the—the source of the problem. But I want to hear about you and Michael Covenant."

For a second, Rosemary looked as though she might press the issue of Audrey's second trip to the Whitcomb mansion. However, she could almost feel her give a mental shrug before she said, "Okay. We were at a psychic fair, like I said. It's a fun way to network. And we'd heard of Michael Covenant, of course, because those circles aren't really that big, you know? He had a booth, too, was selling his books and DVDs. Which, fine, he has his approach to things and we have ours. But then when I was taking a break, went to get some food and bottled water from one of the vendors, I heard him talking loudly about how psychic ability often isn't inborn in us at all, comes from outside entities, and I just couldn't hold it in. I went over and told him that was b.s. and that there are tons of examples of families with psychic talents. Of course, he just smiled at me and said he'd expected I would say something like that, since it's hard to admit that our powers might come from something outside ourselves. I was about to really get into it with him when Isabel came along and pulled me away."

That sounded like the Michael Covenant Audrey had seen on a few interview shows. Funny how in person he didn't come off nearly as arrogant. Or was it simply that he thought he needed her for something, and so was doing his best to play nice? "It's strange he would think that, since he didn't say anything to me about my talents—whatever they are—coming from any place except inside me."

"He probably didn't want to piss you off." Rosemary picked up the half-eaten piece of pepperoni pizza on the plate before her and took another bite. After chewing for a moment, she went on, "Don't get me wrong—of course there are channelers, those who allow a spirit or entity to work through them. But not all psychics are channelers, and I'd argue that not all channelers are psychics, at least not in the way that CeeCee and Isabel and I are. And you, it sounds like."

"I don't know what I am," Audrey said, mentally adding, *Except tired…and frightened.* "Although it seems like I have a talent for picking up on negative energy."

Rosemary set down her pizza and wiped her fingers again. "Well, you've experienced tragedy in your life. That might explain it."

She found that theory just a little unsettling. Wasn't it bad enough to have lost both her parents in a violent and unexpected way? Did that mean she should be doomed to have darkness and bad luck following her wherever she went, like a piece of gum stuck to her shoe?

"I had my first experience a few years before their murders," Audrey pointed out, then allowed herself a much-needed swallow of wine.

"That doesn't necessarily matter," Rosemary said. "We see time as linear, but it really isn't. Actions and reactions can come from anywhere."

It was the sort of thing a physicist might say. Audrey looked at Rosemary as she drank some more wine, at her wild hair and the diamond piercing that glinted from her nose, and wanted to shake her head. In her case, appearances were definitely deceiving.

Rosemary seemed to guess something of Audrey's thoughts—or maybe she'd just outright read them—because she remarked, "I like to read. Makes sense, since I'm part-owner of a bookstore. But a lot of these theories of consciousness circle back around to basically the same principles, if you know what you're looking at. Your first psychic experience was a negative one, even though your life was happy then. What was coming could have still echoed somewhere within you, though. What happened, exactly?"

Audrey explained the odd occurrence in New Orleans, doing her best to be as matter-of-fact and detached about the experience as she could. While she spoke, though, she could feel some of those same shivers work their way down her spine, and she knew that the fear and sickness she'd suffered all those years ago had never left her. Not completely, anyway.

When she was done, Rosemary twisted a curl around her forefinger, idly playing with it as she appeared to think over the story. "You never had anything like that happen to you here in California?"

"No," Audrey replied. "No psychic flashes, no weird feelings, nothing."

"There might not have been anything strong enough to affect you. Everyone's radar—so to speak—is a little different."

"I felt it when my mother died," Audrey blurted out, and Rosemary's big blue eyes widened.

"Oh, God, I'm sorry," she said. "And it was probably harder because you knew something was off, but you didn't dare say anything about it."

"Exactly." Even though they were talking about something pretty dreadful, Audrey could feel some of the tension start to leave her neck and shoulders. It was as if having someone who truly understood what she'd gone through was enough, even though the pain of that moment would continue to resonate within her for the rest of her days.

"Anything after that?"

"No. At least, I don't think so. I'd always been fascinated by the paranormal—the psychic side of it, anyway—and that was why I wanted to focus on parapsychology. Unfortunately, there aren't as many places to do that as there used to be, so that's why I went into psychology."

"But you don't really want to be a shrink."

With someone else, Audrey might have wondered how the other woman had gotten so quickly to the core of her problems. But Rosemary—like her sisters—didn't need a psychology degree to probe at the inner workings of the human psyche.

"Not really," Audrey admitted. "Maybe that was part of why I agreed to do this show with Michael, even if I told myself it was just the money, just having the chance to pay off the balance on my student loans and get the property tax on this house taken care of."

"Is that still a problem?" she asked, and Audrey shook her head.

"No. I got a third of my salary for the show up front, so the taxes won't be an issue, and I'll take care of the loans after I get the final installment of the *Project Demon Hunters* money. If I survive that long," she added with a smile that probably looked more like a grimace.

And clearly, Rosemary wasn't buying it. "Money isn't worth putting yourself in danger, and that's what's happening with this show, no matter what Michael Covenant might have told you."

For some reason, Audrey felt compelled to come to his defense. "He came clean about everything today. And—and he protected me, both times."

"You wouldn't have needed protecting if you hadn't been suckered into doing this show, would you?"

Well, she had a point there. But Michael could have threatened lawsuits and breach of contract and all that if he'd wanted to, and he hadn't. He'd seemed genuinely more interested in getting Audrey to understand why the work was important, why he wanted her to be a part of it.

"'Sucker' is a strong word," she said. "I'll admit I didn't understand everything that working on the show might involve, but after today, I've had a pretty good taste of it."

"And?"

"And I'm staying. Maybe that sounds crazy, but if Michael and I really get this house cleared, then we'll have helped someone. *Really* helped them, in a tangible way."

Rosemary didn't look convinced. "Helped a couple of millionaires."

"Aren't millionaires worthy of help, the same as the rest of us?"

For a moment, she didn't reply. Then she

chuckled, although something about the sound seemed almost reluctant, as though she laughed despite herself. "I suppose you're right. There's just something about Michael Covenant that rubs me the wrong way."

"Well, I can't blame you for feeling that way, after how he acted." Audrey hesitated, not sure how much else she should say. Her feelings on the subject of Michael Covenant were just a little muddled. "But he's not always an arrogant asshole."

"I'll have to take your word for it." Suddenly, she grinned. "It's probably also that he looks a little like one of my exes, which isn't something that tends to endear a guy to me."

Audrey found herself smiling back at her. "No, probably not."

After that, they both seemed to relax a little, and they talked about the store, about how Rosemary and her sisters had grown up in Pasadena but how they'd decided to set up their store in Glendora because rents were so high in their former hometown. Just normal, everyday stuff.

When they were done with their wine and pizza, though, Rosemary fished a card out of her cell phone holder/wallet and gave it to Audrey. It was just a business card for the bookstore, but on the back she'd hand-written a different phone number.

"That's my cell," she said as Audrey looked down at it. "If something weird happens, you call me. I'll rally the troops and come over."

"You all live together?" Audrey asked, touched that she'd be worried enough about her to offer to help.

"God, no," Rosemary said in tones of convincing horror. "Isabel and CeeCee both have kids under five. It's bad enough that I get drafted to do babysitting duty all the time...I don't think I would survive having to actually *live* with them. But their houses are on the same street, and mine's just one up from them, so we can all assemble pretty quickly if we have to."

"I'm sure I'll be fine, but thank you."

Rosemary was quiet for a moment, face so blank, Audrey wondered if she was all right. Apparently, she'd been reaching out with her talent, or at least trying to. "I can't feel anything, but that's the problem with demons. They can really muck up vibrations. Just call if you have to, okay?"

"Okay," Audrey said. "I promise."

That response seemed to satisfy Rosemary, because she nodded before she opened the door and let herself out. Audrey watched her walk down the front path to a little pale green Fiat that was parked in front of the house; apparently, her own place was far enough away that she needed to drive. She gave a final wave before she climbed in, and then Audrey shut the front door.

Even though she was now alone, she didn't feel worried or anxious or afraid. She cleared the plates off the table and put the leftover pizza in a glass storage container with a locking lid, then set it in the refrigerator. A glance at the clock on the microwave told her it was a little after eight, way too early to go to bed.

That was all right. She'd turn on some music, do a bit of reading. Just a quiet, normal night in.

Her cell phone rang. She went to retrieve it from her purse, which was still sitting in the living room. A quick glance at the home screen told her it was Michael calling.

"Audrey. Everything still all right?"

"Just fine," she said. For a second, she contemplated telling him that Rosemary had brought pizza, had promised her and her sisters' help if necessary. Then Audrey realized he didn't have to know that. "Did you talk to Colin?"

"Yes, and he spoke with the owners. They don't care if we have to jackhammer the floor in the basement if it means they can get their house back, so we're set for tomorrow. I can pick you up at seven."

Well, that wasn't quite as ungodly as six-thirty, but still. Audrey wondered if he preferred to drive her to the set so he could be more in control of the situation, then dismissed the thought as uncharitable. There really wasn't a lot of parking on the small side street where the mansion was located, and so it made sense to carpool if possible.

"All right," she said, hoping he hadn't heard the way she'd hesitated before replying. "And if everything works out?"

"Then we'll take a few days off before we hit the road for Tucson."

So much for Santa Barbara. "Aren't we going to fly?"

"It's easier to drive, especially since the crew will have to come in vans because of the equipment they're hauling."

"Your car can make it that far?"

Luckily, he sounded amused rather than taking offense. "No, I'll rent something. We can ride together, if you like."

Seven hours of being stuck in a car with Michael Covenant? Audrey didn't know if that was a good idea. Then again, she also didn't know whether her little Corolla could safely make it all the way to Tucson, either. It seemed kind of foolish for both of them to be renting cars.

"Sure," she said. "It'll be fun. I haven't done a road trip in a while."

"Great. We can talk about it more tomorrow…after."

She didn't have to ask which "after" he was talking about. They were both blithely assuming everything would go well, but these were demons they were dealing with, after all. They didn't exactly play by the rules.

"Okay," Audrey told him. "I'll see you in the morning."

"Seven o'clock. Have a good night."

He hung up then, and she returned the phone to her purse and set it back down on the coffee table. While she didn't have any intention of going to sleep before nine-thirty or ten, she could just as easily read on her Kindle in bed, rather than down here on the couch. That way, she could go to sleep as soon as she felt the time was right.

That matter settled, she flicked on the lights above the stairway, then shut off everything else on the ground floor. The steps creaked a little as she walked up them, but they always did that; the house was nearly a hundred years old. Lights on in the upstairs hallway, and then she was safely in her bedroom, cheered a bit by the warm yellow paint on the walls and the friendly, lived-in antiques that filled the room. It had always felt like a sanctuary in there, and she knew she needed that reassurance now more than ever.

She got out of her clothes and put them in the hamper, then pulled on the T-shirt and knee-length yoga pants she wore to sleep in. A few minutes to wash her face and brush her teeth, and then she was safely in bed, the white noise generator she kept on the nightstand sending out its familiar ocean waves sounds, her Kindle in her hands.

Her usual practice was to alternate reading something nonfiction and a novel, usually a mystery or a thriller. She'd last been reading her nonfiction selection, a pretty dry tome about best standards and practices for psychologists working as independent contractors rather than as part of a clinic. However, after everything she'd been through that day, she wasn't ready to go back to the mystery. Although she hadn't actually seen anyone get murdered at the Whitcomb house, she'd still witnessed enough violence to hold her for a long, long time. With any luck, the standards and practices book would be dull enough to lull her into sleep sooner rather than later, and she could put an end to this seemingly endless day. Not that she was exactly eager to face what waited for her and Michael in the mansion's basement, but at least once that ordeal was over with, she could call herself a full-fledged demon hunter.

Maybe.

Just as she'd thought, her eyelids began to droop before she'd read five pages. She glanced over at the clock. Eight fifty-three. All right, maybe her thirtieth birthday was only six months off, but she was damned if she was going to fall asleep before nine o'clock like an eighty-year-old after a hard night of watching *Jeopardy*. That was ridiculous. Never mind that she'd have to be up around five-thirty in order to be ready when Michael came by to pick her up. She still had her standards.

The letters on the electronic page seemed to blur, bleeding into each other. Audrey blinked, then touched the controls to see if enlarging the font might fix the problem. If anything, that made matters worse. Now there were big black blots on the screen, and they seemed to coalesce, smaller blots joining up with bigger blots, until there was a strange, spinning blackness in the center of the non-reflective glass.

That had to be an optical illusion…didn't it?

The cold struck her body then, washing over her in a wave so icy, it felt as if she'd been dropped into the North Atlantic. Teeth chattering, she stared down at the Kindle, at the apparently bottomless hole that had opened up in the middle of it.

Things were moving in that darkness, ghostly shapes that appeared to be spiraling up out of the abyss. A chorus of thin, screeching wails came with those shapes, growing louder and louder as they got closer and closer. Now Audrey could see skeletal hands reaching out toward her, ghostly fingers somehow pushing their way up past the screen, claws extended toward her face—

She screamed and hurled the Kindle against the wall. The screen shattered on impact, and at once those ghastly voices were gone, along with the apparitions she'd seen. But the destruction of the device wasn't enough to convince her that she was safe. She pushed herself out of bed, jammed her feet into the pair of flip-flops she always kept next to her bed, and bolted down the stairs, flicking on lights as she went, hoping if it was bright enough in there, she would banish any shadows where those entities might be hiding. The briefest pause to grab her purse from where it still sat on the coffee table in the living room, and then she was out the door. Luckily, the doorknob's lock was automatic, and she sure as hell wasn't going to worry about the damn deadbolt.

It was very dark. Her breath coming in sobs, Audrey ran partway down the block until she came to a street lamp. Under its reassuring light, she stopped and pulled her phone out of her purse, and dug back in with shaking fingers, trying to find the business card Rosemary McGuire had given her.

There it was. Audrey brought it out and held it under the light so she could see the numbers clearly. Hands still trembling, she entered the digits and held her breath. Rosemary had to answer. Audrey didn't know what she'd do if she didn't.

But the phone only rang twice before she heard the psychic's voice in my ear. "Hey, it's Rosemary."

"Rosemary," Audrey gasped. "It's Audrey."

No questions, only a sharp, "It happened again."

"Yes," she said. "But worse. Or at least it felt worse."

"Where are you?"

"I—I ran out of the house. I'm about halfway down the block, standing under a streetlight."

"Stay there," Rosemary said quickly. "I'm out the door. I'll be there in less than five minutes."

Right then, five minutes sounded like an eternity. But even though Rosemary seemed to be a strong psychic, it wasn't as though she could wiggle her nose and be here to rescue her instantly. "Okay," Audrey replied, trying to keep her teeth from chattering. She might have been relatively covered up, but her T-shirt, flip-flops, and knee-length yoga pants weren't really enough to hold back the night's damp chill. It felt like the fog was coming in again.

"Just stay in the light. I'm leaving now. And stay on the phone."

"Sure." That felt better. Somehow, knowing

Rosemary was still there, still listening, made Audrey feel a little less alone.

Through the phone's speaker, she heard the rattle of keys, then a creaking, metallic sound that she thought was probably the sound of Rosemary's garage door opening. An engine turning over, and a brief burst of music that was abruptly shut off.

"You still there?" she asked. "I'm coming down Glendora Avenue now."

"Yes, I'm here." Audrey paused and glanced around, but her street was empty. It was a quiet neighborhood most of the time, and now, at after nine on a weeknight, there were no signs of any activity. She didn't know whether that was a good thing or not. On the one hand, she didn't have to worry about any of her neighbors spotting her standing out there, shivering in the cold. On the other, if something decided to claw its way out of the wreckage of her Kindle and come looking for her....

A pair of headlights raked through the darkness. Just a minute later, Rosemary's mint-green Fiat was pulling up next to where Audrey stood by the curb. She let out a little sob of relief and ran to the car, one hand on the door handle before the vehicle had even come to a complete stop. And then she was inside, and Rosemary was pulling away from the curb while Audrey fumbled with the seatbelt.

Once they were safely around the block and headed north—presumably going toward her house—Rosemary said, "What happened?"

"I don't know for sure." Even though the heat was on in her car, Audrey's teeth wanted to chatter, and she had to clench her jaw to force the words out. "I was trying to read on my Kindle, and something came up out of it, was reaching toward me—"

Once again her body was awash in cold. She clung to the seatbelt strap with one hand, the other still clutching the handle of her purse. What would have happened if she hadn't thrown the Kindle at the wall? What if those things had actually *touched* her?

"Damn." Rosemary sounded shaken, but then she said, in slightly too-hearty tones, "Well, you're safe now. My house has all kinds of protection set up."

"More than smudging, I hope." Audrey's voice felt thin and reedy, not like her own at all. "Because that didn't seem to work for shit."

"It's good general protection. It never promised to be absolutely demon-proof."

Now she tells me. But Audrey tried to shake off her resentment. After all, she was the one who'd come up with the smudging idea. Rosemary had probably thought it would be enough, since the house should have been neutral territory.

"I don't have a guest bedroom, but the living room couch is pretty comfy," she went on, apparently deciding it was better not to get wrapped up in an argument about the relative demon-proofing of Audrey's house, or lack thereof. "You'll be safe, and in the morning, you can figure out what to do next."

Right then, the morning felt a very long way off. Audrey knew she didn't want to set foot in her house any time in the near future, and yet she'd have to go back at some point, if only to get some clothes and other necessities.

Worse, she was supposed to be ready in the morning to help Michael dispel the demons in the Whitcomb mansion. She sure as hell didn't see that happening.

The car turned down onto Rosemary's street. The houses here weren't quite as old as Audrey's, instead were probably built in the 1920s—some with vaguely Spanish architecture, others clapboard cottages, well-preserved and neat. She pulled up into the driveway of what looked to be a small, English cottage–style home and turned off the engine.

"Here we are," she said. "Let's get inside."

That sounded like a very good idea. Audrey got out of the car and followed Rosemary into the house, which smelled faintly of incense and had her same sort of cluttery, boho style—a purple velvet couch with embroidered pillows, furniture that looked like a mishmash of stuff she'd gotten at garage sales and at Cost Plus or Pier One. But even though it appeared very different from her own place, Audrey felt safe here, as if somewhere deep inside she could sense the wards Rosemary had put on her home.

"There's the couch," she said, quite unnecessarily, since the purple sofa was sort of the centerpiece of the living room. "I'll go get some blankets and a pillow."

"Okay." Since Audrey's knees were still feeling a bit rubbery, she went over to the couch and sat down, then hugged her purse to herself. Thank God she'd had enough presence of mind to bring it with her. She might have run out of the house with only the clothes on her back, but at least she had her phone and wallet, which meant she still had her I.D. and some cash. It could have been worse.

Then again, it could have been a lot better, too.

From inside her purse, Audrey's phone rang. She startled and almost dropped the bag, then got hold of herself enough to pull out the phone and look at the screen. The number displayed there looked vaguely familiar, although she couldn't quite place it. Still, if someone was calling her at after nine o'clock at night, it must be important.

"Hello?"

"Audrey, it's Michael."

Had he found out about the attack somehow? She couldn't think of how that was possible, but when you were dealing with people who had extrasensory talents, all bets were pretty much off. Before she could say anything, however, he'd continued.

"We're going to have to push back the shoot by a day. Chris walked out."

"He…what?" she responded, some of her current worry replaced by surprise…and a very large amount of relief. At least she wouldn't have to show up at the Whitcomb place tomorrow and face the horrors there. She had enough horrors of her own to deal with.

Michael said, "What he saw this morning really freaked him out. He was holding it together while we were all still there on location, but once he got home and really began to process things, he realized he couldn't go back in that house."

"Hasn't he worked on shoots like this before?"

"Not exactly like this. That is, he's done other shows that Colin has produced, but they never caught anything on camera similar to what we all witnessed this morning."

Audrey could believe that. While she wasn't familiar with everything in Colin Turner's *oeuvre,* she'd seen enough of the shows he'd produced to know that they relied on jump scares and a good deal of fudging to make it seem as if something supernatural was going on, even though closer examination made it pretty obvious that there wasn't much substance to what was being presented.

What had happened this morning, though… that had been real. And frightening. It hadn't been a projection of her mind. It had been something other, something malevolent.

But as terrifying—and as real—as it had been, it was still far, far less troubling than the incident that had just occurred.

Rosemary came back into the living room, holding a folded blanket with a pillow sitting on top. "I'll just put these here," she said, setting them down on an arm of the couch.

"Who was that?" Michael asked, his tone sharpening slightly.

Audrey supposed she could have lied, but the truth would have come out eventually. Besides, she was just too drained right then to hide what had happened to her. "Rosemary McGuire. I'm at her place because there was an attack at my house."

His voice grew even more taut. "Are you all right?"

"I'm fine. I got out in time." Audrey paused there, wondering whether she should provide any more details, then deciding against it. For some reason, it didn't feel right to go into that much detail over the phone. "But obviously I wasn't going to stay there. She gave me a place to crash."

"Let me come get you," he said, the words tight, urgent.

While the offer surprised her, Audrey didn't have any intention of taking him up on it. "You don't have to do that. I'm fine. Rosemary has this house warded."

"Maybe so, but I can guarantee you that the protections she has set up won't be enough. Not against this kind of adversary."

A cold finger of doubt trailed its way down her spine. What if Michael was right? What if Rosemary's wards fell apart the moment a demon came anywhere near her house?

"Michael, I—"

He broke in, cutting off her protests. "Audrey, you have to trust me on this. Let me come get you."

She hesitated. Rosemary, having deposited the blanket and pillow on the couch, was standing off to one side, hands on her hips and her expression somehow both suspicious and resigned. As much as Audrey would have preferred to stay at Rosemary's place, Michael had planted a seed of doubt in her mind. What if the demons actually did follow her here? Could Rosemary really manage to fend off one of their attacks? At the same time, Audrey felt strange about giving Michael Rosemary's address, especially since she'd made it fairly clear that he was not on her list of favorite people.

But Rosemary shrugged. "If the Great White Knight wants to swoop in and rescue you, far be it from me to stop him. The address here is 1750 Laurel Avenue."

For a second, Audrey hesitated. After all, it would be awkward beyond words to have to crash at Michael Covenant's house. Then again, the last thing she wanted was for any harm to come to Rosemary—or to her sisters, who apparently lived close by. They had something she'd lost—a loving, close-knit family—and they'd already helped her enough. She didn't want to be responsible for bringing disaster to their doorstep.

That seemed to decide things, and Audrey repeated the address to Michael, adding, "Where are you coming from?"

"Pasadena," he replied promptly. "I should be there in about twenty minutes. Hang tight."

"I will. See you soon."

She ended the call then, and slowly slipped her phone back into her purse. "I'm sorry," she said, the words coming automatically to her lips as she looked back up at Rosemary. "I really appreciate you trying to give me someplace safe to stay. But if this thing keeps following me, the last thing

I want is for it to come here and try to hurt you. Michael is an expert at handling demons, so…."

Rosemary nodded, although her expression was still grim. "I get it. And I hope he can keep you safe."

"But…?"

The faintest lift of her shoulders. "I'm not sure. It's just that he *says* he's an expert, but has he really come up against anything like this before? Are you sure he really knows what he's doing?"

Audrey didn't have an answer to either of those questions.

She had to hope Michael would.

Chapter 8

MICHAEL SHOWED UP AS PROMISED, ALMOST twenty minutes to the second after Audrey had ended their call. Clearly, he hadn't been anywhere close to getting ready for bed, since he was still wearing the same clothes he'd had on earlier that day.

As Rosemary opened the door for him, she said, "Hi, Michael."

"Hi, Rosemary," he returned, expression neutral. He looked past her to where Audrey stood, purse clutched in one hand. At least Rosemary had loaned her a sweater while they were waiting for Michael to show up, but it still felt strange and horribly awkward to be facing him in basically her pajamas. "Thanks for taking Audrey in until I could get here."

"Not a problem." Rosemary touched Audrey's

arm briefly, a simple, reassuring gesture. "Call me if you need anything, okay?"

"I will," she promised, then went ahead and moved past her so she could meet Michael on the porch. "Thank you for the rescue."

Rosemary grinned. "Hey, we psychics have to stick together, right?"

Audrey nodded, doing her best to smile back at her, and Michael raised a hand in farewell as the two of them walked down the porch steps. His Land Cruiser was waiting at the curb, and he opened the passenger door for her, then waited until she was safely inside before he walked around the front of the SUV to get into his own seat. After he'd started the engine and pulled away from the curb, he said, "I think we should stop by your house."

"Excuse me?" Audrey looked over at him, aghast, but his expression was so neutral, she couldn't get a read on what he might be thinking. Was he joking? Maybe she just hadn't heard him correctly. He couldn't really be suggesting they go back to the place where demons had almost escaped from her Kindle, could he?

"I know it seems risky, but I want to try to get a feel for what happened there, and you probably want to get a few things, don't you?" His gaze traveled toward her for a moment before returning to the road; he didn't say anything else, but it was clear that he could tell she had run out of the house with nothing except her purse.

"Well, maybe, but I'm not sure it's worth risking my life to get some clean underwear."

"You're won't be risking your life. I'll be with you—and you know I can keep the entities from harming you."

Possibly. He'd managed to do so earlier that day, but somehow, what had been trying to climb out of her Kindle had felt even worse than the demons at the Whitcomb house. Maybe it was only that tonight's entities had been inside her own home, and the attack had felt like more of a violation than the others.

Still doubtful, she said, "If you're sure…."

"As sure as I can be," Michael replied. "And I want to see the place where the attack occurred. Possibly I can pick up something from it. I can do my inspection while you're packing your things."

She wanted to ask how much she needed to pack, but she doubted even Michael would know the answer to that question. Probably three days' worth of changes of clothes should be enough; by that point, they'd both have a better idea of whether it was safe for her to get back inside her house.

The real problem was, she didn't know if she really wanted to go back. Not after what had happened tonight. Her house had always been a sanctuary to her, but now it felt…tainted.

Haunted.

They were both quiet for the rest of the short trip. When they pulled up to the house, every-thing appeared tranquil, the light on the front porch shining serenely, the drapes and blinds shut for the evening, with just a hint of the illumina-tion from the lamps inside peeking through.

Appearances could be deceiving, though.

Michael and Audrey got out of his SUV at the same time, although she waited by the passenger door until he came around the front end of the Land Cruiser and stopped next to her. For a moment, he stood there in silence, probably trying to see if he could feel any strange vibes. Then he shrugged and said, "It seems all right. Let's go inside."

She nodded and got her keys out of her purse, and followed him up the front walk to the porch, even though she could feel her stomach beginning to tighten with unease. After she unlocked the door, he went inside first, then paused for a few seconds.

"Do you feel anything now?" she asked.

His response was immediate. "No. Where did it happen?"

"Upstairs, in my bedroom. It's the last door at the end of the hall."

He walked up the stairs, with Audrey trailing reluctantly in his wake. Every other step, he would go still for a moment, obviously reaching out to feel the vibes of the house. As far as she could tell, he wasn't sensing anything out of the ordinary, because he kept going and didn't say anything to her.

Thank God she'd left the lights on. Right now, the upstairs hallway looked innocuous enough, with its shining wood floors and the hand-knotted carpet runner in cheerful shades of blue and cream running down the center of the space.

Under other circumstances, it might have felt awkward to have Michael Covenant entering her bedroom. At the moment, though, she could only be profoundly grateful for his presence. With him there, she didn't feel nearly as afraid. In fact, she could almost believe the whole thing had merely been her imagination playing tricks on her. An expensive trick, because of the smashed Kindle, but still....

It was still lying on the floor, bits of glass from its shattered screen scattered all around it. She wasn't sure what would have been worse—to find it still intact, mocking her attempt to block the creatures that had tried to crawl out of it, or to see it broken as it was now, mute testimony to the terrible events of only an hour earlier.

"I still don't feel anything," Michael said. His

gaze fell on the ruined e-reader, but he only added, "Go ahead and get your things packed. I want to take a look at that while you're packing."

Audrey nodded and got to work, moving quickly to the closet so she could get her week-ender bag off the top shelf. Luckily, the light switch for the closet was on the wall just outside it, so she could turn on the light and reassure herself there weren't any monsters in there before she actually stepped inside. A couple of shirts, one blazer—just in case—and that was it for the closet. Everything else she needed was either in her dresser or the bathroom.

As she hurried over to the dresser, she saw that Michael had now crouched down next to her smashed Kindle and had picked it up—but gingerly, by the edges, so he wouldn't injure himself on the broken glass—and was turning it over in his hands. He was frowning, but that could have meant anything.

While he was preoccupied, Audrey grabbed underwear and a couple of bras, another T-shirt and pair of yoga pants to sleep in, some socks. After that, she went into the bathroom and got out the little bag of travel-sized necessities that she kept under the sink—toothbrush and toothpaste, deodorant, moisturizer. Another bag held dupli-cates of her everyday makeup, and she grabbed that as well.

When she came back out of the bathroom, Michael was now standing up, although he still held the broken Kindle in one hand.

"Did you get anything from it?" Audrey asked.

"No," he replied. "Tell me exactly what happened."

She explained how she'd been reading the world's dullest book on the device and had started to nod off…but then saw that terrible vision of the swirling darkness and the hands reaching out for her.

"And a horrible sensation of cold, just like I experienced at the Whitcomb mansion," she finished. "That was when I threw the thing at the wall and ran."

"Do you think you might have still been asleep when you saw the vision?" he asked. "I mean, it's very possible that your subconscious mind could have been working on you, conjuring images like that because of what you saw in the mirror this morning."

She supposed that could be a possibility, but it had felt far too real. Still, as a psychologist, she knew all too well how powerful the mind could be, how it could make a person see things that weren't there. And really, the hands reaching out of that dizzying darkness hadn't been terribly unlike the ones she'd seen in the bathroom at the

Whitcomb mansion. Maybe it had all been in her mind....

But then Michael let out a hiss of a breath, and Audrey looked over to see the Kindle he held, saw how dark, oily blood was now oozing from the shattered screen. It wasn't Michael's blood; he held the device by its edges, away from the screen, and she couldn't detect any cuts on his hands or fingers.

He looked up, those gray-gilt eyes catching hers. Then he carefully set the Kindle back down on the floor.

"I think," he said quietly, "that it's time for us to leave."

On the drive over to Pasadena, Michael was silent, and Audrey took his lead. Honestly, she didn't know what that strange, dark blood dripping out of her Kindle meant, except that the incident clearly hadn't been the byproduct of a fevered and over-active imagination. Right then, she was just glad that she was well away from her house. While Michael might not have been the most reassuring personality in the world, it still felt good to be there in his ancient Land Cruiser. He was certainly better equipped to deal with this situation than anyone else she could think of.

She had no idea what to expect of his house, because images of everything from a sleek, modern condo to an old converted farmhouse had flitted through her mind. However, they pulled up into the driveway of a large Craftsman-style home, probably around the same vintage as Audrey's own house, except larger and—she guessed, because it was located in Pasadena, not Glendora—much more expensive than hers. The porch light was on, but she couldn't see much exterior detail because the home was painted dark brown, like many other Craftsman houses in the area.

No garage, only a carport. Michael parked the Land Cruiser there and turned off the engine. "We can go in through the back door," he said. "It's closer than going around the front."

She nodded, then, after gathering up her purse and weekender bag, followed him to a modest little stoop at the rear of the house. He unlocked the door, and they went into a decently sized kitchen, one with cheerful yellow and blue tile countertops, a wood floor, and a cute little table for two placed up against a window that must open out on the side yard. In fact, it looked so prosaic, so normal, that Audrey found herself beginning to relax slightly.

"Your bio says you live in L.A.," she blurted out, and he actually smiled.

"Well, that was true when I gave my biography to my publishers. I just haven't updated it lately." A glint in his eyes, and he added, "Besides, a little disinformation helps keep the crazies away."

She didn't chide him for using that particular term. In his line of work, he probably encountered a whole host of people who had a difficult time dealing with reality. Obfuscating his actual city of residence made sense, unfortunately.

"I'm going to make us some chamomile tea," he went on. "I figure we could both use a little help getting to sleep tonight."

"Probably," Audrey agreed. Despite everything that had happened to her that evening, she couldn't quite prevent herself from smiling at the thought of him making the two of them tea.

Not that it was a protracted process, because he had one of those instant hot water spigots installed to the left of the kitchen sink, and so the tea was steeping in a couple of big dark blue glazed mugs within a minute. He handed one to Audrey, saying, "Let's go out to the living room."

"Sure."

The main floor of the house included the living room and dining room and other spaces that appeared to be a library and TV area, along with a sort of enlarged alcove off the living room. In there, Audrey was surprised to see a baby grand piano, constructed of warm, mellow-toned wood rather than the usual black. Antique bookcases with beveled glass fronts lined the walls of the living room, and all those bookcases seemed to be filled to capacity, with more books sitting on top, held in place by geode bookends in natural shades of gray and brown.

It was darker in here than in the kitchen, the original dark wood wainscoting still in place, the same dark wood surrounding the windows and appearing once again in the beams overhead. At one end of the living room was an enormous river stone fireplace with a plain, broad mantel. On that mantel sat more books. One wall held a large cross of intricately carved dark wood. The protection he'd hinted at? Audrey had a feeling that whatever wards he had in place here, most of them wouldn't be visible to the naked eye.

"You can put your bags there," Michael said, pointing with his free hand at the bottom step. "All the bedrooms are upstairs—there's a guest room where you can sleep."

"Okay." Audrey set down her bags in the spot he'd indicated, glad to know that she'd have an actual room to sleep in rather than the couch, which was a big dark brown leather affair that looked imposing rather than comfortable.

He'd gone ahead and taken a seat on that couch. Luckily, there were two armchairs upholstered in dark green velvet placed opposite the couch, so she could sit down across from Michael without it looking too obvious that she was uncomfortable about sitting right next to him.

Mug of chamomile tea held in both hands, its warmth helping to soothe her before she'd taken a single sip, Audrey looked over at him. It felt strange to be alone here with him in his house, but she wanted to do her best to act natural. "What now?"

"Well, we both get a good night's sleep. I'm hoping in the morning I'll have some good news from Colin about getting a replacement camera person." Michael lifted his mug of tea to his lips and took a very small sip; it was probably still too hot to really drink.

"Do you think it will be hard to find some-one?" she asked. In a strange way, it felt good to be talking about a practical problem like finding a new cameraman, rather than returning to the topic of the attack that had occurred at her house not an hour earlier. "I always got the impression that there were ten people for each job in Hollywood."

That comment earned her a smile—a *real* smile, one that seemed to alter his features and make her realize that Michael Covenant actually was a very attractive man. But did she want to acknowledge such an obvious fact? Going in that direction might lead her into dangerous territory, especially considering that she was now sleeping under his roof…if only temporarily.

"I think it depends on the job," he said. "And the problem is that word tends to get around."

"I thought we all had to sign nondisclosure agreements to work on the show."

"We do—or rather, you and the rest of the crew had to sign one. But this isn't like leaking the latest Marvel script to the media. Rumors travel fast, and it can be pretty hard to prove who started them." He let out a little huff of a breath, not quite a sigh, and blew on the surface of his tea. "Anyway, I don't want to punish Chris. Some people can handle this kind of work, and some can't. I just wish he'd figured it out before we started shooting."

Audrey began to agree, then realized she wasn't so very different from Chris, except that clearly, she needed the money more than he did. Would walking away even have helped, though? Somehow, she got the feeling that once a person was unlucky enough to have attracted the demons' attention, it was very difficult to get rid of them. "I'm sure you'll find someone soon," she said, although she didn't sound very convinced, not even to herself.

"I hope so, because I think as soon as we get the Whitcomb house cleared, your home will be cleared as well, and we can put this incident behind us."

Until we go to Tucson, Audrey thought. *What if whatever we encounter there decides to latch on to me as well?*

Although she hadn't spoken aloud, it seemed as though Michael had picked up on what she was thinking. "I'm very sorry about all this," he said quietly. "I've dealt with infestations far worse than the one in the Whitcomb house, and while I might have personally suffered attacks from the entities involved, no one assisting me—and no one on any of my crews—has ever had it affect them directly. If I'd known that was even a possibility here, I would never have asked you to join the show as my co-host."

He sounded so genuinely sorry that Audrey almost wished she was sitting next to him on the couch so she could reach over and place a reassuring hand on his arm. Since she couldn't do that, she said, "Don't worry, Michael. It's fine."

She actually didn't know whether it was fine, but the words were an automatic form of reassurance, a way to let him know she didn't blame him for any of this. And truly, she didn't. Maybe he was putting on an act for her, trying to seem contrite so she would continue to go along with his schemes, but she didn't think that was the case. She didn't know for sure how many of these demonic investigations he'd worked on, although she guessed he'd been involved with enough to know how much risk each one presented. He'd miscalculated in this particular instance, but that wasn't malice, only bad luck.

And, as he'd just pointed out, there was a very good chance everything would go back to normal once they'd gotten the Whitcomb mansion cleansed of its current evil occupants. She had to believe that, because otherwise, she really wasn't sure what she would do.

Or would her house end up on a future episode of *Project Demon Hunters?*

Audrey didn't want to think about that.

For a moment, they were both quiet. The tea had cooled enough that they could take cautious sips now, and it was somehow reassuring to her to sit there and wrap her cold hands around the warm ceramic of the mug she held while she drank the tea. Would the chamomile really help her sleep? It hadn't in the past, but she still appreciated Michael making the drink. It was a sort of peace offering, a way to let her know he was truly sorry for what had happened today.

As she drank, Audrey allowed herself to make a quick survey of the room. The bookcases were the dominant feature, but he also had quite a few abstract and metaphysical paintings hanging on the walls. They should have clashed with the traditional architecture of the house, and yet she found the combination pleasing because of the warm palette all the canvases shared.

She realized then that she couldn't see any photos of family and friends, nothing to show that Michael had a life outside his work. While she realized that not everyone felt the need to display photographs on every surface, their complete absence here was still a little puzzling. It was possible he was an orphan, just as she herself was, but even though Audrey had lost her parents, she still had pictures of her family on the mantel in the living room, and a photo from her parents' wedding on the sideboard in the dining room.

Well, as far as she could tell, Michael had done his best to make himself a mystery, a man without a past. His professional biographies only went back about seven or eight years. Maybe reporters or investigators had tried to dig into his personal history, but if they'd found anything juicy, she hadn't heard anything about it.

"The Tucson case sounds interesting," Michael said then.

"Oh?" Audrey was too tired to inject much enthusiasm into even that one syllable. As far as she was concerned, they needed to get the Whitcomb house wrapped up before they could even begin to think about another paranormal investigation. She needed closure, needed to know that she wouldn't have to face any further attacks.

He didn't seem to notice her diffidence, but went on, "Yes. It's a B&B that's located in an older part of town. The building dates to the mid-1870s. There've been signs of poltergeist activity lately, and the owners want us to come investigate."

She could see why poltergeists might be bad for business, but she couldn't understand why a show that focused on hunting demons would get involved in that sort of situation. After she said something along those lines to Michael, he shrugged.

"'Poltergeist activity' is shorthand for physical objects being affected by unseen forces. The television thrown at us in the basement of the Whitcomb mansion—you could classify that as poltergeist activity, too, even though the TV was being manipulated by a demon."

Great. Audrey sipped some more chamomile tea. "I thought poltergeists were usually associated with children in the house."

"They can be." Michael put his mug of tea down on the coffee table. "Demons often try to work through children because their minds are more open, which is why so many people associate poltergeists with kids or young teenagers. But it's not that these kids have suddenly developed telekinetic abilities, but that they've unwittingly allowed something to enter their homes."

It was warm enough, there in Michael's living, room, but she still shivered. In the *Exorcist* case, that was exactly how the devil had supposedly gotten in—through a pre-pubescent girl playing with a Ouija board. Audrey's parents had certainly never allowed one in their household, although she didn't know how much of that was due to fear of demonic interference or how much of it was the simple belief that there were far better games to keep their daughter occupied.

"There's a child living at the B&B?" she asked.

He shook his head. "No, but there doesn't need to be. A place like that, with people coming and going…it's entirely possible one of their guests let it in."

Pretty bad luck, if that turned out to be the case. She supposed they'd find out the truth eventually…if they were lucky.

For now, though, they had their own problems to focus on.

Audrey yawned, and Michael, rather than being offended, said, "It looks like the chamomile tea is working. Let me show you the guest room."

Not bothering to protest, she set down her half-drunk mug of tea and got up out of the chair where she'd been sitting, felt the heaviness of her limbs. It had been a long, horrible day, and her body was telling her that it needed a chance to recover from all the strain.

They went upstairs. Michael stopped at the first doorway on the right and said, "Here you are. My cleaning crew switches out the sheets every week, just in case I have company, so they're clean. And the bathroom is right next door."

"You have a cleaning crew?" Audrey asked, amused for some reason.

His lips quirked a little. "You think I can keep this house as clean as this without help?"

He had a point. His house was probably about twice the size of hers, and even she felt over-whelmed sometimes, especially if she had a lot going on during the weekend and had to squeeze in the dusting and vacuuming and laundry on a weekday.

"Well, I didn't want to impugn your domestic talents."

His eyes glinted, looking almost gold in the light from the Tiffany-style fixtures overhead. "I have none, I assure you, unless you can count making a good cup of coffee."

"I think that qualifies as a domestic talent," Audrey told him, and was glad to see him smile again. Worn and wrung-out as she was, she thought it would be a good thing to see as many of those smiles as possible.

"You can weigh in tomorrow morning. But

after that first cup of coffee, we should probably go out to breakfast."

"That sounds good." And it did. Audrey honestly couldn't remember the last time she'd had a real restaurant breakfast. Her aunt Deb had taken her out to brunch on her birthday, back in October, but brunch wasn't quite the same thing as breakfast. Beyond all that, though, having breakfast sounded so normal, so mundane. Demon hunters didn't go out for pancakes and bacon, did they?

"Okay, then." He hesitated, and the cheerful expression he wore disappeared, making Audrey wonder if she'd only imagined it. "This house is protected. You're safe here. Don't be afraid to sleep."

He didn't add, *You're going to need that sleep,* but the thought was understood. This was a quiet intermission, nothing else. As soon as he found a replacement for Chris, the cameraman, they'd be back at the Whitcomb mansion.

Audrey said, "After the day I've had, I'm sure I'm going to crash. But thank you for the reassurance—and good night."

"Good night."

He gave her a little tilt of the head, as if that was his way of saying farewell, and then he turned and headed for the door at the end of the hall, presumably the entrance to the master bedroom.

Audrey went into the guest room and closed the door, then put her weekender bag on the armchair tucked into one corner.

It was a cozy room, with Mission-style furniture to match the house, and a quilt in cheerful colors of red and blue and yellow. More Tiffany lamps here, the shades warm cream with amber accents. Had Michael chosen all these things himself, or had he hired a decorator? He'd just admitted he wasn't domestic, but the house certainly didn't reflect that apparent lack.

Well, it wasn't really a concern of hers one way or another. Audrey hung up her shirts in the closet, then took her toiletry kit into the bathroom next door and prepped for bed. About all she had to do was brush her teeth again, since she'd already washed her face and applied moisturizer earlier that evening.

In fact, as she looked at her reflection in the mirror, she realized for the first time that she was completely bare-faced, not a scrap of makeup on, unless you could count the lip balm she always applied before bed. It could have just been the lighting, but the circles under her eyes looked especially pronounced.

Great.

Like it matters, she told herself as she went back to the guest room and shut the door. *Who're you trying to impress?*

The answer was obvious, but Audrey pushed it away. She didn't want to admit to herself that she actually cared what Michael thought of her looks. Because if she did that, she might also have to acknowledge that she found him attractive. He wasn't supposed to be attractive. He was supposed to be her boss—sort of…she guessed it was Colin Turner who actually wrote the checks—and also, why was she allowing herself to be concerned with something as trivial as physical attraction when they were dealing with *demons* here?

You're just tired. Go to sleep. This will all make more sense in the morning.

She wanted to believe that. She also wanted to believe she was safe here.

And mercifully, just a few minutes after she pulled the crisp sheets up to her chin, she was asleep.

Chapter 9

THE LIGHT WAS STRANGE. AUDREY OPENED her eyes and looked up at the ceiling fan overhead.

She didn't have a ceiling fan in her bedroom.

Then she blinked at her unfamiliar surroundings, and she remembered that she was lying in bed in the guest room at Michael Covenant's house. If anyone had told her twenty-four hours ago that this was where she would end up, she sure as hell wouldn't have believed them.

But here she was. This room was much darker than her bedroom at home, probably because there were heavy drapes at the window instead of the cheap faux-wood blinds she'd put up when the previous sets of blinds finally gave up the ghost. Even so, she could see a few specks of bright sunlight beaming in through small gaps in the drapes.

Knowing it was a sunny day made Audrey feel a little better about life. So did the realization that she'd apparently survived a night here without suffering any further demon attacks, or whatever it was that had happened to her Kindle. Luck, or simply the strength of the "protections" Michael had put in place here?

Maybe a little of both.

She got out of bed and made her way over to the closet. After selecting a plain, dark green button-up shirt, she draped it over her arm, collected the rest of the clothes she'd need, and quietly slipped into the guest bath. She'd noticed that Michael's door was still shut, and she hadn't heard any water running. A late sleeper? He didn't seem like the type. She supposed it was possible that he was already up, although she hadn't detected any sounds—or smells of coffee—coming from downstairs, either.

Shrugging off the mystery, Audrey went to the shower and turned the taps. The water got hot almost immediately; the house must have had a good water heater.

And dear lord, it felt so good to get in that shower, to wash off the stink of the Whitcomb house and her own fear—or at least it seemed that way, although in reality, her deodorant had held up pretty well, all things considered. Because she'd washed her hair the day before, she clipped it up and out of the way, and was done with her shower in a little more than five minutes.

Honestly, she'd wanted to stay in that shower enclosure, done in warm-hued tile like the kitchen downstairs, for about a hundred years. But since she didn't have that option—and it would have played hell with Michael's water bill—she tried to be more thoughtful.

Teeth brushed, even though she knew she'd probably be drinking coffee in the near future. Light makeup applied, just enough that there wouldn't be a repeat of her *Night of the Living Dead* impersonation of the evening before. She hadn't thought to pack any jewelry, and she certainly hadn't been wearing any when she ran out of the house in her sleeping attire, so there wasn't much she could do about that. Still, she felt a lot better now that she thought she was slightly presentable.

Audrey went back into the guest room, made the bed, and opened the drapes. The bedroom looked out over a backyard with a neatly mowed lawn and a brick-edged patio, complete with wrought-iron dining set and stainless gas grill. Really, the whole place seemed almost too serenely suburban, and not at all a match for its owner. At least, she really couldn't imagine Michael barbecuing burgers out there while wearing a "Kiss the Cook" apron, but if her work as a psychologist had taught her anything, it was that people could be a bundle of contradictions.

Downstairs, the wooden shutters were all still closed, so the overall impression was dark and heavy, a contrast to the bright morning outside. However, now that she was standing at the foot of the stairs, she could smell the rich, heavy aroma of coffee emanating from the kitchen. She headed in that direction and found Michael in the process of pouring himself a cup. A second mug, glazed a rich, earthy red and dark blue, sat on the tile counter.

"Just in time," he said. He looked cheerful enough this morning; in contrast to the dark clothes he'd been wearing the day before, he now had on a pair of faded jeans and a light gray T-shirt—a shirt that showed off muscles his jacket had hidden the day before. "Coffee?"

"Yes, please," Audrey replied, doing her best not to stare at his biceps as he poured her a cup. Did he have a workout room hidden away some-where in this house? He must, because he didn't seem like the type to spend time at a gym. Taking the mug from him, she added, "Have you heard anything from Colin?"

"No, but I didn't expect to. He's not really a morning person. Insomniac…I'll get emails from him that are time-stamped three or four in the morning, and he can go for days on only a couple said, then was silent for a few seconds as he seemed to listen to Colin's reply to that comment. "Yes, but—" A pause, during which he sat there with his jaw set and the fingers of his free hand drumming on the Formica tabletop. "Right. I know. I know. Okay, then. If you're sure they'll be okay with it." Another pause, longer this time. Then he said, "Four o'clock…sure. We might as well take advantage of the delay and get some night shots in. Okay. Done."

He ended the call, and Audrey sent him a curious glance. "What was all that about?"

An irritated huff of breath before he reached for his cup of coffee. "Colin found a replacement camera guy. Which is great, except that word obviously has gotten out about the location, and so this guy wants extra hazard pay because of how dangerous the shoot could be."

That request didn't sound terribly unreasonable. Actually, she wished she'd had the presence of mind to make a similar request. God knows she would have earned it. "Is that such a big problem?"

"In the grand scheme of things, no, unless the other people on the crew find out about it and start demanding it as well."

"Can they do that?" she asked, genuinely curious. "I mean, we've all signed contracts that didn't include hazard pay, didn't we?"

"Yes, but all it takes is one person calling their union rep and making a complaint, and we could be back to square one." Michael pushed a hand through his jaw-length hair, which still looked slightly damp, as though he'd washed it that morning. For a second, Audrey wondered what it would be like to run her fingers through that hair; all the men she'd dated had had fairly standard short haircuts.

And then she wondered if the strain was starting to get to her. She really needed to stop paying attention to Michael Covenant's physical attributes, no matter how distracting they might be.

She made a sympathetic sound, and he added, "Actually, we'd be worse than back to square one, because if we end up having to replace the whole crew, we'd probably have to give all the new people hazard pay, and it's just not in the budget. We were supposed to be doing this as lean as possible."

"Well, maybe it won't come to that," Audrey told him. "I'm sure if Colin tells this new cameraman that he needs to be discreet, he'll keep his contractual arrangements to himself."

"I have to hope so," Michael said grimly. "Because Colin's letting everyone know that we're going to do a later afternoon into evening shoot, and we need everyone at the top of their game."

of hours of sleep, but when he does crash, he tends to be out of it until at least ten. I've suggested hypnotherapy, but he says he doesn't believe in that stuff."

"It can be effective in certain cases," Audrey allowed, privately amused that Colin Turner seemed to be just fine with TV shows about ghosts and chupacabras and God knows what, but wouldn't see a hypnotherapist for what was, sadly, an all-too-common problem.

"There's milk in the fridge, if you want it," Michael told her, apparently abandoning the topic of Colin's sleep issues. "And sugar here in this bowl." He gestured toward a squat little container with the same red and blue glaze as their mugs.

"Thanks," she said, then used the small spoon in the bowl to give her coffee the precise half-teaspoon she allowed herself.

The coffee was good, strong but not bitter. French roast? Maybe. Audrey had to admit she wasn't a connoisseur, and generally drank what-ever was available, so she'd never been that good at identifying the different varieties.

For a moment, they drank coffee in compan-ionable silence. She liked that Michael didn't ask her whether she'd slept well; it was probably easy enough to tell from a single glance, since she knew she looked vastly improved from the night before.

"I was thinking of going to Andy's Coffee

Shop for breakfast," he said next. "The food is good, especially if you just want something basic. And it's only about ten minutes from here."

Right then, "basic" sounded great. Now that she was rested, Audrey could tell she needed some calories to replace everything she'd burned the day before. Who knew that demon encounters could be such a great workout?

"That sounds fine," she said. After she took another sip of coffee, she forced herself to ask, "Are we going to check out my house, now that it's daytime?"

For a second, his brows drew together in a frown, but then he replied, "If you want. Although I don't think we're going to find that much has changed. Like I said last night, until we handle the Whitcomb mansion, that energy is going to keep reaching out for you."

"Even though I'm here now?"

"Yes. Unfortunately, there have been many documented cases where the demons followed their victims from place to place. Not that I'm going to allow that to happen to you," he added quickly, obviously noting her expression of dismay. "If there's any residue left in your home after we're done with the Whitcomb place, then I'll do a cleansing and banishment there as well. It'll be perfectly safe for you."

Strangely, Audrey did feel somewhat

comforted by his assurances, mostly because she'd just spent a night in his house, and so she knew that Michael Covenant wasn't blowing smoke when it came to his own abilities in cleansing and protecting a property. "All right," she said, figuring she would leave it at that. There wasn't much she could do about the situation except wait and see what happened.

Coffee finished, they headed out to the carport where Michael's Land Cruiser waited. The morning air was brisk, and she wished she'd thought to bring a jacket. Well, with the sun shining brightly in a clear blue sky, the day should warm up quickly. Probably by the time they were done with breakfast, she'd be wishing she had put on a short-sleeved shirt.

The coffee shop was crowded, even for a weekday morning. However, Audrey could tell the management was working hard to make sure that people were seated quickly, because even though she and Michael had five groups ahead of them, they were still guided over to a booth within ten minutes of getting their names on the wait list. Michael asked for more coffee, while Audrey decided to have water; more than one cup of coffee tended to make her jittery, and she was already on edge enough without having extra caffeine in her system.

Once they'd placed their orders—huevos

rancheros for him and an all-American breakfast of eggs, bacon, and pancakes for her—they were left to wait for the food to arrive. Audrey wondered what exactly Michael would bring up as a topic of conversation, since they couldn't really discuss the problem of the Whitcomb mansion out here in public.

But then his cell phone rang, and he shot her an apologetic glance before picking it up from where he'd placed it on the table just a few minutes earlier. "Hi, Colin," he said, and sort of nodded in her direction. So much for Colin's insomnia; it was only a little past nine o'clock. "Well, that's good news," he went on. She experienced a sinking feeling somewhere in her midsection, because that "good news" could only mean Colin had found a replacement camera person, which in turn meant they might be going back to the Whitcomb place a lot sooner than she'd expected. But then Michael paused, a scowl deepening the frown line between his brows. "Hazard pay?" he exclaimed, his tone one of outrage.

The people in the booth next to theirs paused their conversation for a moment, curious glances coming Audrey and Michael's way. Obviously noting the attention he'd just attracted, Michael let out an exasperated breath and continued, albeit with a lowered voice.

"No one else on the show gets hazard pay," he

said, then was silent for a few seconds as he seemed to listen to Colin's reply to that comment. "Yes, but—" A pause, during which he sat there with his jaw set and the fingers of his free hand drumming on the Formica tabletop. "Right. I know. I know. Okay, then. If you're sure they'll be okay with it." Another pause, longer this time. Then he said, "Four o'clock…sure. We might as well take advantage of the delay and get some night shots in. Okay. Done."

He ended the call, and Audrey sent him a curious glance. "What was all that about?"

An irritated huff of breath before he reached for his cup of coffee. "Colin found a replacement camera guy. Which is great, except that word obviously has gotten out about the location, and so this guy wants extra hazard pay because of how dangerous the shoot could be."

That request didn't sound terribly unreasonable. Actually, she wished she'd had the presence of mind to make a similar request. God knows she would have earned it. "Is that such a big problem?"

"In the grand scheme of things, no, unless the other people on the crew find out about it and start demanding it as well."

"Can they do that?" she asked, genuinely curious. "I mean, we've all signed contracts that didn't include hazard pay, didn't we?"

"Yes, but all it takes is one person calling their union rep and making a complaint, and we could be back to square one." Michael pushed a hand through his jaw-length hair, which still looked slightly damp, as though he'd washed it that morning. For a second, Audrey wondered what it would be like to run her fingers through that hair; all the men she'd dated had had fairly standard short haircuts.

And then she wondered if the strain was starting to get to her. She really needed to stop paying attention to Michael Covenant's physical attributes, no matter how distracting they might be.

She made a sympathetic sound, and he added, "Actually, we'd be worse than back to square one, because if we end up having to replace the whole crew, we'd probably have to give all the new people hazard pay, and it's just not in the budget. We were supposed to be doing this as lean as possible."

"Well, maybe it won't come to that," Audrey told him. "I'm sure if Colin tells this new cameraman that he needs to be discreet, he'll keep his contractual arrangements to himself."

"I have to hope so," Michael said grimly. "Because Colin's letting everyone know that we're going to do a later afternoon into evening shoot, and we need everyone at the top of their game."

She'd been sort of hoping she'd misunderstood that part of the conversation, since the only thing less appealing to her than going back to the Whitcomb mansion in the first place was having to be there without the protection of a bright, sunny day. "I thought the original plan was to start shooting in the morning," she said.

"It was, but since we were delayed anyway, Colin figures it's a good idea to get some shots with the setting sun, and then some at dusk. He wants it to look as spooky as possible."

Although Audrey wasn't very happy about the idea—to put it mildly—she could see Colin's rationale for making such a decision. While she knew all too well how frightening the Whitcomb mansion was, the reality needed to be reinforced with visuals for the audience at home.

And really, when one got right down to it, how much did the time of day actually matter? Both attacks on the Whitcomb property had occurred in full daylight. The assault through her Kindle had happened at night, but that could have been more the timing of opportunity than anything else. In a way, that realization upset Audrey the most, simply because it implied there was some kind of malign intelligence behind all this, that they weren't dealing with mere automatic reactions based on being in a certain place at a certain time.

Michael said, his tone gentling a bit, "I know the idea of being there after nightfall is probably frightening, but it will be fine."

"Of course," she said. "I'm not too worried." Then, to change the subject—because if she kept talking about it, she knew she'd only succeed in getting herself worked up over the prospect of facing the Whitcomb mansion after dark—she added, "Do you really think Jeffrey Whitcomb drew all those diagrams on the basement floor? That they somehow survived all these years?"

Michael opened his mouth to speak but was interrupted by the arrival of the waiter with their breakfasts. After their plates were set down in front of the two of them and they were left alone again, he said, "I don't know who else it could have been. And that could explain why the phenomena kept occurring, even though his children had gotten rid of all other evidence of his madness." A pause there as he scooped up a forkful of huevos rancheros and took a bite. Audrey reached down to her own plate to get a piece of bacon, although honestly, her appetite seemed to have deserted her for the moment. Once he was done chewing, Michael went on, "You know how I said that Jeffrey Whitcomb wasn't allowed to close the loop on his spells?"

Audrey nodded. "Because his kids had him sent off to a sanitarium."

"Exactly. Sometimes, destroying the physical evidence of those spells is enough to cut them off. But in this case, since they overlooked the runes and sigils in the basement, the doorway was still open. Probably the Whitcomb children didn't even know they were there—those boards we pulled up looked old, as though their father had them put in not too long after the house was built."

That made sense. If Jeffrey Whitcomb had installed the floor sometime in the teens, it would have probably appeared to have been part of the original fittings of the house. His children wouldn't have noticed anything out of the ordinary, and neither would the subsequent owners of the house.

Audrey finished the rest of her piece of bacon, then said, "And maybe that explains the violent reactions of the entities to our discovering the spell circles. Maybe they're worried that once we destroy them, then they'll be blocked from coming in."

"Very likely." Michael was quiet for a moment, his expression thoughtful. "Of course, they don't have to have been called so formally— which is why anyone with any sense knows it's foolish to use a Ouija board or carelessly repeat incantations, even if they don't believe in them— but in this case, because a formal invitation was made, they may be compelled to play by the rules."

And those rules seemed to indicate that once the spells which had called the demons here were broken, then they would have no way of getting back into the house. Well, that was the theory, anyway.

The question Audrey wanted to ask—why Jeffrey Whitcomb would involve himself in such dark practices in the first place—she could answer for herself. Michael had said that he didn't know for sure whether the Whitcomb fortune had come about through demonic intervention, but it seemed the most obvious explanation. He'd sold his soul to the devil, so to speak, and the price he paid was separation from his family, and eventual madness and death. Just as in cards, the house always wins.

But the people who'd lived there afterward had made no such bargain, and they certainly didn't deserve to be deprived of their home just because of Jeffrey Whitcomb's mistakes. In a way, phrasing the problem like that made Audrey feel more resolved to fix the problem confronting them. Of course, she was still afraid, but she wouldn't allow fear to prevent her from seeing this through to the end.

For a moment, the two of them were quiet as they ate their breakfasts, as if they knew they needed to keep their strength up for the ordeal ahead. The people at the next table finished their meal and got up to leave. One of them, a heavy-set woman probably in her early sixties, flicked a suspicious glance at Michael and Audrey as she went. Had she overheard some of their conversation? Possibly—the noise level in the restaurant was fairly high, which was part of the reason why they'd thought it was safe to discuss the situation at the Whitcomb mansion. However, the diner wasn't so loud that a person couldn't have still overheard what was being said, especially if the person in question was a dedicated eavesdropper.

Well, there wasn't much they could do about it now. With any luck, the woman at the next table had concluded that the two of them were both a little unbalanced and left it at that.

As if he'd guessed what Audrey was thinking, Michael said, "I wouldn't worry about it. People are going to judge—although maybe she'll think back to today when she starts seeing ads for the show."

Possibly, although she guessed that anyone capable of delivering that kind of stink-eye to people discussing something paranormal probably wasn't going to be tuning in to *Project Demon Hunters.*

Audrey shrugged as she took the last bite of scrambled eggs from her plate. "I'm not worried about it. You should have seen the eye rolls I got from my graduate advisor when I said I wanted to take seminars at the Rhine Institute."

He chuckled. "I can imagine. But people are fearful of the unknown. They want things wrapped up in neat, tidy boxes, and unfortunately, that's not how the universe works."

No, it wasn't. She'd learned that lesson early on, but there were plenty of people lucky enough to never have great tragedy impact their lives. About all she could do was lift her shoulders; Michael already knew her family history, so she didn't see the point in commenting further.

"Are you done?" he asked, clearly guessing that she really didn't want to continue the conversation along those paths.

"Yes," Audrey replied. The food was good, and her appetite had recovered enough that she'd eaten almost everything on her plate, but now she was ready to get going.

Luckily, the waiter came by then with the check, and Michael handed him a couple of twenties and told him to keep the change. Under other circumstances, Audrey might have protested and tried to pay for her part of the meal, but in this case, she just went with it. After all, she wouldn't have been driven from her house in the first place if he hadn't gotten her involved with his damn television show.

They went out to his SUV and got in. But instead of turning north toward Orange Heights, where Michael's house was located, he got on the 210 Freeway headed east. Audrey sent him a sideways glance, and he said, "I thought you wanted to check on your house."

"I did," she replied. "But you said there probably wasn't much point until after we were done with the Whitcomb place."

"Maybe not," he agreed, eyes fixed on the sluggish freeway traffic on all sides of his vehicle. It was much worse going west, toward downtown Los Angeles, but there were still enough people headed in the other direction that even going the speed limit was a vain hope. "But we have the time, and I thought you might feel better to see it again."

"Then thank you." Whether she was really grateful or not remained to be seen. Audrey knew Michael was trying to help, but what if they were attacked the second they walked in the door? So far he'd done a fairly good job of protecting her, but....

"Not a problem. I have to make sure my co-host is happy, right?"

She sent him a wan smile and then turned to look out the window. They were passing through Arcadia's northern borders now, the south side of the freeway lush with trees. Just a few more minutes, and they'd be getting off the freeway at Grand Avenue and heading north and east toward the quiet neighborhood where her house was located.

Everything looked so familiar, the shops and restaurants and gas stations, and yet it felt strange to be coming back here, knowing what she knew now. There was a dark corner in this friendly-seeming place, a house that had hidden its secrets for more than a hundred years. Somehow, she didn't think it would be very happy about the two of them dragging its darkness into the light.

But then they were driving up Vista Bonita, and turning onto her street. Everything here looked very much the same—the neighborhood quiet because most people were at work or school. The sprinklers at the Montoya house chugged away, and Audrey thought she caught a glimpse of Anna Montoya, her across-the-street neighbor, disappearing around a corner as she walked her chubby little dachshund.

Despite all that, when Audrey looked out the car window at her own house, painted a soft Dutch blue with creamy white porch and trim, she couldn't help but experience a chill that slowly ran its way down her spine. The house looked just as normal as everything else here on her street, and yet what had happened to her the night before was far from normal.

"Let's take a look," Michael said. He undid his seatbelt and got out, and she was forced to do the same, even though what she really wanted right then was to turn around and drive back to Pasadena and the comparative safety of his house.

As they walked up the front steps, Audrey noticed that he had one hand resting near the front pocket of his jeans. Did he have another vial of holy water secreted away in there? He'd probably come prepared, which meant the answer to that question was most likely yes.

Fingers shaking a little, she got her keys out of the inner pocket in her purse, then forced herself to put the house key in the lock and slowly open the door.

The smell was what hit her first. Not the mildew odor that seemed to come and go in the Whitcomb mansion, but the sharp, penetrating scent of cat urine. Audrey blinked, eyes watering, and then she realized the cat pee was only the tip of the iceberg.

It looked as though a tornado had blown through the house. All the furniture was toppled over or thrown across the room; the end tables had been jammed into the stair railing, breaking some of the finely turned spindles. Pictures were torn from the walls, frames and glass broken.

And there, lying on the rug—which appeared to have large yellow urine stains on it—were the family photographs she treasured so much, their frames also broken. It looked as though something had taken them down off the mantel and then stomped on them.

Audrey let out an incoherent cry and ran over to pick them up, not caring about the shattered glass. Tears began to run down her face as she clutched the crumpled photographs to herself. The rest of the house…that was just things. They could be repaired or replaced. But these pictures were all she had left of her parents.

Almost at once, she felt Michael's arms go around her, pull her away from the fireplace. "Audrey, it's okay. We'll fix this. But we need to get out of here."

"They did this, didn't they?" she asked, forcing the words past the terrible knot in her throat.

"Yes…and they're still here. I can feel them."

He'd barely finished that last sentence before something went screeching overhead, a dark form whose shape was so hideous, her mind didn't want to make sense of it. Wings…scales…glowing yellow eyes. Now she could hear that same screeching laughter tearing at her ears, and she cringed.

With his free hand, Michael pulled a vial from his jeans pocket. As the entity came shrieking back toward the place where they stood by fire-place, he flung the contents of the vial at it, saying, "You were not invited here. I cast you out, send you back to darkness!"

The water hit the demon's flesh and it screamed, smoke rising from welts that had suddenly appeared on its scaly skin. Taking advantage of its distraction, Michael pulled Audrey out of the house and slammed the door behind them, then splashed the remainder of the holy water on the doorframe, as though by doing so he could create another barrier.

They ran to his Land Cruiser and jumped in, and he sped away from the house with a squeal of tires that probably would have brought all her neighbors to their doors…if they'd been home. But because all this was taking place at ten o'clock in the morning, no one was around to see the two of them running from her house as though the Devil himself were after them.

For all Audrey knew, he was.

Once they were on Foothill Boulevard, heading back toward Grand, Michael spoke. "I am so sorry about your house, Audrey. I had no idea they would retaliate in such a way…I thought they would be content with driving you from your home."

She pulled in a hitching little breath, then another. Tears still burned in her eyes, but she tried her best to blink them away. "It's not your fault," she said, her voice barely more than a whisper. She realized then that she still clutched one of her photographs, although the broken frame must have fallen away as she and Michael fled for the door. "You couldn't—couldn't know that was going to happen."

"Still." He shook his head, mouth tight with anger. "We'll take care of the house for you. The show's insurance should cover it. If not, I'll handle it myself."

"It's all right—" Audrey began, but he cut her off.

"No, it's not all right."

They turned onto Grand, going back toward the freeway. She sat in silence, not sure what else she could say. It had been bad enough to know that the demons had tracked her to her house, had forced her to leave. Even then, at least she'd known it would be there waiting for her once she and Michael were done with all this. But now— she didn't even have that hope to cling to. It would probably take weeks to get the mess completely cleaned up, and she didn't know for sure how bad the damage even was. She'd only gotten that quick glimpse of the living room and dining room. What if the demons had trashed the kitchen, destroyed the upstairs as well?

How could she ever feel comfortable there again, even if the insurance took care of everything?

That thought was enough to get the tears flowing again. Audrey sat there, feeling them roll down her cheeks, not bothering to do anything to stop them. Michael reached over and laid his hand on top of hers. He didn't say anything, but right then it was enough to feel the warmth of his skin, to know the reassurance of having someone there next to her.

And beneath the sorrow and loss was anger, a growing rage at these terrible entities who delighted in torture and pain, who didn't care who or what was destroyed as long as they could take some pleasure from it. She could feel her body tensing with that rage, and at once Michael's hand tightened on hers.

"Don't," he said, and she looked over at him in surprise.

"Don't what?"

"Don't let anger take control of you. That's what they want. If you allow negative energy to control you, then you'll be that much more susceptible to them."

Intellectually, Audrey understood what he was saying. It really wasn't that different from the sort of thing she might have said to someone she was counseling. Because rage and resentment could eat away at a person, could turn you into the very thing that hurt you in the first place.

But this was so hard, almost harder than overcoming her anger toward the gunman who'd taken her parents' lives. Because he hadn't targeted them specifically. It hadn't been any kind of personal revenge; they'd merely been in the wrong place at the wrong time. This, though—this destruction had been designed to hit her where it would hurt the most.

This *was* personal.

"I'll do my best," she managed, and Michael squeezed her fingers one more time before he returned his hand to the steering wheel. He was turning onto the freeway on-ramp, and so she could see why he would want to have better control of the vehicle.

"You have to," he said, "because we're going to come up against these things very soon, and I need to know you can handle it."

Audrey swallowed. "You're not going to cancel the shoot?"

"I wish I could," he said. "But we've already been delayed once. I doubt Colin's going to let us push back another day, especially after all the favors he called in to get us another cameraman on such short notice."

Right.

In her misery, she'd forgotten all about that. The show must go on, right? Never mind that her life had been turned upside down. What she needed to do now was take her anger and turn it into resolve, a resolution to face these things down and send them straight back to hell. Because if she and Michael didn't succeed, they'd never leave her alone. She realized that now.

Audrey took another breath, then shifted in her seat so she faced Michael.

"I'm ready," she said.

Chapter 10

THEY DIDN'T TALK MUCH ON THE REST OF THE drive back to Michael's house. He was frowning, but since that seemed to be his usual expression, Audrey really didn't think much of it. As he pulled into the driveway, she could feel that frown mirrored on her own face. Yes, he'd given her a sanctuary here, but that couldn't last forever.

It doesn't have to, she told herself. *Just until we're done at the Whitcomb mansion…and the demons who've followed me home are dealt with.*

Well, clearing the demons out might ensure that she wouldn't suffer any further attacks, but it wouldn't clean up the mess in her house. That was going to require a lot of manpower and elbow grease. Michael had said he'd make sure the production company would take care of it, and yet even if they paid for everything—along with a

hotel for her to stay in until the work was done—
she was still looking at an extended period of
being denied access to her own home.

They went into the kitchen. "Iced tea?"
Michael asked. "You could probably use something stronger, but...."

"Tea is fine," Audrey said firmly. The last
thing she wanted was to be driven to day
drinking.

He nodded and retrieved a couple of glasses
out of a cupboard, filled them about halfway with
ice from the refrigerator door, then got out a big
bottle of Tejava iced tea and poured equal
measures into each glass. After handing one of the
glasses to her, he said, "Do you want to go sit
outside? It warmed up pretty well."

That sounded like a good idea, especially since
the morning was sunny and warm, as if apologizing for the broody, cloudy days she'd experienced earlier that week. "Sure."

They headed outside, to the patio table
Audrey had spotted from her upstairs window
earlier. After they'd both sat down, she sipped at
her iced tea. She was glad that Michael seemed to
like it the same way she did—plain and black, no
froufrou sugar or lemon. After they'd sat there for
a moment in silence, drinking in the sunshine
along with their tea, he spoke.

"Again, I have to apologize. I've never experienced anything like this, not in any of the investigations I've conducted."

It was bright enough that Audrey had extracted her sunglasses from her purse after she sat down. She let them slide down her nose slightly and looked at him over the top of the frames. "Have you ever had an investigation like this, though?"

She thought she saw his jaw tighten slightly, but his tone was neutral as he said, "I've investigated other instances of demonic infestation."

"In a house this old? A place where they've had free rein for so many years?"

He hesitated, and Audrey wondered if he was going to answer her directly, or whether he was going to come up with some kind of excuse. To her surprise, he replied, "No. Nothing like this. I suppose I figured it wouldn't be all that different, except maybe by degree."

"I guess not."

Rubbing at the scruff on his chin in an introspective way, he stared off toward the rosebushes that stood guard along the fence marking the border of the property. They were already starting to show buds, even though it wasn't even March yet. "While there are documented cases of demons following their victims from place to place, that sort of thing only occurs after the people involved have been suffering demonic oppression or even possession for months or years. You'd never been in the Whitcomb mansion before, had you?"

"No," Audrey replied at once. "I'm not sure I'd even heard of it. That is, maybe it was mentioned once or twice, but my interest has always been in paranormal powers of the mind, not ghosts and hauntings, so I never paid all that much attention."

"Which makes the way they've focused on you that much stranger."

She shook her head, then sipped from her glass of iced tea. "Should I be flattered?"

Audrey had thought he might chuckle, but he only frowned, fingers playing with the condensation on the surface of the glass in front of him. "I don't think 'flattered' is exactly the word I would use."

No, probably not. She was quiet for a moment, glad to feel the warmth of the sun on her skin, to see its clear light all around her. In this sunny backyard, it was hard to believe that demons were real, even though she'd seen the terrible evidence of their existence a very short time ago.

"What happened to the Whitcomb family?" she asked then. "That is, you said Jeffrey Whitcomb's wife divorced him, and his grown children had him put in a sanitarium, but what happened to the children?"

"Whitcomb's son never married, and died without children. My best guess is that he was probably gay, although of course the records back then would never have come right out and stated something like that. Still, the phrase 'confirmed bachelor' was thrown around a bit, and that tended to be the euphemism used in those situations back in the day." Michael drank some more tea before continuing. "The daughter married and moved back east. She had children—two daughters. One of them caught polio and died young. The other one married, but it seemed she got divorced sometime in the mid-'40s, changed her name, and moved out of Connecticut, which was where her mother had settled after they left California." He shrugged. "I sort of lost the trail after that, although I suppose I could hire a private investigator to look into it if I thought there was enough need." His eyes met Audrey's, now looking almost golden in the reflected light from the sun overhead. "Do you think it's necessary?"

"Probably not," she said. "I was just wondering. And the family fortune?"

"Most of it was lost in the crash of 1929. Alice Whitcomb had gotten quite a lot in the divorce, and she invested it wisely, so she did well enough for herself. However, Jeffrey's money was pretty much gone, so anything their children inherited, they inherited from their mother."

Jeffrey, who apparently had died raving in a sanitarium. Well, if he really was the one who'd drawn all those symbols and attracted the demons here in the first place, then Audrey didn't have a lot of sympathy for him. "What about the other people who lived in the house?"

"Most of them seemed to have gotten out before the demons really got their claws in them, so to speak. They sold the house, left the area, and apparently lived normal lives. The only real casualty was Abner Crawford, but his children seemed to be okay."

And yet Audrey, who hadn't even spent an hour in the place in total, had demons coming after her from all sides. She would have said that wasn't fair, but she'd learned a long time ago that fairness and the universe weren't exactly on speaking terms.

Michael's cell phone rang, and he pulled it out of his pocket and glanced down at the screen. "Colin," he said shortly, and she nodded. They were probably getting everything firmed up for the late-afternoon shoot. A little chill went through her at the thought of entering that damn house again, although she tried to reassure herself that everything would be done after today, and she'd never have to set foot in the place after they wrapped up shooting tonight.

But then Michael sat up a little straighter in

his chair and said, "What?" in tones so surprised and yet angry at the same time, Audrey took off her sunglasses and sent him an alarmed look.

"What is it?" she mouthed, and he shook his head, as if trying to let her know that he didn't have time to answer right then.

"Are you serious? But we had an agree—" He stopped there, clearly having been cut off by Colin. From the way Michael was angrily drumming the fingers of his free hand on the tabletop, the news couldn't be good. After a long pause, he said, "Okay. Right. No, she's here with me. There was an...incident. No, we're both fine. Right. See you tomorrow."

He put the phone down on the table, then picked up his tea and took a large swallow, all the while looking as though he really wished there was something else in that glass besides plain black tea.

"What's wrong?" Audrey asked.

"The new cameraman—you know, the charming individual who insisted on hazard pay?"

"Yes," she said cautiously.

"Well, apparently regular hazard pay wasn't enough for him. He wanted another two hundred dollars a day as a bonus, after which Colin told him he could kiss his English ass and fired him."

Great. Yet another delay. Yes, there were probably plenty of qualified camera people in L.A. who could take on the job. But with rumors flying this way and that, would any of them be desperate enough to want to do it? "So we have to wait for Colin to find someone else?"

"No," Michael said. Some of the anger was fading from his expression, although he still looked annoyed. "Colin's going to shoot the show himself."

"He can do that?"

"Yes. He actually got started shooting his own productions because he couldn't afford to hire anyone. After a while, he realized he was better at the wheeling and dealing side of things, so he went into producing. But he can do it, although he said he needed some time to refamiliarize himself with the equipment."

"Which means we're not shooting tonight."

"No. Everything's getting pushed back twenty-four hours." He looked at her, sympathy clear in his face. "I'm sorry about that, Audrey. I know it's probably not what you wanted to hear."

No, it wasn't, but she told herself she could handle the delay. It was just one more day, after all. She'd packed enough clothing and toiletries to keep her going for a day after that, but if it turned out they needed to shoot until the very end of the week, she'd either have to venture back into her house—and hope the demons hadn't destroyed her clothing along with the furniture—or she'd have to bite the bullet and go buy a few things to tide her over. Neither prospect was very appealing, and she fervently hoped they'd finally be able to put this thing to bed after they were done shooting the next day.

"It's all right," Audrey said, and thought she actually sounded halfway convincing.

"Which means we have a day to kill," Michael went on. "Is there any chance you could see some of your clients today?"

Immediately, she shook her head. "No, I've already rescheduled them once…I don't want to drag them in on such short notice. I can find a book to read or something."

One eyebrow went up at an ironic angle. "Oh, come on," he said. "I think we can find something more interesting to do than that."

Audrey sat at the small table in Michael's library and shot him a dubious glance. "You know I've done this test before," she said. "Multiple times." She didn't bother to add that those tests had been done mostly for fun, since the Zener card test for psychic ability had long since been disavowed as a valid measurement of clairvoyant talents. Michael probably knew that as well as she did, but the cards still held a certain allure as a quick and dirty way to see if someone measured above the mean in terms of psychic powers.

"True," he replied, "but psychic talent can mature as a person gets older. There are many instances of those powers growing stronger after someone has suffered a traumatic event. I'd say the events of the past few days more than qualify."

Possibly, but if all it took was a traumatic event to set someone off, then Audrey thought she should have been exploding with psychic power right after she lost her parents. It hadn't worked that way, though.

However, she didn't mention that detail to Michael, mostly because she didn't want to see pity in his face again. She'd come to terms with her loss, and she didn't see any reason to keep rehashing it.

"Maybe," she said. "Just don't get your hopes up."

That remark made him flash a smile at her, one that probably shouldn't have sent a pleasant little thrill dancing along her nerve endings. It was a little too cozy, the two of them sitting there only a few feet apart, a mild breeze fluttering the silky drapes at the window, the only perceptible sound the ticking of a clock that hung over one of the bookcases.

"I am going to be entirely neutral," he said. "Now, put on your blindfold."

Audrey hesitated, then picked up the blind-fold—really, just one of those satin sleeping masks you could get at Bed, Bath, and Beyond—and fastened it around her head. A small amount of light seeped through, but she definitely couldn't see Michael or his expression, which was the important thing. Early tests of this kind had been tainted by the subject maintaining eye contact with the test-giver, and many of the positive results had really been due to nothing more than the sorts of nonverbal tells that magicians and fortune tellers had been relying on for centuries.

"Ready," she told him.

A soft rustle seemed to indicate he was shuffling the cards again. Then she heard his voice—really, a nice voice, not particularly deep, but smooth and rounded and rich, the kind of voice that would have done well on radio.

Maybe she just hadn't paid much attention to it before now because she was too busy looking at his face.

"All right," he said. "I'm holding a card. What's on it?"

An image formed in Audrey's mind—not one of the simple outlines drawn on the back of the Zener cards, but of the glowing star that used to sit on top of her family's Christmas tree. It had always been her job to place that star—first by being held up by her father to reach the top of the tree, then later with the help of a footstool. At least, it had been, until the year she lost her parents. Even though her aunt Deb had made sure to decorate the house, Audrey told her she didn't want to use the star anymore, and her aunt had found an angel instead, one with dark hair like her niece's. A little ache went through Audrey; she wasn't sure she even knew where the star was located anymore, although she guessed it was probably packed away in one of the boxes stored in the rafters of the garage.

"A star," Audrey said softly.

"Correct." That was all Michael said, but he sounded pleased. Another shuffle of the deck, then, "What about now?"

This one didn't come to her with any particular imagery, but only the stark outlines of the image as it was drawn on its card. "A plus sign."

"Correct again." He added, amusement clear in his voice, "What was that about me not getting my hopes up?"

"Two cards isn't statistically significant," Audrey said in her primmest voice, and he chuckled.

"No, it isn't. So let's see how many you can get. What am I holding now?"

Once again, the picture of the card came to her with startling clarity. "A circle."

"Correct."

Now, three in a row wasn't statistically significant, either. She'd managed to pull off such a feat before, although her streak ended immediately afterward. Despite that precedent, she couldn't quite ignore the way an uneasy anticipation began to build somewhere in her midsection.

"Now?"

"A star again."

Another shuffling of the cards. "Now?"

"The one with the three squiggly lines."

"And now?"

"A square."

"Now?"

"A circle."

"Now?"

"Another plus sign."

So they went on, no banter this time, only Michael pulling card after card. With the blindfold on, she couldn't see the clock, had no idea how many minutes had passed, but she did her best to mentally keep a count of how many cards they'd gone through. After around eighty-five, though, she began to lose track.

At last she heard a scrape, which she thought might be Michael pushing his chair back away from the table. When he spoke, he said, "You can take off your blindfold now."

Audrey did as he requested. The cards were back in a neat stack to one side of the tabletop, and Michael was standing over by one of the bookcases, his expression one of wonder.

"Do you know how many that was?" he asked.

She stood up as well, mostly because she was beginning to feel a little stiff after sitting in one place, immobile, for so long. "I counted up to eighty-five, but I sort of lost the thread after that."

"One hundred and twenty-five," he said. "I've done a lot of these tests—even though science has done its best to debunk the process—and I never had anyone, not even those who were highly psychic, get more than twenty or thirty in a row. What you just did—getting all of them right—should have been impossible."

How was she supposed to respond to that comment? She managed a weak little laugh, then lifted her shoulders. "Maybe you were providing some sort of auditory tell and just didn't realize it."

"I assure you, I wasn't. You know my intonation didn't change from card to card."

He was right. He'd done his best to keep his tone completely neutral throughout the duration of the test. There was no way in the world she should have been able to get that many cards correct…and yet somehow, improbably, she had.

Audrey had already been feeling uneasy, and now that sensation was ten times worse. While parapsychology fascinated her, she'd never expected to be psychic herself. Or at least, nothing more than the little twinges she'd gotten from time to time, that one incident in New Orleans, or the way she'd seemed to have felt her mother's death, even though she hadn't known what the sensation meant while it was happening. People often did have these flashes; Audrey's friend Bettina had known almost to the minute when her grandmother had died, even though they were hundreds of miles apart at the time, and yet Bettina had otherwise never shown any sign of psychic talent.

But to choose those cards correctly one hundred and twenty-five times in a row? As Michael had just said, it should have been impossible.

"Well, I suppose that explains why I've had such strong reactions to the presence of the demons," Audrey said, doing her best to keep her tone light. "For whatever reason, something seems to have set off my abilities. I suppose if this whole demon-hunting project doesn't take off, we could consider putting together some kind of mentalist act."

Of course she was joking—once she was done with *Project Demon Hunters,* she planned to go back to her practice and live a quiet life—but Michael only nodded in an abstracted way, as if he thought it might actually be a good idea, or at least didn't believe it was a bad one. "I'll have to reconsider our approach from now on, that's for sure."

"What do you mean?"

He came back over to the table and idly shuffled the Zener cards with one hand, making little stacks, then folding them all back together again. "Well, I'd set up the show thinking I was going to be the psychic, and you were going to be the skeptic. But if we're both psychic...." The words trailed off, and he sent Audrey a rueful smile. "We might have to reevaluate things."

A thought occurred to her, and she said, "Maybe it's not so much that I'm psychic, but that you were sending so strongly, I couldn't help but receive the images."

"No, I don't think so." He looked up from the cards. "I've known for a long time that I had some abilities, but they've never been strong enough to pull off anything like that."

For a second, it looked as though he meant to say more. Then he seemed to shrug, and began to put the cards back in the little box they'd come in. Watching him, Audrey couldn't help asking, "When did you know you were psychic?"

"Since I was a little kid, I guess. But most of the time I just tried to ignore it. That whole world felt too weird to me, and I wanted to live a normal life."

This admission surprised her, because Michael seemed to her like the sort of person who had eagerly jumped into the psychic realm with both feet, so to speak. "What changed your mind?" she asked softly.

Although he didn't answer her right away, she could feel a sudden blast of jumbled emotions coming from him. It was so strong that she nearly reached out to grasp a corner of the table to steady herself, but then it faded almost as quickly as it had come, and she had just a second to sort out what she'd felt—confusion, and fear, and worry, and a terrible sort of guilt. "Something that happened a long time ago," he replied, his tone short. "Something with my family."

"What—?"

"I don't want to talk about it."

Now he wasn't looking at her at all, had picked up the little deck of cards and walked over to a writing desk on the opposite side of the room. He shoved the cards into the top drawer and shut it with a noticeable bang.

Audrey knew better than to press the issue. People would only open up on their own timetables; she'd had enough first sessions with clients who stared stonily out the window and didn't say anything to know she couldn't force someone to divulge what they weren't ready to let go. The day before, she'd wondered if Michael might be an orphan, but she thought now that he could just as easily have suffered some sort of abuse in his youth. That would explain the lack of family photos, the way he seemed so reluctant to talk about anything personal. He'd created a world where he was in control, and she guessed he wouldn't be too happy with her for making him realize he wasn't quite as in control as he thought.

"I'm sorry," she said. "I didn't mean to pry."

"It's fine. That's a period in my life I'd prefer not to talk about."

"Then we won't." Hoping she could do something to get that brooding expression off his face, she went over to where he stood by the writing desk. "Since we're waiting on Colin, why don't we get out of here for a few hours? I haven't been to the Norton Simon museum in years—that's not too far away, is it?"

"No, it's not far." His mouth still looked set, unhappy. "But I'm not so sure of the wisdom of going out. Here, we're protected, but my resources are more limited when we're in a public place."

"We went out for breakfast," she pointed out. However, he didn't appear at all convinced by that argument.

"Yes, but that was before I saw what the demons had done to your house. They're clearly willing to reach far beyond the Whitcomb mansion to try to hurt you, or at least frighten you. The last thing we need is for an attack to occur someplace in public."

"Really?" she returned. "Because I would think an incident like that would be great publicity for the show."

He'd been half turned away from her, long, slender fingers playing with some of the papers that sat on top of the desk. Now he shifted so his gaze met hers, and Audrey could see the sudden anger in his face. "Do you really think I would purposely put you in danger like that?"

"No, of course not," she replied hastily, realizing she'd just stepped over a line. "Forget I said it."

A long pause, and then he said, "I'll do my best. But for now, I think we had better stay here."

What could she do except nod? At the same time, though, she couldn't help thinking that it was going to feel like forever, waiting until they could return to the Whitcomb mansion the following afternoon.

Funny how all of a sudden she couldn't wait to get back to the haunted house....

Chapter 11

Trapped here in durance vile. Well, Michael's house was a lot more comfortable than, say, the Tower of London might have been back in the day, but Audrey hated the feeling of being stuck, of not having even a semblance of freedom. He'd directed her to the bookshelves, and said he had Netflix and HBO if she didn't feel like reading, and that seemed to be it. Obviously, her asking about his past had upset him, and he wanted to make sure she was safely occupied elsewhere.

Which was why she spent the rest of the afternoon in his TV room, feet propped up on one of his couches, while she binge-watched the previous season of *American Horror Story* and he stayed hidden away in the library. From time to time, during quiet scenes in the shows she was watching, Audrey could hear his voice, but he was far enough away that she couldn't make out anything of what he might be saying. He'd said he had business to take care of, maybe getting things set up for the other episodes of *Project Demon Hunters,* or making arrangements for speaking engagements once he was done with the show.

She couldn't know for sure, because he hadn't bothered to tell her. That omission made her realize how much she really was just set dressing on the show. She wasn't calling the shots, or even being invited to provide input. No, Michael and Colin would be the ones making decisions. Which was their prerogative, of course, but it only made her feel that much more of an outsider.

While Audrey watched TV, she had her phone plugged into a spare outlet and charging. Thank God she'd started carrying a spare charger in her purse a few years ago or she would have been in a world of hurt...especially since it didn't seem likely that she could have wheedled Michael into taking her to the Apple store in Old Town Pasadena to purchase a new one.

Around six-thirty, just as the last of the daylight began to disappear from the world outside, he appeared at the door to the TV room. She'd long since kicked off her shoes and was reclining there in her sock feet, but so be it. He was the reason she'd been exiled here in the first place.

"Hungry?" he asked, and she picked up the remote and paused the show she was watching.

Actually, she was; they'd let their breakfast do double duty and replace lunch, so it had been more than eight hours since they'd last eaten. "Let me guess...delivery?"

"Of course," he said, looking unperturbed. "I've got take-out menus for Indian, Chinese, Thai, Italian, pizza...whatever you like."

What she would have "liked" was to go out somewhere after being shut up here all day, but she knew that wasn't an option. Since she'd had both pasta and pizza recently, Audrey figured she should try something else. "Does Indian food work for you?"

"Sure. The menus are in the kitchen—let's go take a look."

She removed her feet from the couch, slipped her ankle boots back on, and followed Michael into the kitchen. He went to one of the drawers there and quickly flipped through a stack of papers, obviously looking for the menu in question. "I take it you don't cook," she said dryly.

"No," he replied. "It's easier to order in. Plus, I travel a lot."

Yes, she supposed he did, since he went to so

many conferences and symposiums. No wonder his kitchen looked so spotless—he never used it.

"Here it is," he said as he pulled out a piece of goldenrod-colored paper. "Choose whatever you like—I'm not picky."

While Audrey enjoyed Indian food, she'd never gotten too experimental with it. She figured she probably couldn't go wrong with lamb korma and chicken masala, along with rice and naan and vegetables. When she made those suggestions, Michael nodded.

"That all sounds great. I'll go ahead and place the order."

He pulled out his phone and made the call. She noticed he had the number saved in his contacts, and seemed friendly with whoever was taking the order, so clearly he'd ordered from this place many times before. When he was done, he returned the phone to his jeans pocket and offered her what looked like a genuine smile.

"It'll be here in about fifteen minutes. I'll go ahead and set the table."

"I can help—"

"No, it's fine. It'll only take me a minute."

Which it did, more or less. He got out place mats from a drawer and some paper napkins from a dispenser on the kitchen counter, then headed into the dining room. It was a long, somewhat narrow room, with pretty stained glass windows set high in the east wall and large windows over-looking the front yard to the south. The furniture here was also Mission-style to go with the house, dark but not heavy. Although it wasn't exactly formal, it still felt like a proper dining room, and Audrey wondered a little at it, considering that Michael didn't seem to eat at home very often.

"Sorry to slough you off like that," he said as he went back into the kitchen to get the silverware and dishes—and wine glasses, too. She eyed them but didn't say anything. While a glass of wine sounded great, the idea of drinking wine here with Michael while they were alone together in his house seemed just a bit problematic. "I had a lot of logistics to handle. You managed okay?"

"Oh, sure," Audrey replied airily. "It was relaxing to be able to sit and watch TV. I don't usually have a lot of time for that. And I checked in with my friend Bettina, let her know I was going to be away from the house for a day or two."

"I hope you didn't give her any specifics."

"Of course not," she said, a little offended by the assumption that she couldn't keep the goings-on at her house to herself. The only other person who knew anything about what had happened—why Audrey had been forced to flee the place—was Rosemary McGuire, and since Bettina was not exactly Sister We's target customer, Audrey figured she didn't have to worry about their paths crossing and the two of them possibly comparing notes.

Michael nodded, apparently satisfied by the vehemence in her tone. "You okay with syrah?" he asked, going back to the kitchen. "I've had it with Indian food a few times, and it works fine."

"Sure," she replied. Well, she was all right with the notion of syrah…what she wasn't as sure about was drinking here with Michael Covenant. More than once, she'd thought about what it had felt like when he'd held her, even though nothing had happened between them that could be classified as anything more than friendship. She knew she was feeling alone and vulnerable…and that could turn into a problem.

He fetched the wine in question from a countertop rack, then got out a corkscrew and opened the bottle with an economy of movement that wouldn't have been out of place in a Michelin five-star restaurant. Maybe he was more of a connoisseur than she'd guessed, although if that were the case, one would think he would have more than the four or five bottles she'd noticed in his kitchen's wine rack.

The doorbell rang then, and he went to answer it, taking a quick detour into the dining room so he could put the open wine bottle down on the table there. A quick convo with the delivery person at the door, and a minute later, Michael was back, quickly dispensing the various dishes into serving bowls.

"Go ahead and sit down," he said. "I just want to put this in the trash." He lifted the plastic bag that now held the various Styrofoam containers used to transport the food.

"Okay."

After a brief hesitation, Audrey took the seat at the left, rather than the one at the head of the table. Maybe as his guest she should have sat down in the place of honor, but she wouldn't have felt comfortable there. When he returned a moment later, his gaze flickered toward her for a few seconds. However, he didn't comment, only went to take his own seat and put a paper napkin in his lap.

She followed suit, and then he poured the wine. Not a huge amount, only about halfway filling their wine glasses, but still....

He raised his glass and Audrey clinked hers against it, although she didn't really know what they were toasting. Her newly awakened psychic powers? Being alive and whole and relatively safe, despite everything that had happened over the past few days?

Maybe a little of both.

The two of them sipped some wine, then were quiet for a bit as they both dished up the food.

After they'd had a few bites of lamb and rice, though, Michael said, "I got a call from Colin right as I was finishing up in the study. We're definitely on for tomorrow."

Audrey hadn't known there was a possibility of yet another delay, so this news made her simultaneously worried and relieved. "He'll be able to handle the camera work?"

"He thinks so. Or rather, and I quote, 'You just show up, and I'll make sure this bloody camera gets it all, one way or another.'"

Even though she'd only met the producer that one time, she could almost imagine hearing those words spoken in his quick, lively accent. "He's kind of a force of nature, isn't he?"

"That's a charitable way to put it. I'm sure there are a lot of people in Hollywood who might think of a few other terms to describe him."

Audrey smothered a smile, then reached over to take a sip of syrah. It did go well with the food. Maybe a little too well. She'd have to watch it. "How did you two meet each other?"

Michael drank some wine as well. When he was done, he said, "Colin showed up at a conference where I was giving a talk on demonic oppression and possession, how to spot the warning signs, what to do if you think demonic forces are working on you. He told me he loved my spiel, that he wanted to do a show about it." A shake of the head, and he speared a piece of lamb on his fork, then chewed it thoughtfully before continuing. "It took some convincing before he won me over."

"Why?" she asked, genuinely curious.

"Because I wanted to be as respectful as possible. This is a subject that can be easily sensationalized, and you can lose sight of the fact that, underneath all the phenomena, the spectacle of a house truly being infested by demons, there are usually some very terrified people who need your help. I didn't want to turn it into a sideshow, like those exorcism tours down in Mexico."

"The what?" Audrey stared at Michael. Had she heard him correctly? "Exorcism" and "tours" were not usually words she would put together in the same sentence.

"There's an underbelly to the tourist industry that specializes in tours to all sorts of macabre venues," he explained. "Drug lord houses in Colombia, sites of mass murders here in the U.S. —and tours in Mexico that can take you to observe an honest-to-God exorcism. Or at least, that's what they claim is happening."

"I thought the Catholic church was very secretive about exorcisms." Not that her research had been extensive, but most of the accounts Audrey had read made it sound as though it required a good deal of persuasion and documentation to even get the church to agree to send someone to investigate a case. She couldn't really see the church getting on board with basically selling tickets to watch someone get exorcised.

"It is, but we're often dealing with village priests here, people in poverty-stricken areas. The promise of some much-needed cash is often enough to get them to overlook their misgivings. Also, it's hard to say whether all of these are true exorcisms, or whether they're working with people who simply need psychiatric care. Unfortunately, in some places in the world, it's a lot easier to ask your local priest to perform an exorcism than it is to get to a city and seek real psychiatric help."

Yes, she knew that, all too often, mental illness had been confused with some sort of possession, and the problem persisted even today. And it appeared that practices such as what Michael had just described weren't doing much to remedy the situation.

"That's very unfortunate."

"Yes, it is. And that's why I want to be careful with this show. Of course Colin wants it to be all about jump scares and hyperbole, but I think we'll be able to find a happy medium."

Oh, Audrey was pretty sure the images of that…whatever it was…trying to claw its way out of the mirror in the master suite of the Whitcomb mansion would be enough to scare most people.

Too bad she and Michael hadn't caught the incident in the basement on film, but she had no doubt that the removal of those terrible runes and sigils would be enough to prompt another assault.

And Colin would be filming the whole thing.

"I'm sure you will," she said, and hoped she actually believed those words. Strangely, though, she was glad Colin would be there, if for no other reason than this show was his baby, and he had a vested interest in making sure everything went smoothly. She didn't think she would have been able to put the same amount of trust in someone who was squeezing the production company for hazard pay and who'd thought it was a good idea to extort even more money above and beyond what was already promised.

Michael didn't exactly smile, but he did look more relaxed as he went on to talk about where the team would be going after Tucson. It sounded as though Santa Barbara might be back in the running, although there was a ski lodge in Aspen that he wanted to check out, and a former boarding house in Bisbee, Arizona. That would make four shows out of the six that had been budgeted.

"I'd like to have the final episode be somewhere on the East Coast," he said. "There's so much material in that part of the world. But Colin keeps harping on the budget, so we'll have to see how it shakes out. At least I've got the first four planned, though."

"And one almost done," Audrey commented, with more confidence than she actually felt. It was easy to be blithe about the situation while she was sitting here at the table with Michael, eating Indian food in between sips of syrah. Once they were back down in that terrible basement, they'd be facing a very different set of circumstances.

"Almost, yes." His fingers played with the handle of his knife; although he'd set out knives and forks, they'd only needed the forks so far, so the knife had lain unused through dinner. "But I don't anticipate too many problems, not now that I know what we're up against. Many times, it's figuring out how the demons got in that's the real issue, but we're past that. It's also easier in an empty house."

Audrey could only agree with that. The current owners of the Whitcomb place were miles and miles away in Palm Springs; whatever she and Michael were doing here, it shouldn't touch them. Or at least, she hoped it wouldn't. She asked Michael as much, and he nodded.

"I talked to them this afternoon, let them know we were still on track to have the problem resolved in the next couple of days. As far as I could tell, they were fine—they've been playing golf and swimming, going for hikes. The evil living in their house hasn't followed them."

No, because it had decided to latch on to her, for whatever reason. Was it that the demons had somehow been able to sense her burgeoning psychic powers, and were trying to scare her off before she had time to let them fully develop? Did they somehow see her as a threat?

Audrey found that hard to believe, but then again, she didn't know much about demons' thought processes. And she really didn't want to know.

"Well, that's good," she said as she broke off a piece of naan and dipped it in korma sauce. "I guess they didn't live there long enough for it to really get its hooks into them."

"No, apparently not." Michael was quiet for a moment, although he didn't seem interested in his food or his wine. Instead, he was looking up at the stained-glass windows in the dining room's east wall, expression abstracted. Was he thinking about the McGraths, hoping he could make good on his promise to return their house to them in the near future?

Audrey thought of something then she'd been meaning to ask him, something which had occurred to her as she was watching TV that afternoon. "I know there isn't much we can do about my house until we're done at the Whitcomb mansion, but I realized that we never checked on my car when we were at my house. Do you think we could go look tomorrow, see if it's okay?"

He raised an eyebrow. "Audrey, there's a very good chance that they trashed your car, too."

"Maybe. Or maybe not. It's very possible they were focused on just the house. The garage is detached—you have to walk down the driveway to get to it."

Again, he was quiet. "It's possible it was left alone. We can go look, if it's that important."

"It is. I mean…." She let the words trail off because she had to stop and ponder why this was so important to her. "I don't want you to take this the wrong way, because you've made a lot of effort to keep me safe, but I'd just feel better if I had my car back. Even if I'm only driving it here once we've made sure it's okay."

"I understand. You need some autonomy. Although you know I'll make sure you have some-place to stay while your house is being worked on."

Meaning, she guessed, that he didn't want her here as a house guest of indeterminate duration any more than she wanted to be one. And really, a lot of the work would go on in the background while she was off on location, chasing down demons in Aspen or Santa Barbara or wherever

Michael and Colin determined would make the most interesting shows.

Rather than go into any of that, however, Audrey only said a heartfelt "thank you," and returned her attention to her plate. The rest of dinner was somewhat subdued, and the two of them finished and took their plates into the kitchen in silence.

Once they were done with clean-up, however, Michael turned toward her and said, "I'd like to try another little psychic test with you, if you don't mind."

She wouldn't say she was exactly relaxed, but she did feel a slight detachment from the day's worries, thanks to the two glasses of wine she'd drunk. "I'm not sure I'm in the best shape for reading cards," she told him.

"That's not what I had in mind. More a little…psychometry."

Psychometry, the practice of being able to get impressions about a person or event by touching an item associated with that particular individual or happening. Audrey certainly had never shown any talent for it, but, as the little card-reading session earlier had proved, she wasn't exactly the best judge of her own abilities.

"Sure," she said, hoping she didn't sound quite as reluctant as she felt. An impulse prompted her to add, "But can I ask you something first?"

"Of course," he replied, although his posture suddenly seemed wary, as though he didn't quite trust her to ask something he could answer.

All their talk about psychic powers had reminded Audrey of her conversation with Rosemary McGuire, how she'd argued with Michael about the origins of her family's powers. "I guess I'm trying to figure out how my suddenly getting psychic abilities works with your theory that humans aren't really psychic, that our powers come from someplace outside ourselves."

He shook his head. His expression was more resigned than annoyed. "Rosemary McGuire told you that, didn't she?"

"Well, yes."

"I'm afraid she misunderstood what I was saying. My contention was simply that humanity's psychic powers may very well have come from outside sources—otherworldly entities, so to speak."

Audrey couldn't help raising an eyebrow at him. "What, you mean like aliens?"

Now he did smile. "No, more like fae or djinn or angels."

"Oh, that's all." She supposed that once you were willing to believe in demons, then it wasn't too much of a stretch to include all sorts of other supernatural beings.

Then again, "believe" wasn't probably the

correct word to use when you were confronted by the reality of demons on a daily basis.

"Yes, that's all," he said. "It would help to explain why strong psychic powers tend to run in families. So actually, what I was saying only supported what Rosemary believed about the psychic powers she and her sisters inherited. But that's what happens when you walk into the middle of a lecture and don't try to figure out the context."

About all Audrey could do was shrug. She liked Rosemary, but she could also see how the psychic might have misconstrued what Michael was saying, especially when she was already predisposed to dislike him. And while Audrey wanted to ask whether psychic talents ran in his family, she knew he'd probably shut her down and not give her a straight answer. Better to leave it alone. "I understand," she said. "Thanks for explaining the situation."

He nodded, and they went into the living room, where he asked her to sit down on the couch. She did as requested, then waited as he went to retrieve a book from one of the bookcases that lined the walls. It was clearly an old volume, with its cracked leather binding and worn gold leaf on the spine. She could just barely make out the title.

"*Treasure Island?*" she said, looking up at him.

"It's not the book that's important. It's who it belonged to."

All right, then. Audrey let Michael place the book in her hands, and then she held it with one palm pressed against the front cover and the other flat against the back. Since she wasn't sure what to do, she closed her eyes, thinking that might aid her concentration. For a minute or two, she really didn't see anything. Even so, she was acutely aware of him standing next to the couch, of the clock ticking on the mantel, of the various sighs and creaks of the old house as it settled in for the night.

And then it was as if a brightness grew behind her eyelids, like the sun coming up, even though she knew that wouldn't happen for another ten hours or so. She saw a big, spreading tree, and a stream that meandered beneath it. The tree's leaves were a bright, fresh green, and the sun was warm overhead. Late spring, or early summer. Audrey didn't think the scene displayed behind her closed eyelids was anywhere in California, although she couldn't really say why she had that particular impression.

A woman was sitting on a fallen log next to the stream, the book open in her lap. She was older, probably in her late sixties or early seventies, but her spine was straight as she sat on the log, and the hands that turned the pages didn't shake at all. A mild breeze ruffled her snowy hair, pulling a few strands loose from the ponytail she wore low on her neck, letting them drift around her face, delicate and pale as spiderwebs.

Then the scene faded, and Audrey opened her eyes and blinked up at Michael.

"What did you see?" he asked.

She described the woman and the fallen log, the luxuriant tree—oak?—and the feeling of peace that had lain as thick over the tableau as the golden sunlight slanting through the leaves. Michael nodded, satisfaction clear in his expression...but also something Audrey might have described as fear, if she didn't think that emotion sounded far too melodramatic for the situation.

"Who is she?" she asked.

"My great-grandmother," he replied. "This book was hers. She died when I was barely more than a toddler, so I don't remember her very well. But I remember that spot by the stream, because my mother said it was her grandmother's favorite place to go and read, to steal a few minutes for herself."

"Where is it?" Audrey asked, even though she had a feeling he wouldn't tell her. Providing a location connected to his family would have been giving her far too much information.

"That doesn't matter," he replied, confirming her suspicions. "What matters is that you were able to see the exact location where this book was read, and were able to accurately describe my great-grandmother. There's no way you could have known any of that, except by touching this book."

"Especially since you don't have any family pictures here," she pointed out. "Why?"

"Because I choose not to," he said smoothly. "Not everyone wants to be reminded of their childhood."

"But you gave me this book as a test."

"I needed an object whose provenance was known. That's all."

Audrey pursed her lips in annoyance but didn't bother to reply. It was painfully obvious that Michael would only give her the information he wanted to pass along, and nothing else. Why should she bother to keep beating her head against that brick wall?

Because she wanted him to open up to her. She wanted him to treat her differently from the casual acquaintances who knew so little about him. She wanted...she really wasn't sure if she was ready to acknowledge what she really wanted from him.

Still in silence, she got up from the couch. She handed the book back to Michael and said, "I'm getting tired. I think I'll go to bed now—we have a big day tomorrow."

"You're upset with me."

"No," she replied, even though of course she was. Although maybe "upset" was too strong a word. Frustrated, definitely. Speaking calmly, she went on, "You made it clear to me earlier that you don't like to talk about your personal life. I need to respect that. You don't owe me any answers."

"Maybe not, but...." Whatever he'd meant to say, he apparently had decided against it, because his lips pressed together, as though he needed that physical barrier to prevent the words from slipping out. Then he said, "You're right, though—we do have a big day tomorrow. We should both get some sleep. I'll walk you upstairs."

Audrey wanted to protest that she didn't need a guide, but then she decided it was better to go with the flow. Suddenly, she was very tired, and she didn't see the point in wasting her dwindling energy on useless arguments.

The two of them went upstairs, where she paused in front of the open door to her room. Before she could say good night, however, Michael spoke again.

"You know you're a very extraordinary woman, don't you?"

He was standing very close. Possibly too close, but Audrey found she didn't mind. Maybe she should have minded. There might have been a moment when she could have stepped inside her room, made a quick comment about seeing him in the morning. Whatever that moment was, or could have been, it was lost soon enough, because Michael took another step toward her. Now he was only inches away, those odd, gold-flecked gray eyes focused on her face.

Voice a murmur, he said, "You can tell me to stop."

She knew she should. She knew what was going to come next. But all she could feel was a terrible, aching need, body and soul telling her something her mind had wanted to ignore.

All she could do was shake her head. Not telling him to stop, as he'd said, but letting him know that she didn't want to say those words.

She didn't want him to stop.

And then he was bending toward her, and she felt as if she was falling into those eyes as his mouth touched hers. In that instant, the need within her seemed to flare with a terrible fire, wanting even more than this kiss, wanting him so badly that the strength of her desire shocked her. Had she ever felt this way with anyone else?

She didn't think so, but right then she also wasn't quite capable of rational thought. All she knew was that kissing Michael Covenant felt more right than anything else she'd ever done, even though she knew deep down that they should not be doing this. Not when they were working together. Not when he was being so secretive about his past.

Despite all those thoughts raging through her head, he was the one to end the kiss, not Audrey. He lifted his mouth from hers and took a step backward, then said, "I shouldn't have done that."

Somehow, she managed a shaky laugh. "It wasn't as though I tried to stop you."

"No, but...." One hand went up to push his hair back from his face, and she noticed how he didn't quite want to meet her eyes. "It was unprofessional."

"Technically, you're not my boss, Michael. Colin is."

"True. Even so...."

Audrey put a hand on his arm. It was the first time she'd really touched him like that, and she could feel the strength in those muscles, how solid and firm his body was. Once again, desire flared in her, but she did her best to push it away. "You gave me a chance to stop you. I didn't. That should tell you something." She paused before adding, "Let's just leave it there for now. After tomorrow...after we're done with the Whitcomb house...then we can try to figure out what we're doing. Okay?"

"Okay." He slipped his arm from under her hand, but only so he could wrap his fingers around hers. They were warm and strong, just like him. "Sleep well, Audrey."

He bent and kissed her again, but gently this time, just a brush of his lips against hers. Then he released her hand and turned and walked quickly down the hall, as if he didn't quite trust himself to stay in check if he didn't put some distance between the two of them.

She could relate.

After pulling in a breath, Audrey went into the guest room and shut the door. Her body was still thrumming from his touch, his kiss.

Just when I thought my life couldn't get any more complicated....

Chapter 12

AUDREY HAD WORRIED THAT SHE MIGHT TOSS and turn half the night, fretting about the kisses she and Michael had shared and what she was supposed to do about them, but apparently she was tired enough that her subconscious decided to back off for the night and let her sleep. And that was exactly what she did, so soundly that it was a little after eight o'clock when she woke up.

Eight. Yikes. Good thing they didn't have an early call time this morning.

No sign of Michael when she cracked the door and looked out into the hallway, so she hurriedly got her things together and slipped into the guest bath, then showered and washed her hair. Blow-drying it afterward took up an appreciable chunk of time, enough that it was nearly nine o'clock when she finally went downstairs.

He was sitting at the little table for two in the kitchen, reading something on his phone. A mug of coffee sat in front of him. As soon as Audrey entered the room, he put down the phone and looked over at her. No smile, though; his gaze was troubled. Clearly, he was still worried about the change in their relationship.

So was she, but she didn't want to let that get in the way of what needed to get done today. Trying to sound casual, she asked, "Is there any coffee left?"

"Yes. It's sitting on the warmer."

She smiled at him by way of thank-you, then went to get a mug from the spot where several hung on a rack on the wall next to the coffeemaker. Pouring herself coffee and doctoring it with the little bit of sugar she allowed herself didn't take much time. When she was done, she came over and sat down in the empty chair at the bistro table.

"Any updates on the shoot today?" she asked.

A look of relief passed over his features. In the bright morning sunlight coming through the window, Audrey could see faint shadows under his eyes. Apparently, he hadn't passed as peaceful a night as she had.

"No," he replied. "That is, Colin sent me a text saying we were all still meeting at the property at four, so nothing has changed."

"But we're still going to check on my car this morning."

"I told you we would," he said. "We can go after we have breakfast."

"We should eat in Glendora," she suggested. "There's a restaurant called Flappy Jack's that has great breakfasts."

"Sure." He drank the remainder of the coffee in his mug, then put it back down on the table.

"There's still some left in the carafe, if you want it," she said.

"No, I'm fine." Michael gave her a lopsided smile. "This is awkward, isn't it?"

"Maybe a little," she replied. "But that's okay. Really, like I said last night, we can figure out this…whatever it is between us…later on. Today we have a job to do."

"You're right, of course. Business as usual." From the way his gaze shifted away from hers, however, Audrey had the impression he wasn't sure whether they'd be able to pull off the whole casual thing with any real success. Maybe, maybe not. Even as self-conscious as she currently felt around Michael, she could also sense the energy flaring between them, the way she had to fight to keep herself from getting up, going over, and kissing him again…if for no other reason than to prove the connection they'd experienced was real, wasn't something conjured out of that bottle of wine they'd shared.

But she figured it was better to keep things light for now. The last thing she wanted was for either one of them to be off-balance today. Too much was at stake.

And, in addition to everything else, she really didn't want Colin Turner to suspect anything was going on between her and Michael. Not because she worried that he'd be angry about the situation, but more that he'd try to come up with some way of exploiting the sexual tension between the two of them in order to make the show more interesting.

"As soon as I'm done with this coffee, we can go," she said.

"Okay. There are a few things I need to do first, but I'll take care of those now."

Audrey didn't ask what those "things" were. Returning phone calls, checking his email?

Making sure that all the protections he had put in place in the house were still working properly?

He got up from the table and left the kitchen. She made herself stay where she was, and sipped coffee and looked out the window at the back-yard. The fog had rolled back in again, and the morning was gray and damp. Not the most auspicious beginning to their showdown with the Whitcomb mansion's demons, although she knew that in Southern California, a day might start out gloomy as hell, and be bright and sunny by noon.

She did her best not to think about Michael, about the touch of his lips and the way his hair had brushed against her cheek when they kissed, but, as with most mental exercises like that, the harder she tried to push the memory into the background, the more it seemed to dominate her thoughts. It was idiotic to be obsessing over him like a girl with a high school crush, though. Sometime during her college years, she'd realized she wasn't the sort of person who fell in love easily, whose hormones dictated her actions. In a way, that made life easier, because she wasn't subjected to the kind of heartbreak some of her friends experienced with their own boyfriends. On the other hand, she'd found herself reflecting more than once that it might be fun to experience really falling for someone, falling crazy hard, just to know what it was like.

Well, if her current obsessive thought processes were any indication, that was exactly what was happening now with Michael Covenant. Probably the last person she should have become fixated on, but she realized the universe did like to play these little jokes on her.

In one way, though, she and Michael were supremely compatible—they'd never have to try to explain their interest in the paranormal to the other person. That particular obsession seemed to be hard-wired into both of them.

There were still a few swallows of coffee left in her mug, but it had already gotten lukewarm, so Audrey gave it up as a loss and went over to the sink to rinse out the cup. After placing it in the top rack of the dishwasher, she straightened up, her gaze straying to the window above the sink.

Someone was standing out in the backyard, watching the house.

She startled, then stared back at him. As far as she could tell, she'd never seen the man before—he looked as though he was in his late fifties, tall and almost gaunt, with prominent cheekbones and hollow, sunken-looking eyes. His black coat hung loosely on his frame, as if he had once filled it out much more than he did now.

And then she blinked, and he was gone.

Her heart was beating a mile a minute in her chest. Audrey held on to the edge of the tile countertop, glad for the cool ceramic beneath her fingertips, reminding her that it was real, that she was inside the house and safe. There had been something terrible in the stranger's dark eyes, an abyss of despair and rage and endless, echoing sorrow.

Footsteps sounded on the tile floor and she whirled, then relaxed slightly when she saw it was Michael standing there, looking at her with some concern.

"Audrey, what's the matter?"

"I—" She swallowed, then forced in a breath, telling herself she was all right, that maybe she'd just imagined the man standing in the backyard. "I saw someone. He was standing there." She shifted so she could point at the window over the sink, at the small lawn that formed the center of the yard.

Michael came over to the sink and looked out through the window, brow furrowed. He was so close that Audrey felt his jacket brush against her arm, but right then, she couldn't be concerned with her physical responses to him. "I don't see anyone."

"He—he disappeared. I don't think he was real."

Turning back toward her now, frown deepening. "Describe him."

She rubbed her lips together. They felt dry, sore, even though she'd put on lip gloss before she came downstairs. "Tall and thin...really thin. Dark hair and eyes. He was wearing a long black coat, but it didn't look exactly like an overcoat... more like something you'd see in an old photograph. What did they call those? Frock coats?"

"Jesus."

"What is it?"

Michael turned toward the window again, although the yard remained empty, still and quiet in the foggy morning air. "I think you just saw Jeffrey Whitcomb."

"I *what?*"

He took Audrey by the hand and led her over to the table, had her sit down. "The man you described sounds just like the pictures I've seen of Jeffrey Whitcomb."

"What was he doing in your yard, Michael?" Her hands were shaking, so she knotted them together, hoping that would get them to calm down.

"I don't know. Maybe as a warning…maybe he knows what we have planned for his demon-summoning spells in the basement and is trying to scare us off."

"You're saying his ghost is trying to frighten us?"

"Well, it would have to be his ghost, since he's been dead for almost a hundred years now." Michael shrugged. "That's the only reason I can think of for him to be appearing now. Of all the phenomena reported in the Whitcomb house, I've never come across anything that sounded like it might have been his ghost."

"I thought you said this house was protected," Audrey remarked then, trying not to sound accusatory and probably failing miserably.

"The house is," he replied calmly. "Not the yard. He probably couldn't get any closer than that, which was why he materialized out there, and not in here with you."

Was Michael's explanation supposed to be reassuring? She didn't find it particularly so, not if it meant that the shade of Jeffrey Whitcomb could still wander around the property...that demons might be able to come up on the front porch and leer in the windows.

When she didn't respond, Michael added, "Ghosts can't hurt you, Audrey. Unlike demons, they have no bodies that can interact with the physical plane."

"Maybe," she said, her tone dubious. "But they can still scare the shit out of you."

That remark only made him chuckle. "Come on. You'll feel better after you've had some breakfast."

She wasn't so sure about that. However, going out to breakfast meant putting some distance between her and the spot where she'd seen Jeffrey Whitcomb's ghost lurking, and that sounded like a very good idea to her.

"Sure," she said. "Let's get out of here."

Flappy Jack's was reassuringly normal, and Audrey's appetite recovered enough for her to demolish a Denver omelette and some hashed browns. After she was done eating, though, her stomach wanted to knot itself up all over again, because their next stop was her house. Even though she knew they weren't going inside the house itself, she didn't want to think of what she might see in the garage.

This was your idea, she told herself as Michael pointed his ancient Land Cruiser east along Foothill Boulevard. *Besides, the car's insured. Even if the demons have trashed it, you can get it fixed or replaced.*

That sounded very logical, and was true enough…up to a point. She didn't know whether she'd be able to adequately explain to an insurance adjuster how her car had managed to get damaged while it was sitting inside a locked garage.

They pulled into the driveway. Just as it had been the last time the two of them were here, the exterior of the house looked peaceful, unchanged. A person would have to try to peek past the blinds to see the utter destruction within, and this wasn't that kind of neighborhood. People were too busy living their own lives to snoop like that.

Still, Audrey shivered as she got out of the

SUV and closed the door. She could have blamed the chill she felt on the damp, unappealing morning, but she knew it was much more than that.

Michael came over to her, right hand extended. She took it, glad he was offering her that small amount of comfort. Funny how the touch of someone's hand could be so reassuring... or maybe it was only that she held Michael's hand, and he had a bit more to offer in this sort of situation than your ordinary person.

Still....

Hand in hand, they walked toward the garage. It was small, added to the property in the 1930s, and could only accommodate a single vehicle; Audrey's parents used to take turns parking inside. Rather than undo the padlock on the main door, she went to the side of the building, where there was a separate entry. She got out her keys, went to the green color-coded one—"g" for green and garage—and put it in the lock. It turned easily enough, although she didn't know whether that was a good sign or not.

"I'll go first," Michael said.

She wasn't about to argue. "Okay...but be careful."

He sent her a brief, unsmiling look. "I'm always careful."

Well, almost always, she thought. *You weren't all that careful last night....*

Better not to let her mind follow that particular path. The last thing she wanted right now was to be distracted.

Slowly, he opened the door inward, then fumbled for the light switch on the left side of the door. How he'd known it would be there, Audrey wasn't sure, but she supposed it seemed like the logical location for it.

The lights flared on.

"Well, hell," he said.

All the windows in her Corolla had been smashed in. From what she could see as she peered over Michael's shoulder, it looked as if the upholstery had been torn to shreds. The hood of the car was ripped away from the hinges, those same hinges bent as though something inhumanly strong had pried them apart.

Well, actually, that was probably exactly what had happened. Audrey did her best to look at the scene clinically, to calmly enumerate the damage. Maybe then it would be easier to accept the reality of her poor little car being destroyed.

The hood was still there. It was propped up against the driver-side door of the car, words splashed on it in pale blue paint—the same color as the paint on the exterior of the house. Several spare cans had been stored on a shelf at the back of the garage.

Letters made up of slashes of paint read, *Your next.*

Audrey shook her head. "Apparently, demons have a shaky grasp of grammar."

Michael looked down at her, opened his mouth as though he were going to reply, then shook his head. After a pause, he said, "We'll get you a rental car."

"We can worry about that later," she replied. "At least now I know that the car is a no-go."

"I'm sorry about that."

"Stop apologizing," she told him. "Or rather, there's no need to apologize, unless you came over and did this while sleepwalking or in a fugue state or something."

"No, this was our friends from the Whitcomb mansion." He paused and looked northward, roughly in the direction of where that peculiarly haunted house stood. For a second, Audrey was worried that he might suggest they go over there right now, but instead he added, "I'm glad the production has a large insurance bond. Colin and I argued about that, but I insisted. At this point, though, it's probably better not to mention any of the damage here until we're done with the shoot. Colin's going to be shaky enough, going back to camera work after a long hiatus, and there's no point in upsetting him with insurance claims."

Yes, Audrey could see how that might put a

mercenary like Colin Turner off his stride. Waiting a day or two wasn't going to make much of a difference. At least she had someplace to crash until they got all the logistics sorted out.

All right, staying at Michael's place presented its own set of issues, but nothing the two of them couldn't handle. They were both adults, after all.

"What now?" Audrey asked. A glance down at her watch told her it was barely eleven; they had a long ways to go until their scheduled four o'clock meet-up at the Whitcomb property.

"We'll go back to my house," Michael replied. "And then I'll see how many protection strategies I can teach you before we have to come back here and face those demons."

Not so long ago, she would have dismissed all this as mumbo-jumbo, the sort of psychological chicanery people indulged in to make themselves think they had some sort of control over their environment. But once you'd established that demons were real, and that the ghost of a long-dead man could appear outside your window and stare at you balefully, then you probably had to accept all the rest of it, too.

White sage incense burned from a censer on top of one of the bookcases in the library. It was sweeter and more aromatic than the sage bundle Rosemary had used to smudge Audrey's house, although Michael wasn't using it for the same purpose. White sage helped to clear the mind, to purify a space of negative energies, a necessary prelude to what they would be doing next.

"You aren't particularly religious, are you?" he asked. He'd been rummaging around in a drawer in his writing desk, and now approached with several amulets hanging from leather cords draped over one hand.

"Not really," Audrey replied. "We went to church now and then when I was really little, but my parents stopped taking me when I was around five or six." She paused, giving him a sideways look. She recalled how he'd said during their first meeting that he was an ordained minister, although he hadn't mentioned which denomination. Should she ask? Probably better to wait…it was pretty clear to her that he wasn't Catholic. "Are you going to try to convert me?"

"No," he replied, his expression completely serious, although she'd been teasing him…just a little. "But we're dealing with demons here, and belief in a higher power is absolutely necessary to protecting yourself—and giving yourself the strength to drive them away." He draped one of the necklaces around her throat, a point of some kind of black crystal with a silver cap. "Black tourmaline," he explained. "It can't be matched in terms of protection from negative energies and spirits. I keep a chunk of it in every room, and I always carry a piece in my pocket when I leave the house."

Audrey recalled how she'd seen a rough black stone sitting in one of the bathroom cabinets. At the time, she'd been occupied with other matters, but now she thought she understood why it was there.

"And of course you know what this is," he went on, this time dropping a long chain with an ornate silver cross over her head. "It can serve as a reminder of the higher power we'll invoke to protect us—physically, mentally, and spiritually."

"Okay," she said, hoping she didn't look as foolish as she felt. While she knew all this was real, that the stakes were real, some part of her still couldn't help wondering whether this was all part of some elaborate prank.

"And the prayer of protection," he said. "This is the simplest, and the most used. There are others, but if you memorize this one, it should be enough."

Prayers and charms and chunks of black stone that would protect her from vicious, otherworldly enemies. About all Audrey could do was nod.

"*The light of God surrounds us;*
The love of God enfolds us;

The presence of God watches over us;
Wherever we are, God is!"

She'd been prepared to be amused by such an invocation, but somehow, Michael's voice had deepened as he spoke, and he suddenly seemed taller and broader, as though he should be wearing armor and wielding a spear as he struck down the unrighteous. The gray glint of his eyes was sharp as steel.

The hair had lifted at the back of her neck, and she swallowed.

"Repeat it," he told her.

Feeling foolish, Audrey said the words of the prayer. They sounded weak and ineffective coming from her mouth, but Michael must have been satisfied, because he nodded.

"That should work. But say it again—as many times as you need so you know you have it completely memorized. It's one thing to repeat the prayer here, when you're not under any sort of pressure, but it'll be completely different if you're having to say it while facing an onslaught from a group of demons."

"*The light of God surrounds us,*" Audrey began, then recited the rest of the prayer without a hitch. Luckily, she'd always been good at memorizing things—song lyrics, phone numbers, quotes from movies and books—so this wasn't any kind of a challenge for her. When she was done, she asked, "Why didn't you teach me all this from the beginning? I could have used some of this protection that first time I went into the Whitcomb mansion."

"Because I didn't think you would accept any of it," he replied. He still stood very close to her, and she wished he would pull her into his arms, offer some reassurance that way, but he apparently didn't think that would be a good idea. If only she was brave enough to reach out to him…. He went on, "You were hired to be the show's skeptic, remember? But then your own psychic abilities began to manifest, and I realized you needed to be able to protect yourself, not just have me do it for you. You're now much more open to these energies than you were a few days ago. This—paradoxically—makes you both stronger and more vulnerable. Understand?"

She thought she did. Or at least, she could see why being open to those sorts of vibrations might create a whole new set of problems. If she hadn't been flexing her psychic muscles, so to speak, would she have even seen Jeffrey Whitcomb's shade standing out in Michael's backyard?

"I understand," Audrey said. Her worry must have shown on her face, because he seemed to put his scruples aside and came closer, pulling her against him. She laid her head against his chest, was reassured by the slow, steady beating of his heart. Fiercely, she wished they could stay here like this, just the two of them, safe in his house. Unfortunately, they had a date with a bunch of demons.

Michael ran his hand over her hair, his touch gentle and yet firm. "You can do this. *We* will do this. You've already faced challenges that would have sent most people running for the next state, so I have no doubt that you'll be able to handle this one as well. And it won't be the two of us, either—Colin will be filming, and Susan will take care of the sound."

"Are they going to be draped in crosses and black tourmaline, too?" Audrey asked wryly.

"Actually, yes. That is, I gave Colin a key chain with a cross set with black tourmaline, so he carries it all the time. Susan has a pendant that's very similar. She knows to wear it into situations like this."

To be honest, Audrey hadn't seen a cross around Susan's neck, but it wasn't as though she'd been looking for one, either. She could have had it tucked inside the neckline of her T-shirt; Audrey thought she'd glimpsed the gleam of a silver chain around her neck, but the pendant would have fallen inside her shirt and been invisible to the casual onlooker.

"It sounds like you've thought of everything,"

she remarked, and Michael gave a sad shake of his head.

"Unfortunately, when it comes to dealing with demons, it's almost impossible to think of 'everything.'"

Audrey stared up at him, and fervently hoped he was wrong.

Chapter 13

THEY DIDN'T EAT ANY LUNCH; MICHAEL SAID
it was better to be light and lean when going into
a confrontation like this. Besides, they'd had
breakfast late enough that skipping a meal
wouldn't make that big a difference.

"If everything goes well," he said as the two of
them got into his Land Cruiser, "then Colin and I
will take the crew out to celebrate. That's one
thing I can say for him—he's not afraid to spend
money on a party."

"I thought wrap parties were for the end of a
season," Audrey remarked. She decided she
wouldn't comment on his "if everything goes well"
remark, because she was feeling nervous enough as
it was and didn't need to hear all the reasons why
today's shoot could head south in a hurry.

"Well, this isn't exactly an ordinary show. But

I have a feeling Colin will want to have another party once we've wrapped the season."

Which meant she'd have to go through all this five more times. About all she could do was hope that the other places they were called to investigate wouldn't be quite as intense. She had a feeling that five weeks of this sort of thing would leave her a nervous wreck.

Although....

Audrey glanced over at Michael, his expression intent as he eased his SUV into the heavy traffic on Lake Avenue, and reflected that this job did have its perks. A few days earlier, she would have scoffed at the notion that she and Michael Covenant could ever be romantically involved. And now...now she just wanted this to be over with so he could kiss her again. He was awfully good at it.

They'd given themselves plenty of time to get to the Whitcomb mansion, since traffic eastbound on the 210 Freeway was nightmarish starting at about two in the afternoon and didn't let up until almost eight. Even in the carpool lane, they inched along, but this time Audrey wasn't impatient with the traffic the way she might otherwise have been. At least it was keeping them from getting to their destination too quickly.

Eventually, though, they reached Glendora and the Grand Avenue exit. Surface street traffic was pretty thick, too, but at last they made it to Sierra Madre Boulevard and went right. A few more blocks, and they were turning down the side street where the Whitcomb mansion was located.

Seeing its tall pale shape, the palm trees that marched along the borders of the property, was enough to start Audrey's heart pounding again. On its surface, the house looked gracious and mellow, revealing nothing of the horrors she and Michael had experienced within. Goosebumps lifted on her arms, even though nothing had happened yet.

"It's going to be fine," Michael said, then pulled up into the driveway and parked behind a sleek black Porsche Cayenne SUV.

She didn't have to guess whose vehicle it was, because she saw Colin Turner standing in front of the open lift gate and fussing with what looked like a brand-new, extremely complicated video camera mounted on some sort of Steadicam system. He glanced up as the two of them got out of the Land Cruiser and approached him.

"Nice rig," Michael commented.

"Yeah, it had better be—damn thing cost me thirty thousand quid," Colin groused, fiddling with the controls on one side of the camera.

Thirty thousand dollars? Well, more than that, because a pound was worth more than a dollar. Audrey tried to imagine having the kind of cash lying around where she could just casually scoop up a camera costing that much, and failed miserably.

"Tax write-off," Michael said with a grin. If he was at all worried about what they were about to face in the very near future, he didn't show it. "Everyone else here?"

"If you mean Susan and Kathleen and Daniela, then yeah. Brooke got spooked, too, so Daniela is going to cover for her on P.A. duties." For the first time, Colin looked directly at Audrey. "You'd better go ahead and get worked on, darling —it looks like you could use a bit of extra help."

What the hell was that supposed to mean? All right, she hadn't spent as much time on her hair this morning as she usually did—for obvious reasons—but she'd thought she was looking decent enough, especially if one took into consideration the way she'd been run through the wringer the past few days.

However, she realized it probably wasn't a good idea to get into an argument with the man who signed the checks, so she sent Michael a significant look and then simply said, "Sure. I'll meet you back here when I'm ready."

The guest house they were using for hair, makeup, and wardrobe looked much the same as it had the last time she was there. Kathleen approached Audrey at once, saying for this shoot she wanted her in a tunic and skinny jeans and ankle boots.

Audrey looked at the footwear the wardrobe manager was holding up and shook her head. "Not those heels. This is probably going to get pretty physical. Let's just do jeans and a T-shirt and a leather jacket again...and nothing with more than an inch heel. Otherwise, I could be in trouble."

Kathleen clicked her tongue against the back of her teeth in annoyance. However, after a good look at Audrey's face, she must have realized she was serious, because she didn't offer any arguments, only went back to the rack of clothing she'd brought with her and selected a new set of garments.

"Better?" she asked.

Much better. The jacket wasn't black, but an interesting dark steel blue, the T-shirt a simple pale gray top with a scoop neckline. And the boots had low heels and laced up, sort of like combat boots except more streamlined. Just like the last time, everything fit beautifully.

Time for hair and makeup next, with Daniela once again transforming a blank canvas into something that looked like Audrey, only about twenty times better. She knew it was all for the cameras, for the people who would one day have *Project Demon Hunters* streaming into their homes, but she still felt better once Daniela was done, stronger, more confident.

"I heard you're taking over P.A. duty today," Audrey said to Daniela as she began to put the makeup brushes back in her kit.

"Yeah, Brooke got freaked out over what Chris told her happened. She said dealing with that kind of thing wasn't worth twenty bucks an hour, and she's probably right." A shrug, and Daniela zipped up the little roll of makeup brushes and bent down to put it in the large rolling case she used to stow all her makeup supplies.

"I hope they're paying you more than that," Audrey remarked, and she grinned.

"Oh, yeah, I told Colin the only way I'd do it was if he paid me my regular hourly rate and a half, and he was desperate enough to say okay." She flipped her long, jet-black ponytail over her shoulders as she straightened up.

"You're not frightened?"

Her fingers went to the gold crucifix she wore on a thin leather cord around her neck. "Sure, a little. But it's not like I have to go inside the house with you. I just have to be up here to fetch and carry stuff. I don't know how the rest of you can do it."

Audrey really didn't know, either, but there wasn't much she could do about it at this point. "I guess it's not quite as scary when it's all of us. I honestly don't think I could go in that house by myself."

"No way...not for a million dollars." Her dark eyes twinkled as she added, "Not that Colin is offering me that much."

No, not Audrey, either. She was willing to risk life and limb for a much smaller amount.

Michael poked his head in the door. "Ready, Audrey?"

Her stomach performed a somersault, but she nodded. "Yes, I'm ready."

Daniela looked at him and said, "You're not going on camera with your hair looking like that. And you need some makeup."

"No, I don't," he said as Audrey waited off to one side and did her best to smother a smile, despite her jumpy stomach. "And my hair is fine."

In answer, Daniela crossed the room, comb in hand. Before he could protest, she'd somehow managed to smooth his hair while still allowing it to maintain a certain casual messiness. From a pocket in the smock-like jacket she wore, she produced a big, fluffy makeup brush and some powder, which she dusted on his face. He frowned, but she only raised her eyebrows at him.

"At least you're not so shiny now," she said.

As Michael opened his mouth to speak, Colin appeared behind him, looking annoyed. "If you lot are done messing around, we've got work to do."

"Just coming to find you," Michael said smoothly. "We're all ready here."

This reply didn't seem to mollify the producer too much, because the irritated expression never left his face. However, he only said, "All right—let's go. I want to get some exterior shots before we go in the house."

As much as Audrey wanted to get this over with, she was still relieved to hear she wouldn't have to go inside right away. They all trooped into the garden area, with Colin positioning her and Michael in various spots—in front of a palm tree, near the fountain in the courtyard, on the front steps of the house itself. He seemed to shoot everything looking upward, as if he wanted to make the mansion seem even larger and more imposing than it already was. The one thing that did seem to please him was the way some clouds had moved in, making the day look dark and somewhat foreboding. The wind had begun to pick up as well, and Audrey was glad for her borrowed leather jacket.

Eventually, they moved inside the house. Colin set his expensive camera down on a long side table in the entryway and said, "I went ahead and had someone come in and do part of the floor demolition in the basement. Otherwise, it would've taken you two far too long to get it out of there. You're demon hunters, not a bloody home improvement show."

Audrey looked at him in some surprise. "People went down there, and they didn't get attacked?"

"No, they were fine," Colin replied, looking completely unsurprised by this development.

Michael said, "Demon attacks aren't always consistent. One person might suffer a great deal, while others in the house might not notice anything wrong. They probably left the workmen alone because they didn't disturb what was under the floor."

"Right," Colin said. "They loosened one section but didn't remove it, so that's where you'll work, and that's what we'll film. Then you can go ahead with—well, whatever it is that you plan to do."

Voice grim, Michael said, "We're going to remove those sigils. You got me the paint remover I asked for?"

"Yeah, the stuff they use to get rid of graffiti. Just spray it on."

And work fast, Audrey thought. She had a feeling the demons weren't going to be too thrilled when they saw what she and Michael were up to.

"All right, then," Michael said. He looked over at her, and the hard set of his mouth softened a bit. She got the impression that he would have liked to come over and take her hands, give her the encouragement she needed so desperately right then, but of course he couldn't do that in front of Colin and Susan. She looked tense but not frightened, whereas Audrey could already feel her hands starting to shake.

"I'm going to film you going down the hall toward the kitchen," Colin said, addressing her and Michael. "And also you opening the door to the basement, and walking down the stairs. After that, we're going to take a small break to reposition ourselves so I can put the part of the floor the workmen already tore up behind me, out of camera range. Got it?"

They both nodded, although Audrey had to wonder whether the demons would be so obliging as to wait until Colin had the shot properly framed before they started wreaking havoc. Well, that was what the editing process was for, she supposed.

She and Michael took their positions, while Colin backed away and fiddled with the camera for a few seconds. "Okay," he said in a low murmur. "Action."

"We're going to descend into the heart of darkness, so to speak," Michael announced as he faced the camera. Audrey stood next to him, trying to look calm and confident, and not as though she wanted to drop everything and run as fast as she could out of there. "Further investigation showed that someone painted symbols and signs of summoning on the floor of the basement, opening a gateway into our world. That gateway is the source of the phenomena that have been observed in this house. Once the gateway is closed, the house can be cleansed."

His gaze flickered toward Audrey for the barest second, and she picked up on his cue. "At this time, we don't know for sure who painted the symbols on the basement floor, although the original owner and builder of the house, Jeffrey Whitcomb, is the most likely culprit. It's possible that this deal with the devil he made—literally—was the source of his wealth. For now, the important thing is for us to do whatever we can to make sure the house is freed from these demonic presences so it can be inhabited again."

Michael turned to face her. "Are you ready?"

"Ready," she said, her voice calm. Oddly, she didn't feel quite as nervous right then, possibly because having the camera trained on the two of them—and sharing these not-quite-rehearsed exchanges—lent an air of unreality to the situation.

He put his hand on the doorknob and turned it, then flicked the light switch just inside the doorway. At once, the overhead fixtures came on, illuminating the plain wooden staircase, the scuffed wall next to it. The whole scene appeared completely ordinary, but Audrey knew better.

She knew what lurked down there.

They slowly descended the stairs, Colin and Susan a few steps behind them. As she neared the bottom, Audrey could see that nearly two-thirds of the shabby carpet and wood floor beneath had already been torn up, although the workmen hadn't hauled away the debris. She supposed it would have looked strange to have all the old carpet and wood floorboards gone as if they'd never been there. Now she and Michael could add to the pile, and presumably Colin would be able to splice everything together to make it seem as though they'd been able to tear up the floor in record time.

A couple of pry bars were leaning up against the walls, and next to them on the floor were several spray cans—of graffiti remover, Audrey assumed.

"All right, then," Colin said. He had the camera held on its Steadicam in front of him, but she assumed he wasn't filming yet, was trying to set up the shot. "You two go over to that section that hasn't been torn up yet and start working on it. I'll cut in to make it seem as though you've been doing this for some time."

Michael and Audrey both nodded and made

their way over to the intact section of flooring. The whole time, she kept expecting cold to descend, or for that terrible odor of mildew to surround her, but the basement seemed completely calm right then. She didn't trust it, though…she wasn't about to let the demons lull her into a false sense of security.

As Colin pushed the button to start the camera again, Michael spoke.

"We got permission from the current owner to remove the flooring, so we're going to tear it up and reveal the spell symbols painted on the concrete underneath."

While he was speaking, Audrey took a breath to steady herself, then went over to the corner, grabbed hold of the ugly vomit-green carpet, and began to pull it away from the wall. She didn't know whether the workmen had helped out a little over here as well, or whether the ancient tack strips had long since given up the ghost. Whatever the case, the nasty shag came right up, and within a few minutes, she had a small section exposed.

"Nothing to it," she said with a grin.

Michael smiled back at her, then grabbed one of the pry bars for himself and handed the other one to her. "Let's see what we have under here."

The wood flooring came up almost as easily as the carpet, exposing stained concrete covered with the circles Audrey had caught a glimpse of before, all of them with strange runes and symbols painted around them. With Colin filming the entire time, she and Michael cleared the final section of floor, then tossed the broken floorboards, tack strips, and shredded carpet off to one side, adding to the pile the workmen had started.

Looking grimly satisfied, Michael retrieved one of the cans of graffiti remover, while Audrey bent and got the other one.

"Where do you want to start?" she asked. Part of her wanted to send him a big, toothy grin because this had all been so easy so far, but she knew she needed to look properly serious for the camera.

"With the big circle in the center," he replied. "It's the heart of the gateway."

He began to walk in that direction—and at once the cold descended, even more intense than the times she'd previously experienced it. She heard Colin curse, and Susan let out a gasp.

Heart pounding, Audrey said urgently, "Michael."

"I know." His free hand wrapped around the cross he wore around his neck. "*The light of God surrounds us,*" he began.

Shrieking laughter came from all sides, and Audrey winced. Imitating him, she grasped the cross she wore, along with the amulet of black tourmaline he'd given her. Maybe it was only the contrast with the iciness of her fingers, but it almost felt as if the stone was heating up as she held it, absorbing the dark energies that had come here to do battle.

"*The love of God enfolds us!*" she cried out, brandishing the graffiti remover with the hand that wasn't holding the amulets. She pushed down on the spray tip.

Clear liquid streamed out and downward, hitting the spell circle next to where Audrey stood. At once, the laughter around her and Michael turned to cries of rage. Something struck the can from her hand, sending it flying against the wall, and she gasped and took a step backward. Thank God the thing hadn't touched her, only the can. Even so, her flesh crawled at the thought of something inhuman being close enough to make contact like that.

"*The presence of God watches over us,*" Michael said loudly. He also pointed his can of graffiti remover down at the circle and began to spray at the painted surface.

The shrieking turned into guttural growling, as if a wounded animal crouched somewhere nearby. If anything, this sound was worse; Audrey could feel the hair on the back of her neck standing up, adrenaline surging through her veins, telling her to flee.

But she couldn't. She wouldn't leave Michael here to do this on his own.

The lights went out, and Audrey screamed. To be fair, it was more of a high-pitched gasp than an actual scream, but still. Somewhere up the stairs, she heard Colin curse again, and, incongruously, she hoped they'd be able to edit that out. He was standing next to Susan, so the boom mike had to have picked up everything.

Or maybe they wouldn't get rid of the swearing. This was for cable, after all.

The darkness didn't last long, though, because Colin and Michael clearly had realized this was a possibility and had contingencies planned. A pale glow suddenly drifted down the stairs, and Audrey saw that either Colin or Susan had stuck a couple of tap lights to the walls of the stairwell. The illumination they provided wasn't nearly as bright as what the fixtures overhead had given off, but it was enough to see.

Not that Audrey really wanted to see what was going on right then.

Something was moving in the shadows in the corners. Or rather, the shadows themselves seemed to be moving, growing darker and more solid, coalescing into terrible, monstrous shapes. She couldn't see any details; she didn't want to.

"*Wherever we are, God is!*" Michael shouted. "Audrey, keep going!"

She dropped to her knees and scrabbled for the spray can. Luckily, it had only rolled a foot or so away. Her fingers latched on to it, and she whispered, "*The light of God surrounds us. The light of God surrounds us.*"

Somehow, she couldn't seem to get past that first line. It didn't matter, though, because she had the spray can in her hand now. Gritting her teeth, she pressed down on the nozzle, used the sole of her boot to help erase the outlines of those circles, all those evil-looking symbols and foreign letters.

The pressure had returned, roaring in her ears. Now she couldn't hear what Michael was saying, couldn't focus on anything except doing her best to remove the circles. The largest one was completely gone now, the one next to it more than halfway there. A complete circle still remained, though.

Audrey cast a frantic glance over one shoulder, caught a nightmarish glimpse of some…thing… looming over Michael. He'd let go of the spray can and instead held what she thought was one of his vials of holy water. She couldn't tell for sure in the gloom, but surely that must be what he was using, one of his last defenses against these beings of darkness.

A shriek, followed by more of that horrible, guttural moaning. She guessed that Michael had flung some of the holy water at the demon, although she couldn't stop what she was doing to take a closer look, had to keep working.

Two circles gone, and then the groan Audrey heard must have come from Michael, had emanated from a human throat. She risked a quick glance to her right, saw that he was now on his hands and knees, that thing crouching over him, clawed hands with impossibly long fingers reaching for his neck.

She didn't stop to think. Some mad impulse made her raise the can of graffiti remover she held and spray it full throttle at the demon. All of Michael's instructions about trusting in a higher power flew right out the window as she screamed, "That holy enough for you, you son of a bitch?"

It howled in pain, and Michael took advantage of the creature's distraction to throw another vial of holy water at it. Now it seemed to be shrinking somehow, although in the basement's gloom, Audrey couldn't tell for sure.

"The final circle!" he shouted at her. "Now!"

She nodded and stumbled over to the third circle, the smallest one. Finger pressed desperately on the nozzle of the spray can—and praying there was enough graffiti remover remaining to do the job—she shot the liquid at the old, old red paint on the floor, watched it dissolve and trickle away in rivulets that looked a little too much like blood.

Then it was gone, and the shadowy form of

the demon was gone, too, dissolving like smoke on the wind. The lights flared on, and Audrey and Michael were alone there on the basement floor, looking at each other in shock. For a long moment, no one said anything.

From the stairway above them, Colin chuckled. "Looks like that's a wrap, kids. Michael can do the closing comments later on. Any of you fancy a pint?"

Chapter 14

AFTER THEY PACKED UP THEIR EQUIPMENT and vacated the house—and Michael sprinkled holy water on the entrance to the basement, just to be safe—the crew ended up at a kitschy Polynesian place in Rosemead called The Bahooka. Although Audrey had heard of it, she'd never actually been there, but Michael and Susan—quiet, capable Susan, who'd kept recording the sound during that entire nightmarish encounter—both agreed it was the best place in the area to celebrate.

After the first sip of her piña colada, Audrey was inclined to agree. No canned stuff here; the restaurant used fresh coconut and pineapple juice…along with a healthy measure of rum. At another time, she might have cared more about how strong her drink actually was. But she wasn't driving, and dammit, she'd just faced down a demon and lived to tell the tale. So what if her knees still felt a little shaky now that the adrenaline fueling her during the confrontation was gone? By the time she was done with her first drink, she knew she'd probably be feeling just fine.

Colin was drinking a beer, because he said he was damned if he was going to have any of the froufrou stuff everyone else was consuming. Michael, snugged up next to Audrey in the oversized booth their group had commandeered, was making serious inroads on his zombie. Kathleen had begged off and gone home, saying she didn't drink, but Daniela appeared to be making up for her absence, sipping from a hurricane that seemed bigger than she was. And Susan had a Blue Hawaiian, something that looked as calm and cool as she'd been during the shoot.

"Bloody hell, if I hadn't seen it for myself, I would never have believed it!" Colin exclaimed. Luckily, since it was a Thursday night, the restaurant wasn't too busy. The little grotto that contained their oversized booth—and which had aquariums filled with neon tropical fish embedded in all the walls—was empty except for their party, which meant they all felt a bit more comfortable discussing what they'd just experienced. "I can't wait to get that camera back to my place and start editing this episode. It's going to be spectacular."

"Yes, but you know people are going to say we faked it all," Michael remarked.

The thought had crossed Audrey's mind, but she still raised an eyebrow at him. "I don't know…usually shows like this don't have the budget for those kinds of special effects."

He shrugged. "Some people just have to be skeptics, even when the evidence is practically shoved in their faces."

Colin took a long pull at his bottle of Dos Equis. "Honestly, mate, I don't care, as long as the show pulls in enough ratings to get us renewed."

Audrey really didn't want to think about the prospect of another season. Hell, she really didn't even want to think about the next episode. They were all celebrating now, true, but on Monday they'd have to be back at it again, albeit in a different venue. However, she kept her reservations to herself. Everyone was happy right now, and she didn't want to throw cold water on the party.

Besides, Colin continued, not giving any of the others a chance to comment. "I'll throw together a rough edit over the weekend, see where we're at. We might need to add a few pickup shots, but that shouldn't be a problem."

"'Pickup shots'?" Audrey echoed.

"Things to fill in the narrative, add some detail…maybe make the transitions a bit smoother," Michael explained. He reached for his zombie, the sleeve of his jacket just barely brushing against Audrey's arm. Still, even that light touch was enough to send some happy endorphins flooding through her.

"We'll have to go back to the Whitcomb place for those?" she asked, and couldn't quite keep the alarm out of her voice.

Colin chuckled. "No worries on that front, sweetheart. Chris shot a bunch of footage of the place before he ran out on us. I'd just film you and Michael in front of a green screen in the studio for any bits we might need and put whatever footage looks best behind you. Easy. Same thing for any of our other location shoots—I'll get a library of backgrounds so we can do pickups for every episode as necessary."

She let out a relieved breath. "Oh. That doesn't sound so bad."

"Piece of cake," Colin told her.

Yes, going into a studio and shooting her and Michael doing a few expository bits and pieces sounded infinitely easy compared to their recent confrontation with the demons. Even though she was sitting in a safe place—the restaurant had been around for years and years, but it felt as though only happy energy had collected here—Audrey had to hold back a shudder. Was the world even ready for something like this? Most ghost-hunting shows she'd seen watched only had a few EVPs—electronic voice phenomena—and maybe an object appearing to move on its own as their only real evidence for supernatural activities. Colin had captured a couple of honest-to-God demons on film—or at least, on a memory card. Would people be able to accept what they saw, with all its implications, or would they, as Michael had said, think that the base-ment battle was anything other than Hollywood tricks?

In a way, she hoped it was the latter. Some-times, ignorance truly was bliss.

"And we're set for Tucson," Colin went on. "Got the final sign-off from the B&B's owners, so we all need to caravan there over the weekend."

On Sunday, Audrey thought. *Saturday, I have clients to see.* But she could work all that out with Michael. Now she looked forward to the road trip, even though she'd been dreading it before. Maybe he'd finally feel comfortable opening up to her about his past if they had to spend that much time alone in a car together.

"Where are we staying?" Daniela asked. She was nearly to the bottom of her hurricane and looking a little wistful. Hopefully, the waitress would come by soon for a round of refills, because they'd all made serious inroads on their drinks.

"At the B&B itself," Colin replied. "Not many

paying guests these days, thanks to the distur-bances, so the owners are putting us up for free."

"I'm not sure that's the best idea—" Michael began, but their producer waved a nonchalant hand.

"It'll be fine. From what you've told me, it's all nuisance stuff, anyway—things getting moved around, doors and windows opened and closed, that sort of thing."

"Crosses being turned upside down," Michael said ominously.

"Nothing to it," Colin said. He looked supremely unconcerned, especially for a man who'd just been confronted by the evidence that all of this was real, not something merely being played for ratings. "Besides, if we're all on-site, we won't miss any activity if it happens in the middle of the night, will we?"

Audrey had no idea how Colin could be so blithe about the situation. After all, he'd been down in that basement with the rest of them, had to know what they were up against. Then again, maybe being behind the camera had given him a measure of detachment. And she could guess that he was thrilled about getting everyone free accom-modations, rather than having to spring for hotel rooms for his crew.

For a moment, Michael looked as though he was inclined to argue further. But then he gave a small lift of his shoulders and drank some more of his hurricane. At the rate he was going, he'd be done around the same time as Daniela.

Or Audrey herself. She'd also made a serious dent in her piña colada. Luckily, the waitress appeared then and took orders for another round of drinks and some food to soak up the alcohol. Michael and Susan offered helpful advice on what to get—ribs and crab puffs and a few other highly caloric but tasty-sounding options—and the waitress wandered off toward the kitchen. At least, Audrey assumed that was where she was headed. The restaurant was a maze, full of dark corners and sharp angles and unexpected little alcoves. Good thing that Michael seemed to know the place well, as she had a feeling she'd have to rely on him to guide her out of there by the time the night was over.

They chatted about the upcoming trip to Tucson. Although Audrey had to admit she wasn't overly thrilled about having to sleep in a bed-and-breakfast that might or might not be infested with demons, it was interesting to hear Michael talk about the location, about why it might suddenly be suffering these supernatural activities after so many decades. Apparently, the original building had been constructed in the 1870s and added to over the years, which gave ample opportunities for hauntings. However, by all accounts, things had been quiet there on the paranormal front up until only a year ago, which was when the current phenomena began.

"Has anyone actually seen anything there?" she asked. "Or is it just stuff getting moved around?"

"The owner reported cold spots and strange smells," Michael replied. "That's one of the reasons we decided it would be worth investigating. Otherwise, it's just standard poltergeist activity, something better suited for regular ghost-hunting shows."

Frankly, Audrey had already dealt with enough strange odors to last her a lifetime. But, given the very nature of their project, they had to focus on the more extreme haunting situations and hope the gamble paid off.

The waitress returned with the second round of drinks, and the conversation got even livelier—or at least more ghoulish. Colin and Michael started trading ghost stories, with Daniela chiming in about the time she saw her grand-mother's spirit wandering up and down the hall in the house where she'd lived with Daniela and her parents.

"She was looking for something, but when I tried to talk to her, tried to say, 'Hey, *abuela,* what are you trying to find?', she just disappeared." Daniela shrugged and took a long pull through the straw of her drink. "It was creepy, but I didn't get a bad feeling from her. And then after about a year, she just disappeared."

"She'd probably finished working through whatever issue or problem had kept her on this plane," Michael said. "It's best when it happens that way, when the departed don't need our help to guide them to the next world."

"'Next world'?" Daniela echoed. "You mean like heaven?"

"That's how most people think of it, yes."

Daniela stared at him for a moment, as if trying to process what he'd just said. "Well, how do *you* think of it?"

"I'm not sure yet," he replied. "I just know it's there."

"You are being far too serious," Colin said. Audrey noticed how he'd shifted a little closer to Daniela…and how she wasn't making any effort to move away from him. Fraternizing with the boss? Maybe.

As if she was in any position to comment. They were all adults here…or at least pretending to be.

The food came, and was a lot better than Audrey had expected, given the kitschy nature of the restaurant. Everyone ate, and ordered another round of drinks, then ate some more, and got some more drinks before they all realized they were completely sloshed. Or rather, Colin and Daniela and Michael and Audrey were. Susan had quietly switched to water after her first drink, so she offered to drive Daniela and Colin home, since they both lived in Hollywood, or at least someplace Hollywood-adjacent, like Colin's house in Los Feliz.

Before the age of Uber and Lyft, Michael and Audrey might have been in trouble. But after ascertaining that it was okay to leave his SUV in the parking lot overnight—as long as he came back to retrieve it by opening time the next day, which was eleven o'clock—he used the app on his phone to call for a vehicle. Susan and Daniela and Colin waited with them until their Lyft arrived, and the evening ended with the two of them waving rather blearily at the others as the car pulled out onto Rosemead Boulevard.

Since the driver already had their destination, thanks to the app, he headed northward, toward the 210 Freeway. Audrey didn't remember putting it there, but somehow her head had ended up on Michael's shoulder. Which was fine—it felt good there, felt *right*. He held her hand as they moved along, traffic still thicker than she would have imagined it might be at almost ten o'clock at night.

Eventually, though, they were pulling up into the driveway at Michael's house. He fumbled with his phone so he could leave the driver a tip, and then the two of them got out of the car, stumbling a bit as they made their way up the front walk. More fumbling as he got out his keys and unlocked the front door, but then the two of them were safely inside.

Several of the lights were already on; possibly he had them on timers because he came home at strange hours. They were barely inside the door before he was bending down to kiss her, his mouth sweet with rum and fruit juices, hungry, much more demanding than he had been earlier that day.

Audrey didn't mind, though. She wanted this —no, she *needed* this, needed his lips on hers, his arms around her. They'd both been as circumspect as they could be around the others, not wanting the crew to guess that hers and Michael's relation-ship was no longer quite as professional as they pretended it to be. Now that the two of them were alone at last, they could give in to their need for one another.

They broke apart for a moment, gasping, and Michael took a step toward the stairs. Audrey followed him, knowing what he wanted, knowing she wanted it as badly as he did. They held each other's hands as they went up the steps, helping to steady each other. Maybe this was entirely crazy, to be drunk and stumbling toward his bedroom, and yet she wasn't about to call a halt to the whole thing, wasn't going to stop because she somehow knew she probably wouldn't have had the courage to do this if she were cold sober.

His room was much bigger than the one where she'd been staying, with an *en suite* bathroom and a nice little alcove with a window seat. A hardbound book lay on the cushion there, the tassel of a bookmark hanging out of it, but she couldn't see what the title was.

No time to take a peek, either, because Michael was kissing her again, and she was kissing him back, her fingers tangled in his hair, their bodies pressed together. How long that went on, she wasn't sure, but then she reached for the hem of his shirt, yanked it out of his pants. His skin was warm and smooth under her fingertips, the muscles of his stomach hard and flat. It was too dark to see much detail, but she could feel the ridges of those muscles, knew they were as heavy and strong as his biceps.

He was pulling at her shirt, too, drawing it up and over her head. It got tossed somewhere in the darkness, although Audrey couldn't say where. Not that it mattered, because his hands had closed on her breasts, were stroking her through the thin nylon of her bra. She moaned, feeling her nipples harden at his touch, while a welcome warmth began to throb between her legs.

A few steps to her left, and Audrey felt herself bump into the side of the bed. She and Michael both collapsed onto it, mouths seeking one another yet again, while he found the clasp of her bra and undid it, and she grabbed hold of both his jacket and T-shirt and dragged them over his head. Now that her eyes had begun to adjust to the darkness, she could see something of the contours of his body, the broad shoulders, the sculpted muscles of his arms and chest. He hid all that under loose-fitting jackets and dark T-shirts, but now there were no bulky clothes to conceal how magnificent his body really was.

She didn't get much more than that eyeful, however, because he bent his head and ran his tongue over her nipple and she gasped, hands once more tangled in his hair as she held him close.

"Yes, Michael," she whispered. "Oh, please. Yes."

He made a low, growling sound at the back of his throat, a sound that seemed to thrum through her body. At the same time, his fingers found the button of her jeans and unfastened it, followed by the zipper. Then he worked her pants down, grabbing hold of them and her underwear at the same time.

Now she was naked, but she didn't care, because then he ran his hand up the inside of her thigh, slipped his fingers into her, stroking her, making her moan again and cling to him. Maybe he really was psychic, because he seemed to know just where to touch her, what to do to intensify the waves of pleasure flooding her body.

And, just like that, she came. Came hard, body clamping down on his fingers, her hands clutching him as the force of the orgasm shuddered through her. It had been a while since she'd been with anyone— longer than she wanted to admit—but she thought she probably would have experienced just as intense a climax even if they'd made love only a few hours before.

"Audrey," he whispered, and he kissed her again, lips strong, demanding…and yet gentle at the same time, as though he wanted to make sure he wasn't pushing her into something she didn't want.

Oh, she wanted this. Wanted him—wanted to taste him, wanted to feel him inside her.

Audrey's fingers closed on his belt buckle, and she pulled his belt loose, unfastened his jeans. Soon enough, they were on the floor with the rest of their clothes, and her hand was wrapped around him, feeling how hard he was, how big and ready.

It seemed the most natural thing in the world to take him into her mouth, to run her tongue over his length. Now it was his turn to moan, which he did—right before he shifted his position so his face was between her legs, and he was licking her even as she suckled him.

She couldn't scream with pleasure, not with him filling her mouth, but she did moan at the delicious, intense sensation of his tongue running over her clit, even as she felt the pleasure pulsing through her and realized it wouldn't be long before she came again. This time, it wasn't as abrupt, came over her with the inexorable, steady pace of the tide coming in, and she paused in sucking him to gasp and cry out, her body once again alive with shimmering waves of ecstasy.

A pause, and then he shifted positions again, starting to pull her down on top of him. As his tip began to enter her, though, he stopped and blurted, "Oh, shit. Condoms—"

She wanted to tell him they didn't need them —she was on the pill and not exactly what one could call sexually active—but of course she had no idea how many people he'd been with, or how recently. "Where?"

"Nightstand—top drawer."

Since she was on top, it was easier for her to reach over to the table in question, open the drawer, and extract one of the little foil packets her fingers had been looking for. She tore it open, then slid it down over his shaft, teasing him a bit with her fingers as she did so, just to show that she was all right with this, that she didn't mind the interruption.

"Okay?" she asked, and he nodded.

"Okay."

She pulled him into her mouth again, ignoring the rubbery taste of the condom, and then moved so she could feel him brushing against her once more. A thrill teased its way down her spine at the sensation. Knowing she couldn't wait any longer, she let herself sink down on him, felt him fill her as their bodies joined.

Dear God, that was good. Audrey moved her hips, rocking so he slid in and out, but slowly, deliciously, wanting to wring every moment of pleasure from this encounter. His eyes were half shut, his hands closed on her breasts, caressing.

Maybe she should have been surprised by how well they fit together, how they each seemed to know what the other person wanted. Michael probably would have called it a psychic connection.

Or maybe they were both just drunk enough that all inhibitions had flown out the window, and there was no time to worry or be self-conscious. Whatever the reason, Audrey knew that she'd never had sex like this before, no second-guessing, nothing but two bodies locked together in ecstasy, movements growing faster, until at last he came, hands on her hips as he drove even deeper into her core, her hands on his shoulders, riding the wave, knowing the climax was close, so very close, until at last it hit, shockwaves moving through her body, so good.

So very good.

And then she collapsed onto the bed next to him, breaths coming hard, fast, the warmth of the afterglow surrounding her. He leaned over, brushed a kiss against her lips. "You constantly amaze me, Audrey."

Just as he amazed her, although Audrey wasn't sure she was capable of speech right then. She only stared up at him, caught the glint of his gray eyes in a bit of light from the street that had made it in past the blinds. There was a tenderness in his expression she'd never seen before, something she might not have even thought him capable of. Then again, the Michael Covenant of a few days ago seemed very different from the man who had just made love to her.

Because it had been lovemaking. Once or twice, she'd had sex just for the sake of sex, and she hadn't liked it. This was different. It could have been the alcohol fogging her brain, but she didn't think so. The two of them had joined in a way that made her wonder what this meant for them, for their future together.

It was way too soon to say the words that whispered through her mind, then disappeared.

So she smiled up at him and said, "You're pretty amazing yourself."

He kissed her again, then pulled away so he could get up and go into the bathroom, probably to get rid of the condom. She watched him go, eyes straining against the darkness to see more details of his appearance, maybe to catch a glimpse of his ass before he disappeared into the bathroom.

However, she couldn't see as much as she would have liked. And she realized her eyelids were drooping, the strain of the day and the sex and those multiple piña coladas conspiring to send her into oblivion.

Her eyes shut, and she was gone.

Chapter 15

AUDREY WOKE UP TO THE SOUND OF WATER running, and sunlight doing its best to slip in past the wooden blinds at the window. No morning disorientation for her, though—she knew she was lying in Michael Covenant's bed, and she knew they'd had sex right here in this bed the night before.

Oh, hell.

This was why she should never drink hard alcohol, should stick to beer and wine. How many piña coladas had she drunk at the Bahooka? Three? Four? She couldn't remember for sure, but obviously, it had been enough for her to lose all self-control…and sanity.

Audrey's gaze strayed to the clock on the nightstand. Nine forty-seven. Normally, she didn't sleep that late, but her body must have been doing its best to repair the damage she'd done to it with all that rum. She never got hangovers...but in general, the more she had to drink, the later she slept in.

The water sound she'd heard was the shower in the *en suite* bathroom. She guessed that Michael had gotten tired of her Sleeping Beauty act and had decided to go ahead and get cleaned up. In a way, Audrey supposed that was good, if for no other reason than now she had a chance to get her head together, so to speak, before he emerged from the shower.

First things first. Audrey slid out from under the covers and picked up her discarded clothing, then put it back on. Her purse was sitting on top of the dresser, although she had absolutely no recollection of putting it there. At least she did vaguely remember taking a Lyft home from the restaurant, so they'd retained enough sanity to know that neither one of them should have gotten behind the wheel of a car.

She popped a breath mint—no substitute for brushing her teeth, but better than nothing—and got out the small hairbrush she always carried with her and tried to tidy up as best she could. There was a box of tissues on top of the dresser, and she pulled one out and wiped away the residue of mascara and liner from underneath her eyes. After that, she swiped on some lip gloss, and thought she looked better than she had any right to.

Maybe that would give her the courage to face Michael. Part of her wanted to slink out and call another Lyft so she'd be safely gone before he got out of the shower, but only a coward would do something like that. He deserved better than her slipping away without a word. It wasn't as if he'd seduced her—she'd wanted him just as much as he wanted her. The sex had been beyond good. The problem was....

Well, the problem was that they were working together. And not as co-workers in some safe, boring office job, but doing something that was dangerous and unpredictable. They both needed to be on top of their game. Could they function in such a way and still be lovers behind the scenes? Because Audrey knew they couldn't be honest about their relationship until they were done filming the series. Never mind that she'd seen Colin flirting outrageously with Daniela last night at the restaurant. Colin was the boss and could do what he wanted. It wasn't as though there was some kind of morality clause in the contract or anything, but Audrey didn't like the thought of how it would look if word got out that she and Michael were intimate. The last thing she wanted was to be accused of sleeping her way into this job.

The shower was still running. She guessed that she'd woken up not long after Michael went into the bathroom—for all she knew, it was the sound of him getting out of bed that had pushed her toward consciousness. Her body ached for some coffee, but she thought it was better to wait here until Michael had emerged from the bathroom.

A set of antique bookcases, similar to the ones downstairs but smaller in scale, occupied one wall. Figuring she could pass the time by reading something, Audrey went over to inspect their contents. At first, the collection surprised her a bit—she saw everything from a group of "Goosebumps" paperbacks to what looked like a set of first edition E. Nesbit children's books, clearly very valuable—and then she realized these must have been Michael's childhood books, carefully preserved and kept together in his bedroom bookcases.

Would he be angry if she took out one of the books to look at it? She'd be careful, but she thought it would be fascinating to see the original version of a book she'd loved herself in paperback format.

Very gently, Audrey lifted a red leather–bound copy of *Five Children and It* from one of the shelves. The cover was stamped with gilt, and the leaves were gilt-edged as well. Some of the gilt had worn off, and the red dye had rubbed off the leather in a few places, but overall, the book looked to be in remarkably good shape for a volume that had to be more than a hundred years old.

She opened the book, and at once a piece of paper slipped out from where it had been held between the inside cover and the front page. Frowning, she bent to pick it up, saw that it was a note written in what looked like an older woman's handwriting, the up- and downstrokes crisp but a little shaky. The paper itself was feminine as well, cream-colored with a border of blue flowers, probably supposed to be forget-me-nots.

The note read, *To Michael, for his 10th birthday. Love, Grandma.*

Audrey's first thought was of the woman she'd seen in her vision when she held the book downstairs, but then she remembered that woman had been Michael's great-grandmother, not his grandmother. Clearly, though, the love of reading had been passed down through the generations in his family, and she smiled a little at the thought.

Maybe now that they'd been intimate, Michael might feel more comfortable talking about his family with her.

Then Audrey's gaze strayed back to the book itself. A bookplate had been affixed to the front page, something that would have reduced its value as a collectible, although probably Michael's grandmother hadn't been too worried about that.

What caught her eye, though, was the full name printed on the bookplate.

Michael Anthony Stanek.

At first, Audrey found herself wanting to smile, because obviously Michael had changed his name at some point, maybe because "Covenant" sounded flashier, more in keeping with his public persona. But then her smile began to fade, because "Stanek" seemed oddly familiar to her, as if she'd heard it somewhere before. It wasn't a common surname, though; she couldn't remember crossing paths with anyone with that last name.

Then she went cold, her hands shaking so badly that she almost dropped the book.

The man responsible for the Waikiki Massacre had been named Philip Andrew Stanek. Audrey didn't know why her brain had fumbled over that particular detail, although over the years she'd done her best to put the whole horrifying incident behind her.

And while Stanek wasn't a very common last name, it could have been a coincidence…except that she knew her parents' killer had a younger brother named Michael. He'd been a minor at the time of the incident and his name had never been given to the press or the public, but Audrey knew it because she'd received a letter from Philip's family only a month after the mass murder, telling her how sorry they were about what had happened, and how heartbroken, and how they couldn't understand why any of this had happened. That letter had been signed by Leo, Janet, and Michael and Anna Stanek. Anna was Michael's younger sister.

The door to the bathroom opened, and Michael emerged. He was wearing jeans and a T-shirt, but he was barefoot and still blotting his hair with a towel in an absentminded sort of way. His eyes met Audrey's, and he began to smile… until he looked down at the book she was holding.

Somehow, her voice was steady. "Do you want to tell me about this?"

He didn't reply at first, but came over to her and took the book from her still-shaking hands before replacing it on the bookshelf. When he turned back around, the line between his brows had returned, and his expression was cold and blank. "I don't recall giving you permission to go through my things."

So he was going to make this *her* fault? Audrey crossed her arms and glared at him. "I wouldn't exactly call picking a book up from a shelf 'going through your things.' Don't dodge the question, Michael. Are you—" Now her voice did tremble and threaten to break, and she took in a breath of air to steady herself. "Are you Philip Stanek's brother?"

Another of those pauses. Then, simply, "Yes."

Now rage was flooding through her, hot and powerful. Audrey was glad of her anger, because it gave her the strength to shoot back, "And you didn't think it was important to tell me?"

"I would have...eventually." His lips pressed together. "You have to understand, Audrey—I changed my name, did whatever I could to erase the connection between me and Philip. The last thing I wanted was to be judged by what my brother did."

"Maybe so, but keeping that sort of information away from the general public is not the same thing as keeping it away from me!" Her voice had risen, and she clenched her hands into fists and forced herself to take another breath, to do what she could to avoid giving in to her anger. "We were working together—we just fucking *slept* together! Just when the hell *were* you going to tell me?"

"I—" He shook his head. Throughout all of this, he'd kept his expression studiously blank, as though he knew it was the only way to keep her from completely tearing into him. "Look, Audrey, I never meant for any of this to happen. It was Colin who insisted on casting you—he completely ignored my list of suggestions."

"Oh, so that's supposed to make it better?" she demanded. If he'd thought that kind of revelation would mollify her in any way, he didn't know her very well. "It's all Colin's fault?"

"That's not what I meant. I—" Once again he broke off, only now Audrey was beginning to see some of his own frustration and anger break through. His mouth twisted, and there was a dangerous glint in his eyes. "Do you have any idea what it's like to have something like that hanging over you, to be defined by something you didn't even do?"

She could feel a scowl of her own pulling at her brows. "Considering that I got to be that girl whose parents were murdered by a psychopath, yes, I think I have a vague inkling of what that's all about. You still should have told me the truth—"

"Well, now you know the truth," he broke in. "And this reaction is what I was trying to avoid."

About all Audrey could do was stare at him in disbelief. "I'm not angry at you for what your brother did," she snapped. "Do you honestly think I'd hold you responsible for that? You were a kid, just like me. No," she went on, not allowing him to interrupt again, "I'm angry with you for withholding this information from me. You lied."

"I didn't lie," he replied. "I just didn't tell you the truth. Because I knew you wouldn't be able to handle it."

"I could have handled it just fine if you'd been

honest from the beginning." She paused there, staring at him, attempting to see if she could detect any contrition at all in his expression. But she didn't see anything like that, only the same frustration and anger she'd noted earlier. "How long were you going to let this charade go on?"

"Until I thought it would be safe to tell you," he said. "Whenever that turned out to be. It's not like I had a timeline mapped out in my head, but probably after we were done shooting."

And right there, Audrey understood. He wasn't going to apologize, because he didn't think he'd done anything wrong. It was more important to him to make sure they finished filming the show than to tell her that oh, by the way, my crazy older brother killed your parents and a bunch of other people while staying on the eleventh floor of the Hyatt Waikiki.

"Oh, we're done, all right," she retorted. Without saying anything else, she went over to get her purse from the dresser and slung it over her shoulder.

Now Michael looked alarmed. "Where are you going? You can't go back to your house—"

While this was a valid point, Audrey sure as hell wasn't going to tell him that. "I don't think that's any concern of yours. I'm a grown woman —I'll figure it out."

"Audrey—"

She gritted her teeth and ignored the pleading in his voice. No, she was not going to be rational and sensible and stay to hear him out. If he hadn't outright lied to her, he'd definitely misrepresented the situation, misrepresented who he was. She knew she could never trust him again.

Without replying, Audrey went out into the hallway and marched down the stairs. Once she got to the bottom floor, she pulled her phone out of her purse. Thank God it still had some battery life left. With shaking fingers, she pulled up the Lyft app, then requested a pickup. A car was only a few blocks away, so it should be here soon enough. The last thing she wanted was to be standing on the sidewalk in front of Michael's house for any amount of time. She definitely didn't want him to have the opportunity to come and plead with her some more.

He hadn't followed her down the stairs, though. Nor did he emerge from the house after she slammed the front door. What he was thinking, she didn't know…and didn't care to.

Audrey had no idea whether the Lyft driver— a thick-set Hispanic man in his late thirties— knew she was doing her own hellish walk of shame right then. "Twenty-three Meda Avenue in Glendora," she told him as she climbed into the back seat of his Toyota RAV-4, completely forgetting that the app would have already informed him of her destination.

Luckily, the driver didn't seem inclined to comment, only nodded in acknowledgment and pulled away from the curb. Although she told herself not to, she couldn't quite keep herself from looking back at Michael's house as they drove off. Although he'd never emerged, she thought she caught a glimpse of him standing at one of the upstairs windows, staring down at the street.

Like a ghost himself, because when Audrey turned back to look a second time, he was gone.

After that, she faced forward and told herself to forget about him. What all this meant in terms of the show, she didn't know. There was no way in hell she would ever work with Michael again, so she'd have to find some way to wriggle out of that damn contract. Could such a gross omission of vital information be enough to claim a breach?

She wasn't a lawyer. She didn't know. Maybe Bettina would, but then Audrey would have to tell her about what had happened. What had seemed so magical, so transformative, the night before now felt sordid, shameful. It hadn't exactly been a one-night stand, and yet....

Of more pressing concern was what she planned to do with herself. The house was trashed, not really habitable. She could go stay in a hotel or an Airbnb somewhere, but she couldn't afford to do that for very long, especially if she walked out on *Project Demon Hunters* and had to return the thirty-three thousand she'd been paid already.

One step at a time, Audrey told herself. *Go home, and hope it's safe enough to go inside and get what you need.* She realized then that a bunch of her things were still at Michael's place, but it was all second-string travel stuff, not anything she needed to survive.

The Lyft driver stopped in front of her house. To her surprise, there was a mint-green Fiat compact parked there already. As soon as Audrey got out of the Lyft, the driver-side door on the Fiat opened and Rosemary McGuire emerged.

Audrey stared at her in shock, barely noticing the Lyft pulling away from the curb. "What are you doing here?" she blurted.

Rosemary grinned as she walked over to where Audrey stood. "Psychic, remember? Of course, it helps that you're such a good transmitter. Not quite as loud as a police siren, but close."

For some reason, her comment made the blood rush to Audrey's cheeks. "I'm sorry about that—"

"Don't be sorry. I could tell you needed help." Now that Rosemary was close enough to see Audrey's face, she went suddenly sober, worry obvious in her clear, sky-blue eyes. "What happened?"

"I thought you were a psychic."

She raised an eyebrow. "I'm getting emotions pinging all over the place, but no details."

"It's a long story. Let's just say that Michael Covenant and I aren't exactly on speaking terms at the moment." Audrey let out a breath, then turned to look at the house. As far as she could tell, it appeared unaltered from the last time she'd been here, but who knew what fresh hell the demons had unleashed inside? "But I need to go in there, get a few things, even though the thought scares the hell out of me."

"I can imagine." Rosemary's chin went up. "Still, it's daylight. I'll help you."

Audrey realized then she was thinking of the attack that had come through the e-reader. Because she hadn't spoken with the psychic since the night Michael came to pick her up, Rosemary didn't know anything about the second attack, the way the demons had trashed the place.

"It's pretty bad in there," Audrey warned her. "I had some…visitors…show up and make it really clear that they didn't appreciate my interference, if you know what I mean."

For a second, Rosemary stared at her, and then comprehension seemed to dawn in her eyes. Although she looked visibly paler, her voice was firm enough as she said, "Then we'll just make this fast, won't we? And you can come crash on my couch—for real this time."

"No, I can't do that," Audrey replied. "I don't know how long it's going to take to get my house fixed up. I'll probably go and stay with my aunt Deb over in Claremont." Even as she spoke, though, she realized she really didn't want to do that. After years and years of putting her life on hold to give Audrey security, and more years of getting back in the rhythm of living in her own house and having a world separate from her niece's, Deb had started dating again. From what she'd said, it sounded as if things were getting pretty serious with Tom, the man she'd been seeing for the past six months. It wouldn't be fair for Audrey to interrupt her aunt's life after she'd already given so much of it so selflessly.

"I don't think your aunt can give you the protection you need right now," Rosemary said. "CeeCee—my sister Cecily—has a guest house that's vacant right now. She and her husband's last tenant moved out and they're deciding whether to rent it long-term again or turn it into an Airbnb, and I'm sure she'd let you stay there for a bit until you get everything worked out."

"If it's all right—" Audrey began, and Rosemary nodded.

"I know it will be. But let's get your stuff out of the house here first."

If money hadn't been so tight, she honestly would have asked Rosemary to take her shopping for some clothes and toiletries. But it seemed silly to do something like that when everything Audrey needed was just a few yards away. Assuming, of course, that the demons hadn't destroyed everything. They'd gone in the garage and torn her car apart, so it was entirely possible that they'd also wreaked havoc in the closet and in the bathroom drawers and cabinets.

Only one way to find out, though.

"Let's go," Audrey said.

They went up the front steps. Rosemary waited while Audrey got out her keys and opened the front door. She pulled in a breath and held it, mentally bracing herself for the chaos that was about to greet her. As the door swung inward, however, she could only stand there on the threshold and stare at her living room in disbelief.

It was fine, not a single picture or coaster out of place. If she hadn't seen the destruction for herself, Audrey would never have believed that her house could have been so thoroughly ravaged. Now, though…now it looked as though she'd just had a cleaning crew come in.

"I thought you said—" Rosemary began, and Audrey shook her head.

"I know," she broke in. "They tore it apart—

and I mean that literally. As in, the stuffing was pulled out of the couch and chairs."

Everything was back where it should be... including the photo of her and her parents that was the one thing Audrey had rescued from the destruction. As far as she knew, it should have been back at Michael's house, tucked into her weekender bag. That it was here now, in its frame, unwrinkled and good as new...she wasn't sure what to think about that.

Rosemary walked over to the fireplace, looked at the photos there, then turned around and studied the rest of the space. Her expression was puzzled, and, judging by the way her brow wrinkled, it seemed she wasn't sure what to make of all this, either.

"I guess I'd better check upstairs," Audrey went on. "When—when Michael and I came back here, we never made it that far, so I don't know whether it was in just as bad shape as the rest of the house or not."

"Right behind you," Rosemary said. Audrey couldn't tell whether her friend was worried or not, but at least she didn't try to stop her.

They both climbed the stairs to the second floor. Everything here appeared to be in perfect order as well—mail was piled neatly in the little letterbox that sat on Audrey's desk in the office, and when she went into the master bedroom, the bed was made, all the throw pillows arranged just so. The bathroom was likewise in perfect shape.

She took a second look, realizing that the debris of her shattered e-reader had been cleared away. That detail seemed to prove she wasn't making this up, that someone or something had come in here and restored the house to an almost preternaturally neat state.

"Well, maybe I don't need to crash in your sister's guest house after all," Audrey said slowly, her attention returning to Rosemary. "I mean, everything looks fine here."

"Too fine," she returned. Her arms were crossed, and she was still frowning. "It's like…they *want* you to think it's safe to come home. They want you to be alone here."

A little shiver ran down Audrey's spine. "You can sense that?"

"Not exactly. But…there's something here. Something watching. It doesn't like me being here, which is probably why it hasn't done anything to us. You'll be much better off at CeeCee's place."

Part of her wanted to protest. After all, she hadn't really felt anything in the house, although logically she knew there was no way any human being could have restored it so quickly. And she was tired, and wanted to sleep in her own bed.

But that bed wouldn't be any refuge if Rosemary was right about the demons—or whoever was responsible—trying to lure her into a false sense of security. As much as she hated to take advantage of Rosemary's sister, Audrey knew that the guest house was her best option.

"All right," she said wearily. "Let me pack my things."

While Rosemary hovered off to one side, Audrey got out her hard-sided suitcase and a tote bag, since her weekender bag was still at Michael's. She didn't know exactly what she should pack, but she figured a few pairs of jeans, some tops, and a skirt and blouse for meeting her Saturday clients should get her through the next week. After that…she'd just have to see what happened.

As Audrey was cramming her blow-dryer into the tote bag, Rosemary spoke. "So…what happened between you and Michael, anyway?"

She hesitated. Although Rosemary had proven herself to be an amazing friend in a very short period of time, still, Audrey really didn't know her that well. She'd never been the type to confide in people—ironic, she supposed, considering what she did for a living—and she had no desire to air her dirty laundry to her or anyone else. And even though she was still furious with him, she didn't want to reveal Michael's secret, not when he'd gone to so much trouble to conceal who he really was, his connection to one of the worst mass murderers in U.S. history.

"I made a mistake," Audrey said. "A big one. And now I have to figure out what to do about the aftermath. I just know that I'm done with *Project Demon Hunters.*"

To her relief, Rosemary didn't press for any details. For all Audrey knew, the psychic had been able to pick up enough that she could partially guess at what might have happened, even if she couldn't know anything of the secret Michael had been hiding for so many years. "Will that be difficult?" she asked, her expression concerned. "I mean, I assume you had to sign a contract."

"I did," Audrey said wearily. "And I don't know what it's going to take to get out of it. But if Michael continues with the show, he's going to have to do it with a different co-host."

A nod. "I wish one of us could help you with that, but there aren't any lawyers in my family."

"None in mine, either. I'll figure something out."

Audrey bent and grasped the handle of her travel case, and Rosemary hurried over and picked up the overstuffed tote bag. As she went down the stairs, Audrey held on to the banister tightly, braced for some kind of invisible attack, thinking unseen hands might push both of them down during a moment when they were vulnerable.

They reached the bottom safely, though, and then both hurried to the front door. As Audrey closed it behind her and locked the deadbolt, she allowed herself a small sigh of relief. It wasn't until she was back outside that she realized she'd been sensing an unseen pressure on her body the entire time she was inside, a pressure only noticeable once it was gone.

Rosemary seemed to have experienced much the same thing, because she sent a worried little glance back at the house as she walked over to the car. However, she was quiet as she opened the passenger-side door and set Audrey's tote bag on the back seat.

"The trunk's full of stuff," she told her. "Go ahead and put your suitcase back there, too."

It was a bit of a squeeze, but Audrey was able to wedge her case into the back seat, then push the passenger seat back to its regular upright position. As Rosemary went around to enter on the driver's side of the car, Audrey got in and fastened her seatbelt. Something made her glance over at the house just before they began to pull away from the curb, and once more a trickle of cold ran down her back.

Maybe she was seeing things…maybe it was just a trick of the light…but she could have sworn she saw the shape of a man standing up there, staring down at her.

Audrey made herself look forward, even though she wanted nothing more than to turn in her seat and stare back at the house. But then they were safely away, and she released a breath she hadn't even known she was holding.

Once again, she wondered if she would ever be able to go home.

Chapter 16

ROSEMARY'S SISTER CECILY WAS SIMILAR TO her in appearance, with long curly brown hair and big blue eyes. Unlike her sister, she had her magnificent hair pulled back into a loose ponytail, and looked a little harassed as she jounced a fretful one-year-old on her hip.

"Here are the keys to the guest house," she said, handing them over to Audrey. The baby tried to make a grab for them, but she was able to get them safely tucked away in her purse before they were intercepted. Luckily, the baby seemed more interested in the way she'd made the keys disappear than realizing he'd been thwarted in his attempt to get them to play with, so at least he showed no signs of throwing a tantrum. "You'll have to pull in the driveway at night, since there's no overnight parking."

"That's all right," Audrey said hastily. "My car's in the shop, so I've been using Lyft to get around."

"Even better." Cecily smiled at her, clearly glad she wouldn't have to deal with the complications of juggling cars in the driveway. "I can't promise we'll be quiet, not with this one around"—she transferred the baby to her other hip—"but he mostly sleeps through the night now."

"It's fine," Audrey told her. "Really, I'm just grateful for a place to crash."

"I'm glad we had it for you to use." She glanced over at her sister. "If you could show Audrey around—"

"Sure," said Rosemary. "I'll give her the grand tour. Of course, since the guest house is only about five hundred square feet, that shouldn't take very long."

Cecily only shook her head, then waved at Audrey in an off-hand way and headed back to her house, which was a handsome Craftsman-style cottage, sturdy and square. From what Audrey could tell, the guest house was much newer construction, probably built in the '50s or '60s. There wasn't much to it, as Rosemary had pointed out, but it was neat and clean, with laminate floors and wood blinds at the windows, a kitchenette, and a small but immaculate bathroom. Everything looked fresh and new, as if it had been remodeled recently.

Audrey set her suitcase down near the foot of the bed. "This is just perfect. Thanks so much."

Rosemary put the tote bag on the floor next to the suitcase. "It's not a problem. You've been through a lot—you need someplace to stay and get yourself together. And it is safe. Cecily's property is protected. Nothing should bother you here."

She had to hope Rosemary was right. Nothing here set off any alarms, but Audrey would be the first to admit that her nascent psychic powers—if they were even real, and not something Michael had made up to make her believe she would have any chance of prevailing against a demon attack—weren't exactly trustworthy when it came to determining whether a place was safe to stay in or not. "Well, that's good to know."

"So, what's your next step?"

Go to bed and sleep for a hundred years, she thought, but Audrey knew that was no solution. If nothing else, she had to meet with her clients the next day, keep up her end of the bargain.

Before she could reply, her phone rang from within her purse. She contemplated not answering it, but that wasn't really an option. While she had no wish to talk to Michael—and she thought it likely he would be the one calling—she used a service to answer client calls, and it was entirely possible her phone was ringing now because one of her clients needed to get in touch with her.

The call was from somewhere in the 213 area code. Audrey didn't recognize it, but touched the screen to accept the call anyway. "Hello?"

Colin's voice, clipped and furious. "Michael told me how you walked out on him this morning. What you two little lovebirds do in the bedroom is your own business, but if you think this is going to keep you from going to Tucson for the next shoot—"

Audrey had to hold back her own wave of anger. Speaking as calmly as she could, she said, "I'm sorry, Colin, but circumstances have changed. I don't think I can do any more shows."

Rosemary, looking subdued, mimicked holding a phone to her ear and mouthed, *I'll call you,* before she headed out the door. While Audrey possibly could have used her moral support, this was probably a conversation better played out in private.

Sounding angrier than ever, Colin spat out, "Do I have to remind you that you signed a contract? Or that you've already been paid one-third of the sum stipulated in the contract? You can't just back out like you're changing your mind about what you ordered for dinner."

"I know I signed a contract," Audrey said wearily. "And I haven't spent any of the money. I can get a cashier's check and return it all to you." Technically, this was all true. She'd written the check for the property tax and had planned to mail it, but the sealed envelope was still tucked inside the desk in her office.

"That's not the point!" Colin snapped. "Even if we could find a replacement for you at the last minute, there's the little matter of the episode we've already shot. There is no way we could edit you out and put someone else in."

Audrey wanted to say that there had to be some way, Hollywood effects wizardry being what it was, but she guessed that any solution would be costly, and therefore not something Colin would want to pursue. There was the footage they'd gotten of that thing trying to crawl its way out of the mirror, and then hers and Michael's battle with the demons in the basement...both of those scenes would be incredibly difficult to replicate.

"Did the contract cover threats to life and limb and property?" Audrey asked, her tone acid. "I mean, there were the medical provisions, but that doesn't count the damage done to my house and car, or—"

"What damage?" Colin demanded.

She hesitated. After all, the damage had been repaired, or at least it looked as if it had been. Maybe that had all been an illusion. At this point, it was so hard to tell reality from fantasy, she just didn't know anymore.

"Someone trashed my house, and vandalized my car," Audrey said briefly. "Michael can corroborate that. He saw the damage, too." Which was true enough, although it didn't tell the whole story.

"I'm sorry to hear that, but can you prove that the damage is connected to your work on the show?"

"Well, no, but—"

"But nothing." Colin's voice hardened. "Let me tell you, Ms. Barrett—if you try to renege on this contract, if you try to pull out of the show and leave us all holding the bag, you will be in a world of hurt. My lawyer eats sharks for breakfast, and I have no doubt that he will have no compunction about turning your life into a living hell."

Was it possible to be scared to death and yet angry as hell at the same time? It must be, because that was how she felt right then—frightened over the prospect of what Colin and his lawyer might do to her, and furious that she'd been put in this position in the first place. "Do you know about Michael?" Audrey asked, playing the only card she had left.

This response was clearly not what Colin had been expecting, because there was a pause before he responded. "What am I supposed to know about Michael?"

Oh, hell. Mad as she was at him, did she really want to betray his secret? Because although neither of them had mentioned any specifics, Audrey was almost positive that Colin didn't know anything about Michael's past, didn't know that the two of them were already connected by a shared tragedy long before they'd ever met. Maybe Colin wouldn't be fazed by knowing that Michael was related to a man who'd killed so many people, but even if the news didn't bother him personally, it was very likely that sooner or later he'd let the information slip, and the identity Michael had spent more than a decade building would be wiped out, just like that.

For the longest moment, Audrey hesitated. Then she realized that even if she could gain some kind of advantage by telling Colin the truth about Michael, she wasn't sure whether she could live with herself afterward. She remembered how he'd said that it had been Colin's idea to recruit her for the show, that he'd done what he could to suggest other possibilities. They were both victims of circumstance here.

Even so, that didn't mean Audrey could continue working with him. Not when he'd kept such a horrible truth from her.

"Nothing," she said. "Just that…I don't think either of you were completely truthful with me."

"We were as truthful as we could be. Neither of us could possibly know what we were up against at the Whitcomb mansion." Colin paused for a few seconds, then added, "And while I understand that a drunken tumble might make things awkward on set, I don't have time for your theatrics. You'll be at the Thunderbird B&B in Tucson on Monday morning, or you will hear from my lawyer."

She knew it wasn't an idle threat. The real question was, could she even find anyone to defend her in such an obvious breach of contract case? And, if not, could she find it in herself to endure five more weeks of shooting the damn show, of being around Michael Covenant?

Michael Stanek, she thought. *Brother of Philip. Philip Stanek, who shot your parents for no reason except he'd decided to set the world on fire that particular day.*

Five weeks wasn't so long, was it? All right, these past few days had felt like weeks, and she had no idea what sort of horrors awaited in Tucson, or the other locations where Colin planned to film the show. But better to endure those weeks than to have her life ruined by a lawsuit she couldn't afford. She might lose the house, the only thing she had left from her parents. Her existence wasn't a perfect one, but it seemed idyllic compared to what it might be if she lost what little she possessed in this world.

"All right," Audrey said, not bothering to hide the defeat in her voice. "I'll be there."

Of course, the planned road trip with Michael was out of the question. She did a little research, found out she could fly Southwest from Ontario into Phoenix, and then do a short hop from Phoenix to Tucson. Since she didn't have any real alternatives, Audrey forwarded this information in a text to Colin, letting him know of her plans and the time her flight would be getting in on Sunday. In response, she got a message that said, *Good. Will have Susan pick U up @ airport at 3 p.m.*

Obviously, P.A. Brooke was history, and everyone left was doing double duty. Audrey couldn't really blame the girl; she'd tried to run, too, but Colin had neatly outmaneuvered her.

Well, at least he was being diplomatic enough to have Susan show up to fetch her rather than Michael. But possibly Colin had realized that the whole affair was resting on some very thin ice, and so he didn't want to push things any more than he had.

Once Audrey was done with those plans, she

called Rosemary. She'd barely said "hello" before Audrey told her, "Colin threatened to sue me into the next century if I didn't do the show, so I caved. I'll be going to Tucson on Sunday—I had to wait until then because I'm seeing clients on Saturday."

"Are you sure?" she said, her tone doubtful. In the background, Audrey heard people talking, which meant Rosemary had probably gone to work at the store after she was done dropping Audrey off at her sister's house. "I mean, the situation at the Whitcomb mansion was rough enough, and that was with you and Michael working together. If you're going to be continually fighting each other—"

"We're not," Audrey cut in. "That is, we'll just have to be adults and work together as professionals. Then, when this is all over, we can promise not to talk to each other ever again."

Rosemary let out a sigh that was loud enough to come through clearly on Audrey's cell phone's speaker. "I'm not just talking about acting like adults. I'm talking about going up against otherworldly forces when your energies are out of rhythm. That could make for a very dangerous situation."

Possibly she was right, but Audrey had already agreed to this whole mess and had no way to back out now. Maybe, just maybe, if things got bad enough, even Colin would come to the conclusion that they couldn't continue.

Right.

"I'll be careful," Audrey said. "There isn't much more I can do than that. Anyway, I'll be here tonight and Saturday night, but then I'll be out of town until the following weekend. What do you want me to do with the key to the guest house?"

"Just leave it under the mat when you leave on Sunday," Rosemary replied, sounding resigned. "I'll let CeeCee know. I'd have you give it to me, but I have to go to a retreat I signed up for months ago, and I need to head out to Idyllwild tonight. Shitty timing."

That was for sure. It would have been nice to have Rosemary around for moral support this weekend, especially since Audrey knew she really couldn't tell her friend Bettina about any of the things that had happened over the past few days. Well, she was going to be busy Saturday from nine to six, and after that she'd probably want to collapse anyway, so it wasn't as if she would have had the time and energy for much socializing anyway.

"It's okay," Audrey said. "I have to work all day tomorrow, and then I'll be heading out of town. But have fun at your retreat."

"I'll try to. Can you call or text from your

location in Tucson? I know I—and my sisters—would feel better if we knew everything was going okay."

"Of course," Audrey replied. "At least, I don't see why not, unless the cell reception is bad there. But even if that's the case, I'll figure something out."

"Good." The voices in the background of Rosemary's phone got a bit louder, and she added, "I have to go—the cash register is getting swamped. Take care of yourself, Audrey."

"I will," Audrey said—an automatic response without any real conviction in it. "'Bye, Rosemary."

The call ended there, probably because Rosemary had to shove her phone in her pocket and get to work. Audrey looked around at the guest house, at the unfamiliar furnishings, and let out a sigh.

Well, at least she didn't have to worry about packing for her trip to Tucson. Thank God she could take the tote bag as a carry-on.

Unfortunately, that was about the only positive thing she could find about her current situation.

The next day and a half went faster than she

thought it would. She spent that first afternoon getting her office tidied up in readiness for all her client meetings the next day—luckily, the office was in walking distance from Cecily's house—then got takeout that night and went to bed early. Saturday was spent in seeing clients, taking notes, and getting all their appointments set up for the following weekend. Audrey had to hope the shooting schedule in Tucson would be basically the same as it had been here in Glendora, with everything wrapped up by Friday. She and Michael hadn't really talked about it, and she sure as hell wasn't going to call him—or Colin—now. She'd just have to wait and see, and hope for the best.

She didn't sleep particularly well, but she still dutifully rolled out of bed at seven o'clock the next morning and got herself together. Her flight to Phoenix didn't leave until eleven-thirty. Still, she wanted to make sure she got to the airport in plenty of time, especially since she had to take a shuttle, thanks to her car being out of commission.

Or maybe it was actually fine; she hadn't gone back to the house to check. However, if her home wasn't safe to stay in, then her car probably fell into that same category. At some point, she'd have to get all that sorted out—she couldn't stay in Cecily's guest house forever, after all—but for right now she would allow herself to be focused on the week ahead, on the uncomfortable prospect of spending way more time than she would like in Michael Covenant's company.

For some reason, it was easier to think of him that way. "Michael" on its own was too intimate, made Audrey remember the touch of his lips, the sound of his voice…the way their bodies had become one in a moment that had felt so right and yet was completely, terribly wrong. She hated how she reacted to those memories, the flush of need that went through her, even as angry as she still was.

Maybe some dry desert air would clear her head.

The ride to the airport was uneventful, as was the flight from Ontario to Phoenix, so short that the jet barely reached cruising altitude before it began to descend once again. Two hours' layover at Phoenix International Airport, a huge maze of a place, as confusing in its own way as LAX. Then boarding a 737 for the short hop down to Tucson, the whole time her stomach growing tighter and tighter with dread and anticipation.

Audrey had thought she could do this. But could she? Right then, she didn't know what intimidated her more—facing demons, or facing Michael Covenant.

Well, she was here now, watching the sharp-edged mountains that formed Tucson's border to the east come into focus as the plane descended toward Tucson International Airport. Not so many minutes later, they were taxiing up to the terminal, and then there came the inevitable wait as the plane was connected to the tube that would allow the passengers to disembark.

Not a long enough wait, though. Even though Audrey remained in her seat while everyone else jostled to get their luggage out of the overhead compartments, eventually she had to get up, retrieve her tote bag, and make her way off the plane. She followed the signs to baggage claim and collected her little rolling suitcase, then trundled it out to the main terminal. Nothing here actually stood out to her—in terms of architecture, Tucson International bore a striking resemblance to the airport in Ontario, bland and utilitarian—but she wasn't really looking at the building. Her eyes scanned the crowd, searching for Susan's tall, lanky form, her long dirty-blonde ponytail.

There she was. Their eyes met at almost the same moment, and the sound operator waved and gave Audrey a relieved smile. She came over to her, and Susan said, "How was your flight?"

"Fine," Audrey replied. Not much else to say about it, and the topic felt awkward in general, considering just a few days earlier they'd all thought they would be caravanning together.

"I'm parked just across the way," Susan said, pointing to the lot across the street. "Do you need help with any of that?"

Audrey handed over the tote bag with some gratitude, since it was awkward trying to manage it, her purse, and the rolling suitcase all at the same time. "Thanks, Susan."

"No problem."

The two women threaded their way through the crowd in the terminal, then went outside to wait for a green light so they could safely cross the access road that separated the terminal from the parking lot. The car surprised Audrey a bit; it was a big black Lincoln with heavily tinted windows, the kind of car she associated with limousine services, not private drivers.

Susan must have noticed her reaction, because after she closed the trunk, she explained, "I had car trouble on the way here, so it's at a repair shop in town while we do the shoot. This one was the only thing the car rental place had available on such short notice."

"Ah," Audrey said. The last time she'd rented a car, they'd given her a Hyundai Sonata, but she had to admit she wasn't too savvy about the sorts of cars rental services tended to use.

"Why don't you go ahead and get in the back?" Susan asked. "I have a lot of equipment piled on the front seat."

Audrey almost made a comment about her playing limo driver, but then she gave a mental shrug and told herself to go with it. Susan got in behind the wheel, and Audrey opened the rear door and slid into the back seat, then fastened her seatbelt.

Susan started the engine. Before she began to back out of the parking space, however, the rear passenger door opened, and a tall man in a black suit got in. For just the barest second—probably because of the suit—Audrey thought it was Michael, and irritation began to flare.

But then the man turned toward her, and she realized she was looking at the face of a stranger. Or rather, Audrey thought she didn't recognize him…at first. Then she focused on the deep-set dark eyes, the thick black bars of brows, the thin mouth and long nose. She'd seen that face before, staring mournfully at the kitchen window of Michael's house, gazing down at her from her own upstairs bedroom.

The man in the back seat was Jeffrey Whitcomb, the late owner of Whitcomb mansion.

The story continues in *Unbound Spirits,* releasing in March 2019.

(Paranormal Romance)

Darkangel

Darknight

Darkmoon

Sympathetic Magic

Protector

Spellbound

A Cleopatra Hill Christmas

Impractical Magic

Strange Magic

The Arrangement

Defender

Bad Blood

Deep Magic

Darktide

Books 1-3 and Books 4-6 of this series are also available in two separate omnibus editions at special boxed set prices. Chronicles of Cleopatra Hill includes the series' two "back in time" novellas, *Bad Blood* and *The Arrangement*.

THE DJINN WARS

(Paranormal Romance)